Fragments That Fit

ARIA GLAZKI

ANIKA PRESS

Fragments That Fit

Chapter 1

S *ON OF A—*

Not that Shoshi should have been surprised, really. Of *course* on the day she'd been running late for work, and there'd been no parking at the Chestnut Hill stop—so she'd had to shell out twenty bucks to park in the city—her car would die. And her ancient cell phone's battery would, too.

Shoshi dropped the useless thing in her purse and trudged toward the only place that looked open, which was—of course— a bar. Not exactly the best place to find herself stranded alone after midnight.

But it was her best hope for a phone, and to avoid freezing to death in the middle of the street.

Shoshi pulled the door open and stepped into the darkened room, stamping her boots free of snow on the waiting mat. A few patrons glanced her way, but otherwise no one seemed to pay her any attention, thank G-d.

She walked over to the bar and tugged off her gloves. When the bartender looked up, she shot him a tight smile, her cheeks still tingling from the change in temperature. He frowned, sizing her up, but made his way over.

"Hi," she exhaled when he reached her.

"What can I get you?" he asked in a weary monotone.

Could she ask for the phone without ordering something? Best-case scenario, his eyes would shoot daggers her way the entire time she was here. What was the cheapest drink she could stomach nursing while she waited for help? "Just half a pint of whatever cider you have on tap."

He nodded, tossing a cardboard coaster onto the bar.

"Wait," she added as he started moving away. "Listen, I'm really sorry, but my cell's dead and my car won't start. Is there a phone here I could use?"

He stared at her for a few pounding heartbeats then turned to pick up a handset. Shoshi sighed, pushing her hair back from her face and trying to smooth down the grease-coated frizz before he turned back around. She aimed for a grateful smile when he handed her the phone. "Thank you."

He didn't respond.

Nat's voicemail greeted Shoshi's first attempt to rouse her potential savior from sleep. She hung up and hit redial. The bartender set her cider down before shifting toward a man who came up to trade his empty glass for a fresh drink. Shoshi angled her body away.

Right before the rings clicked off onto voicemail for a third time, a groggy voice muttered, "Who's this?"

Shoshi stifled the pang of guilt. "Nat, I'm so sorry, but it's Shoshana." She waited, but there was only silence. "You there?"

"What's wrong?" It wasn't even really a question.

"My car's dead. I need a tow, and I'd call triple A or someone, but you know they take forever at night, and I have this super important interview tomorrow that I'm woefully under-qualified for, so not sleeping definitely wouldn't help, and—" Shoshi bit back the flow of words. "I'll make it up to you," she promised.

"Yeah, yeah. Where are you?"

A wave of relief eased the tension thrumming through her. "Dalton and Scotia." She glanced around for the name of the bar. "At the Roaring Serpent."

"Got it," Nat said and unceremoniously hung up.

Shoshi set the phone on the edge of the bar and took a deep breath, letting it out slowly before sipping the cider. It wasn't awful. She unzipped her jacket a little, settling in for the wait. It would take Nat at least twenty minutes to get here, but that still meant Shoshi would make it home in about an hour and a half. Hopefully. Other than the fact that her car being out of commission meant she had no way to get to her interview tomorrow, it was all fine. She could handle it.

When the bartender came by to pick up the handset, the man she'd noticed earlier moved closer, looking her up and down. Shoshi shot him a polite half smile and refocused on her cider.

"Rough night?" The man's deep, sleek voice interrupted her scrutiny of the stream of bubbles in her glass. His self-assured smirk and a disquieting glint in his eyes killed any remaining interest she might have had in being social.

"I'm fine," Shoshi brushed off.

His eyes trained on the region of her chest, focusing on the vee of skin exposed between the edges of her coat. "If you're worried about getting to bed, my place is only a short walk away."

"That's charming." Her head shook unevenly. *Un-friggin'-believable.* "Because what I need to top off this crappy, crappy day are the drunk advances of someone with nothing better to do than hang out alone in a bar in the middle of a Tuesday night, who couldn't even be bothered to ask my name before suggesting we sleep together. Not that that basic human courtesy would have changed anything. But lucky me, your place is nearby."

Unfazed, he raised his tumbler to his lips and sipped the dark liquid, gaze trained on her. "I didn't say anything about sleep."

Shoshi rolled her eyes, turning away once again. A long sip of her cider did little to clear the bad taste of the brief exchange.

"And your name is Shoshana," the man added.

Her head snapped toward him. *How...?*

Then her brain caught up. "Eavesdropping. You're just full of impressive traits, aren't you. Haven't you ever heard of manners? I mean really, do these half-assed lines ever even work?"

One of his eyebrows crooked, emphasizing his pale eyes. Eyes that were once again examining her, lingering over the messy mass of her hair, the collar of her Wendy's uniform, the unmanicured hand resting on the bar. His head turned slightly, indicating toward the room behind him.

Shoshi glanced in the same direction. There were no other women in the bar, at least none that she could see.

"Slow night," he said, as if his gesture needed further explanation. She was nothing more than a last resort.

Sure, she was no knockout even on her best day. After a nine-hour shift that left her smelling like grease—even though she'd mostly been on register tonight—and months subsisting on fast food meals, *sexy* would be the last way to describe her.

Meanwhile, this man with his square jaw, chiseled cheeks, and impossibly symmetrical dark features juxtaposing his light skin—not to mention broad shoulders and fit build beneath a nice, if slightly rumpled, suit—would be appreciated by any straight woman with a pulse. Until he started speaking, anyway.

But that really wasn't the point. "Shocking how the women of Boston have something better to do than wait around to service you, isn't it?" Shoshi deadpanned.

The corner of his lips quirked up, and his eyes ran over her body again, assessing rather than appreciating.

One of them was saved from further comment by the blinking lights of a tow truck pulling up outside. Shoshi dug into her purse for her last ten-dollar bill and set it by her unfinished drink. "Thanks for all your help," she called to the bartender, who'd stayed strategically away from the two of them, before heading outside.

All she had to do was make it to her place, and then she could officially put this night behind her. At least until she had to figure out how to get to her interview. And how to make this up to Nat. And how to cover the bill for her car repairs.

Yeah. Everything was totally under control.

Chapter 2

Y OU'RE NOT WHAT I'M LOOKING FOR," LUC DAVIN SAID without even looking up when a secretary showed Shoshi into his office the next morning.

She froze half a step inside the door. "I don't understand," she admitted after a touch too long.

When the regional vice president of one of the biggest venture capital firms in Boston did look up, recognition momentarily dropped Shoshi's jaw. She snapped it closed. "Oh. Now I do."

Davin's eyebrows jerked upward, and his eyes trailed over her body for the umpteenth time in twelve hours. He was really going to deny her a job because she'd turned down his coarse come-on? She'd wasted money on cab fare for this!

His gaze dropped to the tablet he held before coming back to her. "Shana Glass." He paused. "You applied under a fake name?"

"It's the name I use professionally." Neutral enough not to sound "ethnic" and a perfectly reasonable shortening of her full name. "I'm sure your birth certificate says *Luc* on it, right?"

He let the tablet displaying what had to be her résumé drift down onto the lacquered desk. "As I said, you aren't right for this position." He turned to the computer angled toward him. The dismissal was unmistakable.

"Then why ask me in for an interview?" Shoshi challenged, stepping a bit further into the room. Her fingers dug into the portfolio she held so she wouldn't fiddle nervously with the charm around her neck. This was the first interview she'd gotten in months of applying to positions that would actually use her master's degree in finance. She couldn't afford to simply walk away.

He sighed, then leaned back in his chair. Unlike last night, his suit was crisp, the slate tie carefully knotted. "HR handles pre-screenings for positions. Someone must have made a mistake. How was it you put it? You're *woefully underqualified*."

So there wasn't going to be even a hint of professionalism. Then again, with his reputation, Luc Davin could do whatever the hell he wanted. His methodical—though now she suspected ruthless—rise to regional VP of Griffith & Moore was incomparable. *Admirable*, she would have said before meeting him. He must not have been as drunk as she'd thought if he could quote her words back at her so easily. Was there any way to salvage this?

"Look, Mr. Davin, despite my private comment to a friend last night and completely natural pre-interview nerves, I can assure you, I am more than capable enough to be your next finance director." *Liar.* This job was way out of her league. It was also her only option, one she couldn't let slip away, even if someone's mistake was the only reason she stood there now. "I may not have as many years of experience as some of your other candidates, but I am determined, efficient, and adaptive. If we could both agree to move on past last night's unfortunate—"

"Enough."

Shoshi's lips clamped shut. The lascivious drinker from the night before had nothing in common with the calculating, astute, and obviously capable man in front of her now. A man who saw right through her practiced bravado.

"We both know you were reaching when you applied for this job. Director of finance? With four months at Keres Financial as your most relevant experience? Doesn't exactly recommend you."

At least she'd anticipated that being brought up. "I'm sure you can understand attributing that situation to me is about as reasonable as blaming your junior associates for any of your hypothetical misconduct."

"Ignorance isn't a particularly desirable attribute in an employee. No one in their right mind would hire you for a position like this." He glanced at the tablet again. "Though I see you left Wendy's off your résumé."

The derision in his expression notched her chin up a fraction. Heat filled her cheeks, and malicious enjoyment touched his eyes. There was no question he was relishing dressing her down after the night before, even if he was right—on paper, this job was so far out of her reach. She'd only applied out of a growing desperation to escape the fast food world.

"It didn't seem relevant," Shoshi managed in response to his dig.

"And even if you *were* otherwise qualified," he continued, "the way you comported yourself last night proves you're not ready for a position that would require you to represent a company such as ours with all manner of professionals from all over the world."

"And what about your behavior last night?" she asked, her tone remaining remarkably even. "How well did that reflect on this company?"

His expression didn't change.

She held his sharp gaze a moment longer in the resulting silence. "Thanks for your time and consideration," she said on autopilot before heading out the door.

Shoshi kept it together until she made it out of the firm's office space and ducked into the hallway bathroom, which was thankfully single-occupancy. She locked the door and leaned against it, blowing her breath out in a steady stream as her eyes prickled. When that didn't help, she pounded her fist gently against the door, her other hand fingering the hamsa charm her dad had given her for her Bat Mitzvah. She'd worn it for luck and courage, a reminder of the encouragement he would have offered had he known about the interview. It hadn't been enough. Because *she* wasn't enough. None of this was supposed to be this hard.

Shoshi'd had a plan. Her father's life insurance money had mostly been spent on covering his healthcare bills, so freshman year of college, she'd sold the house. That money had run out midway through her senior year, but loans and part-time work had seen her through her master's. Landing the job at Keres Financial was supposed to mean a stable future, even if it was a commission-based position. That was when she'd left her education off her résumé and picked up some shifts at Wendy's.

It was only supposed to be temporary, a way to survive while she proved herself. An offer from Keres had been everyone's dream. Until it turned out the firm's executives had engaged in some extremely shady—read: illegal—practices. Not that anyone else at the company had been aware, much less Shoshi, who'd only been there a few months when everything came to light. But she also hadn't been there long enough to establish her own reputation, and now no one wanted to hire her.

Shoshi had done everything "right," but so what? She was still stuck two years later, balancing her hours at Wendy's and her "side job" at Dunkin' Donuts while sending her résumé to every moderately relevant listing she could find.

She wasn't alone in the endless job hunt, of course. Plenty of recent graduates struggled to find positions related to their field of study, relying on their parents or moving home.

Shoshi had neither.

Just a worthless degree, a mountain of debt, and two dead-end jobs. At least she could eat half her meals at work, though G-d only knew what the repercussions for *that* would be down the line.

Not that it mattered now. Since coming here had turned out to be a waste of time, she had to get out of this bathroom and back to Riverside so she could call a cab, get to the mechanic's, and hopefully get her car before she had to head to work. Lingering disinfectant coated the inside of her nose, like the building itself was eager to wipe any trace of her from the premises, but Shoshi was happy to oblige. She splashed some water on her cheeks then ran her fingers over her hair to catch the frizz no styling product could entirely control, even if she could have afforded one. With a fresh coat of lip balm slathered over her lips, she tugged on her coat and picked up the faux-leather portfolio Bentley had given them all right before graduation. As if the thin folder would help them land jobs.

The hallway was silent, Griffith & Moore's secretary perfectly centered behind their glass doors. Shoshi turned and headed to the bank of elevators. Luc Davin may be one of the most successful men in Boston's financial world, but there was no way she could have worked with him, not after her brief but all too informative glimpse into his personality.

This was for the best, she told herself as the elevator descended. It had to be.

Luc tapped the screen and dragged Shoshana Glass's application file into the REJECTED folder. He'd have to have a talk with whoever had passed her through to this interview. He would have thought it was a poor excuse for a prank, if she hadn't actually shown up with that barely buried disgust in her eyes.

Not that anyone in the company would prank Luc Davin. No, someone had made a stupid or thoughtless mistake and wasted his time.

Shoshana Glass was inexperienced, with a degree whose shine had quickly worn off and an aura of desperation. She might have hidden it better today than the night before, but it was there. Along with a seething disdain for him, and just enough of a backbone to make her interesting.

Shoshi's phone buzzed against her hip as she made her way to the Green Line. The number was local but not one her phone recognized. Could it actually be another interview? With her luck, it would be some spambot.

Holding her breath, she ducked into the next recessed door-way to answer the call away from the wind. "Hello?"

"Miss Glass? This is Priscilla Klein from Griffith & Moore."

Oh, no. Had Shoshi forgotten something at their office? Maybe it was something she could live without. But then, what were the chances of running into Davin if she did go back? Shaking her head slightly, Shoshi pressed the phone closer in case she'd heard wrong. "Yes?"

"Mr. Davin would like to see you in for a follow-up inter-view this afternoon at three."

Had she slipped somewhere on the ice? There was no way Davin wanted to hire her; he'd made that abundantly clear. Did he have nothing better to do than humiliate her further? Who would've thought a man in his position had so much free time to treat others as playthings.

"Miss Glass?" the secretary asked in her silence. If this was a hallucination, it was a vivid one.

"Oh, yes?"

"This is *extremely* rare," Priscilla Klein informed her, as if she'd expected Shoshi to shriek in excitement. "Shall I tell Mr. Davin to expect you at three?"

Did she really have a choice? Even if he offered her some other job low down in the ranks, it had to be better than wasting away—mentally, not physically—serving up a steady rotation of burgers and donuts. Taking it might shred whatever molecules remained of her pride, but she didn't have the luxury of walk-ing away. "Yes," she heard herself saying. "I'll be there."

Chapter 3

JUST BEFORE THREE, SHOSHI SWIPED A MOIST PAPER TOWEL over her face. After getting someone to cover the first couple hours of her shift, she'd called Nat, only to learn her car needed much more work than just replacing the battery. So instead of going to pick it up or wasting money on the cab fare home, especially since she would have to rely on a cab after tonight's shift, she'd hopped off the T at the Prudential stop and headed to the library to kill the time. She'd splurged on lunch at the Newsroom Café and settled in with a new dystopian. It had almost even worked to distract her from mulling over what Luc Davin could possibly want with her.

On her way back, she'd detoured to CVS to grab a travel-sized bottle of hairspray and some mascara to go with the tiny tube of lip gloss in her bag. She'd reached the Griffith & Moore building with enough time to lock herself back in the bathroom outside the office doors and do what she could to smooth back the frizz in her hair and touch up her makeup. If she had to face Davin again, she would do her best to look the part.

Priscilla Klein pursed her lips as she took Shoshi's coat and bag once more, clearly unimpressed with Shoshi's efforts. This time the woman didn't announce Shoshi's arrival, merely waving one hand toward Davin's office with a reserved, "He's expecting you."

Shoshi took a deep breath, then another one. She could do this. A job at Griffith & Moore—any job—would be life-changing. Maybe she could work her way up or transfer internally to one of the company's other locations. There wasn't much keeping her in Boston.

Steeling herself for whatever awaited her inside, she resettled her necklace so the charm sat dead center and knocked decisively on the wooden door.

"Yes," he called, managing to sound imperious in that one syllable.

Shoshi's damp palm slipped on the handle before she got the door open. "Mr. Davin." His light, piercing eyes found her, and Shoshi swallowed her discomfort. "Nice to see you again," she forced out.

One eyebrow crooked, but otherwise he didn't acknowledge the obviously false pleasantry. "Shut the door," he directed.

She obeyed and stepped further into his office, resisting the urge to fiddle with the hamsa or smooth the line of her top. Fidgeting betrayed nerves, and he didn't need visible confirmation of the unease zinging through her.

Luc Davin observed her for a prolonged moment, not speaking. Was he judging the small changes in her appearance? The silence was clearly a power play, intended to disorient her or maybe intensify her anxiety.

But she had nothing to lose in this game. "You asked to see me?"

"I have a proposition for you." Was that choice of words deliberate? He gestured to the high-backed chairs set across from him.

Shoshi walked toward his desk, her heart pounding so loudly he could probably hear it. She lowered herself to the edge of one chair and waited.

"I need an assistant," he said finally.

She dug her fingertips into her thigh to help keep her professionally blank expression in place. She'd been half-right: he *was* offering her a job. But being his assistant would mean dealing with him constantly—and politely deferring to him at all times. Well, unless he crossed a line in front of witnesses so she could take a grievance to HR, but the man had to be smarter than that.

"You'd have a variety of responsibilities, everything from taking care of my dry cleaning to preparing materials for investors, facilitating meetings, and miscellaneous other projects," he elaborated, maybe taking her silence for a tactical maneuver rather than shock. "The hours won't be traditional, and you'll generally be on call at all times."

"Why me?" she interjected when he paused, and instantly kicked herself mentally. She couldn't afford for him to rethink his offer. Then again, could she stomach taking the job? "You made it quite clear that you don't appreciate my limited work experience." Even if her degree qualified her for at least a Senior Associate role.

"On the contrary, your current position has given you invaluable experience for this. I imagine you've mastered the question, 'Is there anything else I can get you, sir?'" He stopped, cold eyes searching out Shoshi's response. As her face heated, he continued, "You also have the background to understand what the job requires, or so you assured me. And you're desperate enough to accept the unconventional hours."

Shoshi's eyes widened, and her head tipped back before she caught herself. No equivocating, no hiding his assessment, just flat out: *desperate.* He wasn't wrong.

But if the position was salaried, that could give her some breathing room to continue searching for a real one, one actually utilizing her degree. Surely Davin would maintain a level of professionalism if she were to work for him.

"You do understand there's a difference between a secretary and an executive assistant," she half asked.

His head tilted and one index finger lifted off the desk.

"I would expect a salary commensurate with such a difference, if I accept." Not that she had any idea what a reasonable salary for an executive assistant was. Even a lowball offer had to be more than she was making now. At least her voice had come out steady.

His lips pulled into a half smirk, and a predatory humor came into his eyes. "What's living cost here nowadays," he mused, "thirty-five grand? I'll start you at seventy."

Shoshi's heart stopped. Even forty would've been a small improvement, but *seventy*?

"You'll also have health insurance and other benefits, a company car…"

"I have a car, as you know." And if she accepted, she could cover the repairs to keep it running. Maybe even get some extra work done so it'd be more reliable.

Davin's jaw tightened, but she resolutely kept his gaze. He was probably unused to anyone challenging anything he said, but cowering before him now would set a precedent decisively not in her favor. Desperate or not, she would not let him walk all over her.

Wait, was she actually considering this?

"Fine, then," he said eventually. "I'll tack on three grand as a signing bonus. If you deign to accept, of course."

Shoshi didn't miss the sarcasm. Pulse whooshing in her ears, she inclined her head, mimicking his earlier motion.

"You can use it to get your car fixed." Before she could protest, he added, "You'll be using that car for work, errands, et cetera. You have a responsibility to ensure your vehicle is safe." Steel laced the words, allowing no room for argument.

The dictatorial manner scraped along her nerves, even if that was exactly what she'd planned to do. Shoshi uncurled her toes in her boots. Imperious or not, he was offering her a lifeline. Before last night, she would have been thrilled at an offer to learn from the man, given his reputation. Maybe the best choice was to forget their uncomfortable encounter at the bar and start fresh, take this opportunity for what it could be.

"Priscilla will set up an appointment for you to come in tomorrow to handle the paperwork." His eyes skimmed over her once again before he turned a few degrees away and picked up his tablet. "That'll be all."

Shoshi stood. The absurdity of the situation made her add, "I haven't said I'll take the job."

Davin lowered the device and looked back at her with an unsettling blend of challenge and satisfaction. "Won't you?"

How could she not? Who knew what was crazier—passing up this opportunity, or agreeing to work for him, doing goodness knew what at all hours. He'd undoubtedly derive pleasure from assigning her ridiculous, menial tasks with impossible deadlines, fully embracing the caricature of a terrible boss. But being *desperate* only made her more tenacious. And resilience was bred in her bones. "We'll see," she bluffed then strode to the door, a spike of adrenaline pumping through her.

Even without glancing back, Shoshi would have bet that predatory smirk of his had returned. But if Luc Davin thought he could chew her up and spit her out, he had another thing coming.

Luc tossed back his scotch, lifting two fingers to the passing waitress. It didn't take long for her to slip a fresh tumbler onto his table. He swirled it in a couple circles between his palms before downing this one as well.

A trio of women clustered around a cocktail table near the bar kept eyeing him one by one in an attempt at discretion. But it was the one who'd stalked out of his office twice today that he couldn't get off his mind.

His memory of meeting her the night before was hazy at best. The distaste that radiated off her in his presence, overshadowing even her desperation, was crystal clear.

It was rare anyone saw Luc as he truly was. Somehow Shoshana Glass did. Once she took the job, both she and her low opinion of him would be inescapable.

Was it cruel to invent a position simply for the sake of tormenting her, provoking that simmering dislike into a roiling hatred? Perhaps. But Luc was damned sure bastard enough to do it.

Chapter 4

*H*EY, NAT," SHOSHI CALLED THE NEXT MORNING, WALKING up to the small garage that currently housed her car. A constant stream of customers at Wendy's had kept her from really thinking through Davin's offer last night. Accepting seemed crazy. But if the car repairs were more than the couple hundred bucks she could squeeze onto her credit cards, she truly might not have a choice. Should she apply for another zero-percent card to tide her over? Would anywhere else even give her one?

As it was, the best she could do in exchange for Nat's help was a hot thermos of Shoshi's last packet of instant coffee.

"Shoshana." Nat wiped her hands on a rag and stiffly crossed the smooth concrete of the garage, fixing one of the straps of her overalls. The other hung forward unfastened, revealing her fading I'M SPEAKING tee shirt. She eyed the thermos Shoshi held, and her posture eased. "Thanks," she said with a small smile, accepting the coffee.

"I will make this up to you," Shoshi assured. "I promise." With people moving away after school and others pulling away after Keres Financial went under—as if just knowing Shoshi would somehow taint them—Nat was pretty much the only friend she had left. Not that she'd had all that many to start with. She'd been so busy with schoolwork and *work* work that socializing hadn't been much of a priority. By the time she could bear to talk to any of her old friends from back home, they'd all moved on.

"Thanks, you didn't have to," Nat said, setting the coffee aside to shrug on her jacket. "And it's not that. Something weird happened."

They walked a couple steps outside, away from both the noise and prying ears of the garage. "Weird how?" Shoshi asked. "Are you okay?"

"Me?" Nat twisted the thermos between her palms. "Oh yeah, it's not me. It's you. Your car."

"My car?" *Shit.* She could maybe get a rental for a couple days, charging that instead of the car repairs, but then that signing bonus Davin had promised would have to go to scouring used car ads. And that definitely meant taking the job.

"Yeah, someone paid for a bunch of repairs," Nat said.

How long would she have to work for Davin before she could justify accepting the bonus?

"Wait." She refocused on Nat's disconcerted expression. "What?"

"Someone called, asking about a car brought in in the middle of the night Tuesday. Paid for all sorts of things—your brakes, new tires, timing belt. Even your AC."

"It's winter."

Nat's chin dipped, her eyebrows shot up, and one hip jutted to the side.

Shoshi shook her head. Nat was right: that wasn't the point. *Bizarre couple of days.* "You didn't do it, though, right? I mean, it's my car." Why the hell would someone pay for repairs—expensive ones—for someone else's car?

Nat's expression turned sheepish, her shoulders rising. "Tino's the boss. He took the money, and I'm pretty sure he got a bonus for it, too."

Shoshi sagged against the brick wall of the shop, her breath puffing out.

"Look on the bright side," Nat said. "Whoever it was paid extra to get the job done fast, so it'll be done by tomorrow, maybe day after. And the work did have to be done. No offense, but that thing was falling apart."

Shoshi didn't answer, staring down at the tips of her boots. Nat had a point about her car, but this wasn't some random act of kindness.

Davin was the only one besides Nat who even knew Shoshi's car was in the shop. He could have easily seen the mechanic's name on the tow truck. What was he trying to prove? That money talked? Everyone knew that. And what the hell entitled him to make decisions about her car?!

But that was it. Money wasn't the issue here, just power. If she accepted this job, she'd be under his thumb—at his beck and call professionally, sure, but also subject to his whim. *Desperate.* He could dangle the fruit of stability in front of her and yank it away at any moment. Seventy thousand dollars sounded too good to pass up, but Massachusetts was an employment-at-will state. What if she took the job only for him to fire her a week or two later? Too soon for her to even get that signing bonus he'd promised, most likely.

"Earth to Shoshi," Nat said, waving her hand in front of Shoshi's face.

She grimaced. "Sorry. Weird couple of days."

"No kidding." Nat narrowed her eyes but otherwise let it slide. "How'd that interview go?" she asked as they headed back inside.

How much should Shoshi tell her? Davin's offer didn't exactly paint Shoshi in the best light. And if she shared everything but took the job anyway? She didn't need Nat's judgment on top of her own. "It was a disaster. That job was way out of my league," she admitted. "But I have a shot at another position in the company, apparently. It's more administrative though."

"Better than what you're doing now?" Nat asked, flicking one of her side ponytails over her shoulder.

"Less flexible." An important point Shoshi hadn't considered. It was nice to talk this through, even without the details. "So if I did manage to get an interview somewhere else, that might cause problems."

Nat shrugged, picking up a wrench or something and heading toward Shoshi's poor car. She'd driven it since her senior year in high school, and it hadn't been new then.

"That's what sick days and long lunches are for," Nat said. "And you haven't exactly been getting lots of interview requests."

Nothing she could say to that.

After a couple of minutes of silence underscored by the clangs and hisses of the shop around them, Nat asked, "It's still a finance company, isn't it?"

Shoshi nodded. Since Nat couldn't see with her head buried under the car's hood, Shoshi added, "Yeah, sort of. Venture capital."

"Learning opportunity? Administrative work shows you the ins and outs of things. Still sounds like a better call than juggling food service jobs. And benefits, right? Nice ones, unless those car repairs are a result of you turning tricks."

Shoshi lightly smacked Nat's arm, then sighed. Those were practical, well-reasoned points. If you took Davin out of the equation, it was a no-brainer.

"What is it?" Luc asked when the door to his office opened following a short, precise knock.

"I'm sorry, Mr. Davin," Priscilla said, hovering by the door with a pinched expression.

Luc dropped his pen. She was fantastic at keeping the office running smoothly, only anxious when something didn't go to plan and she couldn't handle whatever it was herself. Not many things fell into that category.

"Miss Glass is insisting she speak with you before heading to HR. I've told her you aren't available, but—"

"It's all right, Priscilla. Thank you."

Luc leaned back in his chair, squarely facing the door as Priscilla showed in the frazzled brunette. If she intended to turn down the position he'd invented, there would have been no need for her to come in. If she intended to accept, no reason for her to be in his office rather than signing the generous contract. This had to be about the car. He waited for her to speak.

Shoshana stared at him with her fingers curved into loose fists. She wore the same faded slacks as she had the day before and a blouse that strained around her bust, as if it had shrunk or she'd gained weight. They'd have to discuss her buying a more appropriate wardrobe.

"I wanted to go over a few things before making a final decision about your"—she swallowed, briefly breaking eye contact—"offer."

Her discomfort was obvious, though she chose her words well. Most would have jumped at the opportunity in her position. She was still trying to establish a sense of autonomy, or preserve a semblance of dignity. Intriguing. Luc arched an eyebrow.

"First, while working as your assistant may require me to integrate myself in certain parts of your life to keep everything running smoothly, *my* life outside of the professional setting will remain off-limits."

He masked his satisfaction with a slow blink. It was about the car.

Her tongue snaked out to lick her bottom lip, betraying her nerves. Then she squared her shoulders and continued, "Stunts like what you pulled with my car will *not* happen again."

Luc waited a beat before responding. "As I mentioned, Miss Glass, your vehicle will be necessary for a variety of professional uses, including my own transportation on occasion. Nor will I accept mechanical trouble as an excuse for tardiness or failure. Ensuring the vehicle's safety was entirely within the professional realm."

Her cheeks flushed. Flustering her was perhaps too easy.

But her voice came out evenly. "We had agreed I would take care of that. If you cannot trust me to follow through, I have no business working for you."

Right the first time. She most definitely had no business working for him, but Luc didn't give a damn about what was best for her. "Was there anything else?"

She hesitated, eyelids flickering as her gaze flitted to various points in his office before coming back to him. "I would like a written document, in addition to the standard contract, stating that you won't fire me for a reason an impartial member of Human Resources wouldn't find appropriate."

Luc's eyes narrowed. Clever, but the request was incredibly unorthodox. Negotiating in her position, however… That backbone, her apparent integrity, was the reason she stood there now. "Why's that?" he prodded, as if it wasn't abundantly clear.

One hand started reaching up toward her face before she caught herself and clasped both in front of her. "If I upend my life to accept this position, I would want assurances you won't change your mind on a whim, as long as I fulfill my duties."

"To my satisfaction."

Her lips tensed into a parody of a smile. "Thus the impartial third party."

Griffith & Moore had a handful of guidelines in place that limited groundless termination, but even those didn't kick in until after a probationary period. She was negotiating for additional assurances. Definitely clever. "Agreed," Luc said. "With a limit of three months."

She visibly exhaled, notching her chin up. "Six."

Luc stopped short of shrugging. "Fine." She wouldn't last that long regardless.

Silence stretched between them, but he had the advantage. He could wait her out.

"And if you do fire me without cause?" she asked eventually.

A corner of Luc's lips tugged up. He had her. "Aside from a wrongful termination case? I'm guessing you still have student loans." He didn't wait for her to confirm it. "If I fire you within that time, without an HR-approved cause, I'll cover what's left of them. So long as you agree to keep the company out of it."

Her lips parted with her surprise, her eyes growing wide.

It would never happen. When he got tired of her, he'd simply get her to quit. But the enticement meant she didn't see the loophole.

As if there was any question, Luc prompted, "Well?"

Chapter 5

SHE'D REALLY DONE IT. SHOSHI'S SIGNATURE STARED UP AT her from the final page of her copy of the contract. There was a knock on the conference room's door, and someone slid an envelope in front of her. "Thank you," she murmured automatically.

Alone again, she pulled out the sheet inside. As she unfolded it, a slip fell out. Shoshi caught it before it could flutter to the floor and slid it beside the contract. The page was a printed copy of the company dress code. A couple lines were underscored with unhesitating swipes of a pen.

> Employees must at all times appear neat, well groomed, and professional. Frayed, disheveled, ripped, or casual clothing (including denim) is not permitted.

Shoshi flushed, glancing down at her outfit and smoothing her hair out of habit. She'd dressed so she could simply switch out her top for the mandatory Wendy's one, with snow boots hidden under her well-worn slacks and her hair pulled back into a ponytail that was already starting to droop. Davin's opinion on that was about as subtle as the rest of him.

She dropped the dress code sheet near the other slip. *A check.* Her hand hovered over it, not daring to turn it over. The message was clear: use the money for new clothes.

When she flipped the check, the sight of her full signing bonus dropped her jaw. She'd thought she would have to wait until her first paycheck, but here it was: three thousand dollars. She could pay this month's rent, make a divot in her credit card bills, buy *fresh* food. Get a phone that worked. And a comforter that wasn't so threadbare Shoshi had to sleep in three layers and use bath towels as blankets to keep warm. Maybe replace the furniture she'd had to sell a few months ago to scrape rent together.

And he wanted her to buy *clothes*? She'd definitely go shopping this weekend, but work clothes were the last thing on her list. She still had a few outfits from her time at Keres, even if the weight she'd gained from all the fast food made them strain around her body. Winter layers were on her side for now. She'd follow the letter of the dress code, and Davin would have to deal.

Shoshi folded up the check, tucked it into an inside, zippered pocket of her purse, and gathered her things. She could deposit it on the way to work—to *Wendy's*, where she could finally quit. Her lips twisted humorlessly. With her account history, the teller might think she stole the money, or forged the check. She wouldn't even blame them.

Three thousand dollars. And that was just for signing. The whole thing was almost Faustian. Good thing Shoshi didn't believe in hell.

When she finally made it home, Shoshi dropped her bag and coat on the kitchen counter with a sigh. Kitchen necessities, a cheap mattress on a cheaper metal frame, and cardboard boxes she'd stacked into a makeshift storage space were all that remained in her little studio. Then again, that, a few stacks of books plus a library card, and her laptop—which mercifully still functioned—was all she needed.

She pulled off her boots then rushed across the room to her bed, plopping down to avoid the cold floor. *Technically* one of the benefits to her studio was having heat and electricity included, but the ancient radiator in the corner by the bathroom barely combatted the cold seeping in through the window above it. She peeled off her uniform shirt and immediately replaced it with her dad's old, worn-out Northwestern sweater, pulling her bra straps off as she went. She switched her slacks out for her yoga-and-sweat-pants double-layer combo before finishing taking off her bra. Maybe she could splurge on an electric space heater now. How much would that set her back—fifty bucks? More?

Ratty slippers offered a figment of protection from the chill as she crossed to her kitchen and filled a pot with water in her nightly ritual. At least her stove was electric and therefore covered in her rent. As she waited for the water to boil, Shoshi's eyes landed on the half-consumed bag of Krave on the counter. She'd eaten during her shift tonight—she'd felt too guilty to quit with absolutely no notice, leaving the others shorthanded, so she'd worked her shift plus promised to come back for a last one tomorrow. But for once, she didn't absolutely have to ration.

She could have tomorrow's breakfast portion for a snack as she unwound from all the craziness of the last few days.

The chocolate-filled rectangles clattered against the bowl, overlaying the hissing of the water as it approached boiling. Shoshi forced herself to carry the cereal to her bed first, giving the water more time. A shiver swept through her as she crossed back to the stove. She brought the pot to the end of the mattress, pulled a bath towel over it, and lowered carefully, curling her feet against the makeshift bed warmer.

Tension dropped from her shoulders as the heat radiated up her legs, and another shiver worked its way through her torso before she scooped up some cereal and opened her laptop.

Davin might try to make her miserable in her new position, but overall things were looking up. They had to be.

Chapter 6

PRISCILLA KLEIN TAPPED A PERFECTLY MANICURED FINGER on the manila folder she held. Shoshi curled her own fingers to hide her bare nails. So far, nothing the office manager had described was even remotely related to finance, but being Davin's shadow—and chauffeur, apparently—had to mean getting an inside look at market analysis, investment strategies, discovery tricks, term negotiation, and the many other details of managing a fund, right? Maybe she could even network with some of Davin's or the firm's connections. To be fair, she was mostly basing her knowledge of being an executive assistant on the movie *Set It Up* and a quick web search. It wasn't like Davin had provided a formal job description.

But either way, she'd be getting a salary. Managing Davin's schedule, running his errands, planning meetings, and compiling expense reports—these were all doable. It was the "miscellaneous projects" where he had room to get creative. But whatever Davin might have in store, she wouldn't let it overshadow the anticipation thrumming through her at being back at a desk, rather than a register or a grill. Today was day one of getting her life back on track.

So far this morning she hadn't even seen him, which was fine by her. Priscilla had led Shoshi into a small conference room connected to Davin's office and handed her a variety of paperwork. Now she dropped the folder atop the other documents. "I printed out this week's schedule for you, but you'll want to start familiarizing yourself with the firm's accounts and things like Mr. Davin's board commitments, unless he gives you other instructions."

"Is there a computer I can use to get started?"

"They should have your desk set up later today," the blonde said, glancing out the doors to a bare desk that had appeared outside Davin's office.

The rest of this alcove was set aside for senior staff offices and an additional conference room—with glass walls, unlike Davin's personal one—where Shoshi had signed her contract. Priscilla's half-circle desk separated the senior staff from the analysts, associates, and other employees, as well as the break room.

"Okay, thanks," Shoshi said, leafing through the paperwork. "So...do you enjoy working here?"

Priscilla arched an impeccably plucked eyebrow and offered a tight smile. Blue eyes, perfect sleek chignon, and smooth skin that was pale but not washed out even under the office lights all seemed to say that Shoshi wasn't going to last long enough for it to matter. "It's not for everyone," she said, confirming the impression.

Shoshi's own eyebrows shot up. Before she could ask what the problem was, the other woman gave Shoshi's outfit a quick onceover and left.

"Well, then," Shoshi said to the empty room. *What a warm and heartfelt welcome.* Since it was clearly the best she was going to get, there was nothing left to do but get to work.

By midday, Davin still hadn't made it back from the meetings listed on the schedule Priscilla had provided. Shoshi waded into the firm's records, learning what she could about the portfolios he managed. Her new desk had a clever design in the top-right corner—an almost shelf-like barrier that would block any sensitive documents from view of prying eyes. The phone stood directly to the left of that nook, and her desktop computer stood further left, the screen angled toward her, leaving space in front of her for anything that still required paper. The drawers were empty except for her purse, but since this desk was *hers*, she'd soon get to change that.

Other than her tapping at the muted keyboard, this side of the office had remained eerily quiet. Maybe when she got a little more comfortable, she could bring in headphones so the constant silence didn't drive her crazy. But otherwise, the calm day suited her fine. She may need time to familiarize herself with the particulars of the firm's processes and of Davin's scheduling needs, but that didn't seem unmanageable. Priscilla's brusque manner aside, there was the tiniest chance taking this job had been a good idea.

A pair of women strode in through the main doors, veering to the other half of the office, and Shoshi's eyes flicked to the upper corner of her computer screen. *Two thirty.* She'd forgotten about lunch, and her body was so accustomed to sporadic meals, it hadn't even reminded her. Sighing, she locked her user account and pushed back from the desk. She'd brought an honest-to-goodness salad—with fresh vegetables and everything—from her newly stocked kitchen, but she had yet to check out the employee break room. Going in search of a fork seemed like the perfect excuse, even though she'd also brought one with her.

She pulled the salad from her bag and crossed to the other side of the office suite. For the moment, Priscilla's desk sat empty. Beyond it, modernized cubicles—desks blocked off with tack boards from each other, though not from general view—were grouped in sets of six. Two sets of two workspaces offered their employees higher barriers and more privacy, and conference rooms of varying sizes edged the space.

Low chatter from phone calls, keys tapping, and a miscellany of other office sounds filled the air, but the break room tucked into the corner was empty. Shoshi set her lunch on the counter and started opening cabinets to get an idea of the system. In addition to a selection of tea, coffee, various sugar and sugar-substitute packets, plasticware, and paper plates, the shelves held boxes of granola bars, packets of cookies, and single-serving bags of at least five varieties of chips. The higher shelves were stuffed full of refills for everything. One of the lower ones had been set aside for haphazardly placed coffee mugs, all unique.

Against one wall sat a rack of drinks, from soda to smart water, and a fancy coffee machine dominated one end of the counter. Different types of milk lined the door of the fridge, and the top shelf here offered individual servings of cream cheese, hummus, string cheese, and neat stacks of yogurt—dairy *and* coconut-based. A handful of bags lay on the other shelves, without any clear system. At least no one here seemed to worry about food being stolen, which made sense considering the sheer amount Griffith & Moore provided.

Steps sounded on the laminate floor behind her, and Shoshi twisted sharply to glance over her shoulder.

"Sorry," the newcomer said, throwing his hands up. His pale-gray suit nicely offset his dark-brown skin, and he moved in it with easy comfort as he continued to the coffee machine.

She exhaled, letting the tension drop from her posture, and shot him a smile. "Hello."

"Hi." He paused a moment before adding, "You're Luc Davin's new secretary, right?"

"Assistant," Shoshi corrected on autopilot, then shook herself mentally. That wasn't the point. "I'm Shana."

"Sebastian," he answered with a small nod. "Have to say, we're all a bit surprised Luc brought you on board."

"Oh?" She raised her eyebrows in a hopefully curious yet unaffected way, waiting for him to elaborate.

"Oh, don't get me wrong." Sebastian brought down a mug without even looking in the cupboard and set it on the rack in the coffee machine. He pressed some buttons, and a grinding noise underlay his next words. "It's nothing to do with you, but Luc always goes over everything himself. The man's a maniac, keeps everything on a tight leash. Him trusting anyone else, with anything…" Sebastian shrugged, shooting her a look that screamed *good luck*.

Shoshi nodded slowly. "Maybe he's realized he needs some additional support," she said, willing her cheek muscles to curve her lips. She'd been wondering herself what had prompted Davin to suddenly need an assistant—a position that hadn't been listed on any job boards she could find.

Sebastian's head tipped to the side as he considered her, as if he was sizing her up for an office pool on how long she'd last. When the coffee machine stopped hissing, he tilted his full mug at her without a word and walked away, leaving her alone again in the break room.

Shoshi grabbed a bottle of water and a fork then settled at one of the three round tables. After shaking the dressing she'd brought into the salad, she speared an artichoke heart with a slice of cucumber and a cherry tomato. Her eyes drifted shut as the fresh juices hit her tongue.

Soft sounds of laughter drifted into the room, snapping her eyes open. If anyone caught her mooning over a bite of crisp vegetables, she'd have no chance of making a decent first impression. Shoshi swallowed and pulled out her cell phone, which was still holding on, making a new one too much of a luxury. She scrolled through her contacts, searching for someone she could text, just for some company. Aside from Nat, who'd be busy at the garage, Shoshi hadn't been in touch with anyone in ages. Social media sufficed to watch the gap between her former friends' lives and her own yawn ever larger.

When she reached the last name, she puffed her breath out and slipped the phone back into her pocket. Maybe eventually she'd find friends among her new coworkers and start rebuilding some semblance of a social life. *One step at a time, Shosh.*

Back at her desk, an email popped up from Davin with a list of meetings to shuffle around—written in shorthand, of course— and terse instructions to book a trip to New York for next month. It took longer than she might've liked, but Shoshi muddled through deciphering the message, contacting those affected, and making reservations.

Since Davin still hadn't returned, she headed into his office. The space was filled with dark greens and rich browns to match the luxurious carved wooden desk. Two mahogany file cabinets stood discreetly out of the way against the wall separating his office from the dedicated conference room. The opposite wall featured what appeared to be a well-stocked liquor sideboard.

Shoshi opened one of the top cabinet drawers and got to work piecing together the connections between the paper files. As she neared the last folder in the second drawer, a chill voice came from behind her.

"What do you think you're doing?"

She spun toward the door, letting the file drop back into its hanging folder. Davin stood watching her, his severe expression enhancing his sharp bone structure.

"Familiarizing myself with your files and system," Shoshi explained as her heartbeat settled.

He stalked toward her. "Those are confidential."

Letting go of the little hamsa charm she'd grabbed on instinct, Shoshi clasped her hands in front of her, the bite of her nails helping to steady her voice. "It was my understanding that that's why you had me sign a nondisclosure agreement."

He didn't speak, rounding his desk and settling in the leather chair.

She swiveled to keep him in view. "I've emailed you the reservation information for—"

"No need, in the future," he cut off. "Those details are now your responsibility."

"Of course, Mr. Davin."

When she didn't move, he turned his head just barely, crooking an eyebrow at her. Shoshi slid the drawer of files closed and made her way out of the office, shutting the door gently despite the tremble in her hand. She slumped into her chair, dropping her forehead onto her hands. Davin's appearance had startled her enough that her limbs were still jittery, which made no sense since she'd been in *his* office. His presence shouldn't have come as a surprise. But his predatory aura had prickled along her skin, ratcheting up her unease as it pinned her in place.

Shoshi counted the seconds of her breath until the quivery feeling faded. At least her first day was almost done. And with Davin spending most of it out of the office, it hadn't even been all that bad.

The little voice warning he'd been lulling her into a false sense of security was nothing more than nerves. Davin had hired her for a reason. The whole dynamic was simply new to both of them. So what if it took more than one day to find their rhythm? Shoshi wasn't giving this job up for anything.

Chapter 7

TUESDAY SHOSHI REACHED THE OFFICE PROMPTLY AT EIGHT. She hung up her coat in the hidden closet tucked behind the reception desk and dropped her purse into her own desk's drawer. Then, because it was slightly open, she rapped her knuckles on Davin's door, right under the gold-embossed lettering of his name. The door swung partially away from the pressure.

"You're late," he said.

Good morning to you, too. The digital employee handbook that had been waiting in her office email account had *suggested* arriving at 8 AM, and only a handful of her new coworkers had already made it in. But of course he expected her to magically know some unwritten rule he had.

Then again, her grouchiness might have more to do with the early hour than with him. She definitely couldn't let it affect her work. "I'm sorry, Mr. Davin. What time would you prefer I came in?" There, that had sounded suitably professional, right?

He dropped his pen to look at her, eyes trailing over today's outfit—the same charcoal herringbone slacks as the day before but with a nice knit sweater. His gaze stalled on the necklace she'd worn again before dropping to the pale-blue nail polish she'd applied last night. "Seven thirty," he said finally. "At the latest."

Eesh, that was going to be rough. Even eight was pushing it now that she'd gotten used to late shifts. But if that was what it took, she would suffer through alarms blaring and getting up before the sun. "Of course. Since you don't have a lunch meeting scheduled today, what would you like to have?" Apparently ensuring meals were available—precisely at twelve fifteen, as if he was intentionally emulating some movie cliché—was an integral part of her new position. At least Priscilla had included a list of Davin's favorite restaurants with yesterday's documents.

"Italian," he said, looking away. "Get me the file on the Norling property, and be ready at a quarter to four."

Of course. She'd barely gotten started on exploring his file system yesterday before he'd objected, but now he wanted her to intuit where everything was. The name didn't ring a bell, so the file probably wasn't in the two drawers she'd gone through, but there were so many she couldn't be sure. Shoshi pulled out the top drawer from the cabinet she hadn't touched yesterday, sending up a silent prayer that she had chosen correctly. Her fingers ran over the file tabs, searching for NORLING.

The oppressive sense of Davin at her back grew as she shut the drawer and opened the lower one. Shoshi swallowed down the anxiety. How long would it take to get used to Davin's proximity, his irritated impatience? Two thirds of the way through this drawer, her hand finally landed on the right file. She withdrew the folder and set it quietly on the edge of his desk, within reach but out of the way.

"Is there anything else I can help you with, Mr. Davin?" she asked, careful not to echo the question he'd mocked while offering her the job.

His eyes flicked to the file before he refocused on his computer. "Not convinced you've managed to help with anything yet." Irritation ticked at the edge of his jaw. "Are you planning to hover there all day," he added, "or will you perhaps attempt to make yourself useful?"

"Of—of course, Mr. Davin," she stammered like a complete moron, moving toward the door.

How was it Shoshi'd shrugged off countless demeaning remarks in her past jobs—not to mention in grad school—yet every time her new boss opened his mouth, he threw her off-balance? Made her feel like she'd already failed in some way that was obvious to everyone but her.

But feelings weren't facts. No matter how shaken Shoshi felt, she'd prove to Davin just how useful she could be.

Despite the nerve-racking start, Shoshi's day was again mostly quiet. She followed up on rescheduling with those who hadn't responded, sat in on a meeting with the associates, ordered Davin's lunch, and printed directions to the Norling property, since presumably that was where they were headed later in the afternoon. She ate her own lunch—a mixed-veggie and pastrami sandwich—at a more reasonable hour, though alone at her desk as she continued sorting through Davin's workload and responsibilities. It was intimidating, seeing the funds and high-profile endowments he oversaw. By all accounts, he did so extremely well.

The phone rang for the first time around three, and Shoshi picked up automatically before her brain faltered. What was she supposed to say? "Uh… Luc Davin's office," she finally managed.

"Yes, is Mr. Davin in?" a young male voice asked.

"What is this regarding?" Screening calls was what assistants did, right?

"This is Parker Jones of InterPlay. I've come across an interesting opportunity I'd like to discuss with him."

"Of course. If you would hold, Mr. Jones, let me check if he's available." After scanning the office phone's many options, Shoshi hit one gray button and held her breath. A red light blinked beside LINE 1. *Straightforward enough.* She rose and knocked on Davin's door.

"What now?" he called. He'd seemed annoyed even by her bringing in his lunch earlier. Like he hadn't wanted an assistant in the first place, despite this whole thing having been his idea.

Shoshi cracked the door open. "A call for you, Mr. Davin, from—"

"I'm unavailable," he cut off brusquely. When she didn't leave, he fixed her with a stare, then let out an exasperated sigh. "I suppose I'll have to draw up a list of people you can put through. Otherwise, I am unavailable. Take a message. Perhaps you'll even manage to discern which of those I care to see."

"Of course," Shoshi forced out with a small nod and shut his door. *Too busy for the hoi polloi.* When she picked up the phone, pressing the Line 1 button, the light beside it kept blinking. *Uh-oh.* How likely was she to hang up accidentally? She couldn't keep the man on hold all day. Twisting her lips to the side, Shoshi tried hitting the original Hold button again.

Nothing happened. Sticky sweat coated her palms. She'd aced grad school, but now she was frozen. Working a phone really wasn't supposed to be this hard. Davin couldn't fire her for dropping one call, could he?

Don't be ridiculous. Shoshi exhaled, shaking the nerves out of her free hand. She needed to stop psyching herself out. *Third time's the charm.* She hit the Line button, followed by the Hold button. The light blinked once more, then stopped, shining evenly. Shoshi's eyes shut in relief, and she silently counted to three to steady her voice before saying, "Mr. Jones, I'm sorry, but Mr. Davin is unavailable. May I take a message for you?"

He stammered out a disjointed message about an investment opportunity. Maybe Davin had good reason for not taking the call. She really should do better at giving him the benefit of the doubt. After all, he had to have a pretty solid idea of what he was doing, with his track record and senior partnership at Griffith & Moore at a relatively young age—mid-thirties, maybe? He'd been curt with her, but nothing that could strictly speaking be considered crossing a line, ever since she'd signed the contract, anyway. Once she got her bearings, she'd have to smooth things over between them. The steady salary was invaluable, but it didn't mean she couldn't also leverage the position for something more.

At three forty, Shoshi knocked lightly on Davin's office and poked her head in.

"Yes, five minutes, I know," Davin said without looking up. "My coat, and be ready to go."

Shoshi shut his door and crossed to the closet. Priscilla glanced her way, and Shoshi shot her a smile, determined to be friendly. "How's your day going?"

She could have sworn Priscilla wanted to roll her eyes, but professionalism won out, and the woman merely resumed her work. Shoshi opened the closet and grabbed her coat, leaving four others. The women's jacket was out, at least—probably Priscilla's. So the choice was between a tan coat with large pockets, a pea coat in a subtle plaid, and two black coats of differing lengths. Shoshi went with her gut, pulling the shorter black coat off its hanger.

When she turned back from the closet, Davin's door had opened. His eyes dropped to the coats in her hands, and a dark eyebrow crooked.

"I'm sorry, is this not—" Shoshi cut herself off, stepping out of the way as he crossed to reach into the closet himself.

He took out the second dark coat, smoothly pulling on the deep-gray fabric. She scrambled to hang up the wrong one and hurried back to her desk to get the directions and her purse.

"Priscilla," Davin said meanwhile, "how's Jamie?"

"She's good," the office manager said, decisively more upbeat than Shoshi had ever heard her. "A bit stressed with their upcoming release, so I only ever see her when she's passed out next to me, but good."

"Glad to hear it. All that hard work will be worth it, you'll see."

"Maybe if you finally take me up on that dinner invitation, I'll actually get to spend some time in the same room as her."

"And jeopardize my investment?"

Davin's pleasant tone stopped Shoshi in her tracks. He glanced over his shoulder, any trace of congeniality disappearing as he took in her hip-length hoodie-like coat—an awesomely comfortable find. Shoshi shot him her well-practiced customer service smile despite his scrutiny.

He turned and headed toward the elevators. "Did you confirm dinner tomorrow night? And push lunch on Thursday, they're not ready." He spoke in an even tone, not waiting for any kind of acknowledgment or reply.

Shoshi flipped over the printed directions and pulled a pen from her purse to scribble down the details.

"Get Andrew to cover discovery on that integrated ad company, I want it by tomorrow at five. And the Scholshire group is coming in the morning, so have three cappuccinos, a mocha for Lucy, a pitcher of coffee—I assume you know your way around a coffee machine?—and an assortment of pastries, including vegan options."

By the time he paused, they had reached her car, its dull paint making it instantly stick out in the row of gleaming, much newer vehicles parked in Griffith & Moore's dedicated spots. To be fair, after Davin's demanded repairs, her car was in drastically better shape on the inside, where it counted.

"I'm reconsidering already," he commented dryly. "Let's hope looks can be deceiving." It wasn't clear if he meant the car or Shoshi.

A few more moments passed before Davin strode to the passenger side and looked at her expectantly. Finally moving herself, Shoshi hit the remote unlock button twice, and the car's chirp echoed in the garage. Somehow it was still less audible than his sigh.

She shook her head and slid into the seat, swinging her purse into the back. Having reclined the passenger seat to his satisfaction, Davin pulled out his phone and tapped away without another word. Until she unfolded the directions.

"What is that?"

She glanced at him as she maneuvered the car through the garage. "Directions." It came out almost like a question. The property was an hour outside the city, without traffic.

"Pull up GPS on your phone," he instructed. "It's more reliable."

Shoshi bit her lip to hold back her own sigh. She counted to five and back down again before explaining, "I have a basic phone." And the simplest, cheapest plan possible. "It doesn't have GPS. But I assure you, reading a map…" She trailed off as a mechanical voice instructed her to turn right in three hundred feet. Davin held his phone out, clearly displaying their location.

Shoshi dropped the paper directions behind her and took the device. He reached into his briefcase and withdrew a tablet to continue his work, scowling at the screen. She didn't dare even switch on the radio for the ride. It didn't take a genius to have figured out Davin preferred her unseen and unheard.

Luc grit his teeth and reread the same line of notes for the fifth time. He needed the time this trip would take to refresh his mind on the details of the Norling property. Instead, he kept glancing up, tracking how Shoshana drove, making sure she wouldn't miss any threats coming out of nowhere. He'd ensured the vehicle was in working order, but he knew nothing about her driving skills. So rather than him doing his job, his eyes kept bouncing between her loose grip on the wheel, the other cars around them, and the passenger-side mirror.

He should have stuck with the car service, but he needed some justifiable use to come from having hired her. Besides, the added expense didn't make sense when driving him would irritate her. And it was, her fingers tapping out a rhythm on the wheel every few minutes until she caught herself, squeezed to stop the motion, and sighed.

Problem was, it was irritating him more.

Chapter 8

GRIFFITH & MOORE'S OFFICES WERE EERILY VACANT WHEN Shoshi arrived—at seven twenty-five—the next morning. She had mostly faded into the background during last night's meeting while Davin discussed architectural designs and the parking situation for potential future tenants, along with a myriad other details. She took notes on it all, though it didn't seem like he had any problems remembering everything. Sebastian had been right: why exactly did Davin need her?

The company had a preferred car service, so it definitely couldn't be for the sake of riding around in her crummy little Honda. But if he wanted to use her essentially like an Uber driver and answering service, the salary she'd be getting was more than worth it. At least once she managed to tune out his constant irritation.

After the meeting, Davin had had her drop him off near the bar where they'd met. It wasn't clear if he ever slept, but he didn't look anything less than immaculate when he walked in a few minutes after her. He dropped his coat on her desk and went into his office without a word. So apparently executives actually did like to do that.

Shoshi shook her head, hung the coat up beside her own, then started up her computer. After finally getting home last night, she'd researched local pastry shops—not included with the other information the office manager had provided—and found one that both had vegan options and delivered. When she'd called to confirm the order this morning, they'd promised to arrive promptly at eight.

With just under an hour before the Scholshire group was due, Shoshi went over to the break room and pulled out a stack of plates and napkins. She brought them into Davin's private conference room and crossed to the cabinet set in the corner. He'd specifically said "pitcher" for the coffee, and there wasn't one in the break room. The cabinet's upper shelves were mostly empty, except for three neat rows of champagne flutes. Shoshi crouched to check lower.

"Paper plates?" Davin's voice sliced through the silence.

She spun so fast she lost her balance and smacked her head into the wood.

"Are you kidding me? What do you think this is, a child's birthday party?"

Shoshi blinked rapidly and pulled herself up, bracing against the cabinet. She opened her mouth, but before she could apologize, Davin spoke again.

"This is a three-hundred-*million*-dollar endowment, do you even understand what that means?" he demanded. "Did they teach you to count that high at Bentley?"

Shoshi swallowed down the urge to inform him "setting up conference rooms" wasn't exactly a course she or any of her peers had taken. She had messed up, still too accustomed to the casual fast food world. She hadn't been thinking. So, she would make up for it. Presumably they had china somewhere.

Davin glared at her a moment longer then spun and stalked out of the room. At least this time he had good reason to be annoyed.

Shoshi blew her breath out in a shaky stream and crouched again, rubbing over the side of her head that still smarted. A silver pitcher and serving tray as well as porcelain coffee cups stood on one shelf, along with matching saucers and dark-green cloth napkins on the one below. There were no plates. She would *not* make the mistake of assuming the Scholshire group would use the saucers for their pastries. The early hour may have left cobwebs in her brain, but she had attended meetings with important clients, once upon a time.

Before those clients had been bilked out of their money.

Shoshi shoved the thought away. There had to be plates somewhere, but first things first. She set eight places, leaving the coffee cups slightly off-center, then grabbed the paper plates and pitcher and headed back to the break room. She paused upon seeing Priscilla.

"Yes?" the woman asked, slipping elegantly out of her peach coat. She didn't wait for a response before stepping away to the closet.

"Good morning, Priscilla. Would you point me in the direction of the china for Mr. Davin's meeting?"

The office manager let the closet door drift shut with a soft thud. Her gaze landed on the paper plates. This time, she couldn't hold back her eye roll, pairing it with a little smirk.

When she took a key from her desk and walked over to a locked door in the corner beside the second conference room, humiliation swirled in Shoshi's gut. Sure, the paper plates had been her mistake, but how the hell could she have guessed this closet—which no one had even mentioned, much less offered her a key to—would have anything to do with her job? Davin had made it clear from day one, and Priscilla had obviously chosen a side: they were both content to set her up to fail.

And she couldn't give either of them the satisfaction, no matter how many hidden landmines she'd have to evade.

Priscilla left the door open and started back to her desk.

"Thank you," Shoshi forced out, digging her nails into her palm. "And when you get a chance—"

The other woman paused midstride with a little headshake.

"—please get me a copy of that key."

Priscilla didn't move for a few seconds, but then she nodded curtly and kept walking.

Shoshi set the pitcher and plates on her desk and pulled her phone out of the pocket of today's brown slacks to check the time. The coffee would need to be hot, and she needed to have time to make the special drinks Davin had listed, but it was probably more important to finish setting up the conference room to ensure a good first impression. Easier to bring coffee in a little late than to be moving plates around. She may have gotten a rough start, but that didn't mean she couldn't pull this off in time. Nothing focused the mind quite as quickly as needing to prove those two were wrong to underestimate her.

As efficiently as possible, Shoshi set each place with a small plate, a water glass, and a fork and knife laid atop a folded napkin. She also set out two serving plates in preparation for the pastries. *My delivery.*

Shoshi checked the time again and frowned. 8:07. She walked out of the conference room in time to see Priscilla opening one of the boxes from the bakery, as if they'd appeared in the office by some lucky coincidence. Stuffing down her frustration, Shoshi rushed over, calling, "Thank you."

Priscilla looked up, the corners of her lips downturned, her perfectly manicured coral fingernails popping against the pale teal of the box like she'd planned it that way.

"You're welcome to take one before I plate the rest," Shoshi added pointedly.

"No." The woman added a pinched smile. "That's all right." She shut the box and lifted both for Shoshi.

After hurriedly setting out the pastries in the conference room, Shoshi grabbed the silver tray and four additional cups, switched the empty boxes for the pitcher waiting on her desk, and crossed back to the break room yet again. And they said office jobs were sedentary.

Sebastian stood by the coffee machine, this time in a black suit. A purple tie stood out sharply against his crisp light-gray shirt. "Still here, I see," he said with a semi-friendly smirk.

"Sorry to disappoint," Shoshi quipped. She set everything on the counter and opened the freezer. She could set the coffee machine going, fill the water glasses, then worry about making the special drinks. All in sixteen minutes.

Sebastian was still watching her when she turned with the ice. "Want some help?" he asked more seriously.

Shoshi's shoulders dropped with her relief. She hadn't interacted much with her other coworkers yet, and Sebastian was the only one to be even remotely friendly. Low bar, but she'd take it. "Please," she admitted.

He set his mug down on one of the tables. "Sure. Today's not my day in the pool, anyway."

Shoshi let out a light chuckle. So she hadn't been wrong about there being a pool. Whatever his reasons, she could use the extra hands.

By eight twenty-five, they'd gotten almost everything done. All that was left was finishing up the cappuccinos. It helped that the machine could work on more than one drink simultaneously. And that Shoshi'd learned to make various coffee drinks at Dunkin's, not that Davin knew that.

And that Sebastian had offered her a hand. She definitely owed him first pick of any leftover pastries.

Balancing the tray carefully, Shoshi walked back into the conference room as Davin opened the connecting door to his office.

He swept a glance over the table but didn't comment, so apparently she'd managed to avoid any more glaring faux pas. His silence, it seemed, was going to be the clearest indicator of her success. A moment later, he crossed to the main conference room doors, his voice carrying as he greeted the Scholshire board members. Shoshi shut her eyes and took a deep breath, then pasted on a smile, turning toward her three-hundred-million-dollar learning opportunity.

When the Scholshire board had gone and Davin's conference room was once again spotless, Shoshi rewarded herself with a delightfully decadent pastry topped with raspberries. Almost all the others had remained untouched, the assortment necessary for appearances more than anything else, but hopefully they wouldn't go to waste. She grabbed the boxes and ventured into the other half of the suite in search of Sebastian. As he made his choice—a vegan almond croissant—several of the others paused to partake and even said hello, eyeing Shoshi with more curiosity than animosity. So progress, of sorts. Food did always make socializing easier.

More confirmations of scheduling changes followed, along with more phone calls, more lies about Davin being unavailable, and more messages, which Shoshi methodically logged into a new spreadsheet she'd created. Until she learned to read his mind, Davin could decide which ones mattered himself.

As she searched the network files for an expense report form, Priscilla dropped a slip of paper and a small box on her desk and stalked back silently. *Ominous.*

The white box was clearly labeled as an iPhone, and clearly open. Was it Davin's? Shoshi reached for it, her fingers catching on a Post-it attached on top.

This is *your work life*, it read. The word *is* was underlined three times. Subtlety didn't seem to be her new boss's strong suit.

Sure enough, the phone inside was on and connected to a network. This wasn't like meddling with her car—many people had dedicated work phones, right? She may not want to be on call twenty-four seven, but Davin had been upfront about that before she accepted the job. Having constant access to work files and email would probably make her life easier, even.

Still, something about it didn't feel like a *nice* gesture. He was saying that he found her phone inadequate. Sure, the thing was old and falling apart. She'd been weighing the necessity of replacing it for months, but even then she would have gone with a basic device, both for ease of use and because of the mercenary added cost of a required data plan. This one would be covered by Griffith & Moore. In a way, it wouldn't even really be her phone or number.

Shoshi forcibly relaxed her twisted lips and passed a hand over her face to smooth away the frustration. The slip of paper Priscilla had brought with the phone was a claim check for a dry cleaning service, so after figuring out how to forward calls from the office—*thank you, Google*—Shoshi logged out of her computer and tucked the iPhone into her purse. There wasn't anything pressing waiting to be done, and if Davin needed her, he could now reach her whenever he wanted. *Super.* But at least she could go run his errands without worrying she'd miss something important. Plus she could turn on music in the car.

Less than an hour later, Davin's dry cleaning hung in the closet beside his coat. It wouldn't have even been all that bad if Shoshi'd had more errands to run—more time away from the suffocating sense of Davin, just behind his office door, and the interminable silence in this half of the office suite. Constantly dealing with people at her last jobs had been draining, but the contrast with this one was too stark, almost like jumping into a sensory deprivation tank. She didn't even want to imagine what Davin would say if he caught her using headphones at her desk, so that was out. Still, she'd take the silence over long shifts on her feet dealing with unreasonable customers and grease splatter.

A little before five, a graying man who had to be the Andrew on Davin's calendar approached Shoshi's desk. She stood, offering him a small smile. He hesitated, taking a small step back at her movement, his eyes flicking to Davin's door.

"Is that the information on the integrated advertising company?" At his nod, she added, "I know Mr. Davin is expecting that. Let me check if he's available for you."

Andrew's salt-and-pepper eyebrows drifted together, but he muttered a tight, "Okay, thanks."

Doing her best to emulate the polished, inconspicuous assistants she'd seen in other offices, Shoshi knocked on Davin's door then opened it, stepping just inside. "Mr. Davin?"

This time he glanced at her right away.

"Andrew is here with the discovery you requested."

Davin scanned something on his screen then nodded. "All right. Show him in."

"Is there anything else you need before I head home?" She was meeting Nat for an honest-to-goodness night out, one where she could afford more than tap water.

Davin's head barely turned, but suddenly all his attention was on her. "The Clements dinner is tonight. Or are you quitting already?" The penetrating intensity of his gaze belied his unaffected tone.

"I… I'm sorry, I must have misunderstood. The restaurant is only a few blocks away, but—"

"You'll be taking notes at this meeting. Is that sufficiently clear?"

Shoshi pressed her lips together to hide her sigh and nodded. She backed out to show Andrew in then sent Nat a text. Rescheduling was a bummer, but the promise of a steady paycheck easily won out. It always would.

Still, the dinner in question wasn't until seven thirty, a full twelve hours since she'd gotten to the office, likely making this her second sixteen-hour day in a row. It felt even longer.

Davin wasn't asking anything of her in that regard that he wasn't doing himself, though. Shoshi would just have to adjust, and maybe stock up on some energy drinks to supplement the office's coffee supply. How much caffeine was too much?

Chapter 9

Buying energy drinks shot to the top of Shoshi's To Do list as she dragged herself out of bed Thursday morning. Maybe she would even dedicate an entire desk drawer to them.

Being in the office by seven thirty meant getting up before six, and she hadn't made it home until midnight. Worse, dinner had consisted of a myriad of inappropriate jokes, barely legitimized by a smidgeon of business talk. Shoshi had bitten the inside of her lip to keep herself from calling out the pompous, entitled jackasses.

Davin had caught her gaze a couple times, the challenge in his eyes clear. He never quite crossed the line himself, but he certainly wasn't going to chastise the others, either. The crooked smirk he offered her easily turned into a conspiratorial smile as he schmoozed the other men, who were apparently wealthy enough people genuinely let them get away with anything. Shoshi'd tried to catch the server's attention to convey a silent apology, but she hadn't been able to do much beyond repeatedly murmuring her thanks.

The only tolerable part had been the exquisite duck medallions in a delicate plum sauce, even if Davin had ordered on her behalf as if scared she didn't know how to read a menu.

Shoshi shook her hands out, letting the gesture roll up to her shoulders to work out the tight muscles, then went to get some coffee. A few sips later, she felt more like a human being. Five hours of sleep wasn't much, but it was only one night. Well, two nights.

Back at her desk, the iPhone chimed with a new message. `Where's my dry cleaning?` Davin's number asked.

`In the office,` Shoshi wrote back. She'd mentioned it to him the night before, but apparently the alcohol or the crude jokes had wiped that memory away.

`150 Huntington Ave. Now.`

The terse reply was quickly followed by an apartment number.

Shoshi gulped down half her coffee and grabbed her purse. It wasn't like Davin desperately needed the suits right that second. He had to have plenty more. What was the big deal, other than the "inconvenience" of carrying them home himself? He hadn't even had an assistant until a few days ago, but bossing her around about the most inconsequential things was already second nature.

Davin's apartment building wasn't far, and Shoshi could have taken the T, but it was cold enough outside that she chose to drive. Stupidly, as it turned out, since she spent nearly fifteen minutes circling around searching for parking. He hadn't waited for her. Instead the doorman presented her with a key and a guest parking pass that probably wasn't actually meant to mock her for wasting all that time.

It was so strange, unlocking Davin's apartment, walking into his personal space in his absence. How did other assistants handle this creeping sense of crossing intimate boundaries?

The long hallway opened into a living room, or at least a leather couch implied that was the case. The light of the overcast day filtered in through the far windows. Where did he want his dry cleaning—in the hall closet? Or should she find his bedroom? That felt incredibly invasive, but wasn't that in fact the job? Unobtrusively infiltrating his life to help things run smoothly. Otherwise he could have brought the clothes home himself.

Shoshi glanced at the closet to her left, then down at her boots, their worn, dark leather contrasting with the pale wood floor. Trekking dirt and slush from outdoors into his home didn't seem like the smart call. She didn't need to give Davin any more reason to be annoyed with her. With a small sigh, Shoshi stifled the flicker of curiosity and hung the garment bag in the closet. If the parking pass was any indication, she'd be seeing plenty of his apartment in the future. Probably more than she could ever want.

A soft knock brushed Luc's office door, its pattern already familiar. Shoshana had quickly stopped waiting for acknowledgment when he was alone, and the door soon opened. Without a word she set a bag from a nearby Thai place on the corner of his desk, along with a plate and silverware.

Luc finished the sentence he was typing and turned to her as she straightened the silverware atop a precisely folded napkin. Her nail polish was chipped, and today's blouse threatened to pop open if she breathed too deeply. He didn't let his eyes linger.

She hadn't said anything about last night, though the pinched tension around her lips hadn't disappeared either. Her disapproval had been abundantly clear in the flush that hadn't left her cheeks throughout the dinner and the ritual clenching and unclenching of one of her fists. Luc dealt with all sorts. All he cared about were their portfolios, not their morals. Who was he to judge?

When especially flustered, Shoshana had tugged on the same little charm she'd worn to her interview and nearly every day since. At this rate, she wouldn't last a month. More than enough time to prove, yet again, that he deserved what he had coming to him.

And her naïve indignation had given him an idea.

As she headed out, he called, "Shana."

She stopped, her shoulders rising before she forced them down and turned around with an expression that just missed the mark on professionally blank. "Yes, Mr. Davin?"

"I have a special project for you."

Her eyes widened, and a hand crept up toward that necklace before resolutely dropping back down.

Her discomfort pulled his lips into a smirk. "Follow me."

He stood and crossed to the adjoining conference room. She stopped inside the double doors, eyes glued to the white boxes stacked on the conference table as if she expected something to jump out and bite her.

"As you saw last night, this job relies on connecting with people on an individual level." Her gaze jumped to him, anticipating a trap, maybe. But she wouldn't expect this. "They must trust us, engage with us, know they can rely on us."

"Of course," she said stiffly in his pause.

"When it comes to individual investors, as opposed to groups or institutions, this occasionally requires performing certain small favors, to cement their comfort with the relationship." Luc hadn't done any such thing in years, and at most he had occasionally used his connections to procure restaurant reservations or event tickets. Nothing like this, but Fuller would appreciate it. He'd commented several times on how unfortunate it was his collection was languishing in cardboard boxes. And Shoshana would find the task abhorrent. Two birds and all. "These boxes contain issues of *Playboy*, I assume you've heard of the magazine?"

Her eyebrows flattened, drawing together over her dark eyes, but she remained rooted to the spot.

"You'll need to arrange them by decade, hair color of the centerfold, and then alphabetically within hair colors. You'll also need to procure any missing issues, though I don't believe there are any. They'll need to be organized in binders with protective sleeves. Talk to Priscilla about those."

Shoshana's jaw shifted. At her side, her right hand clenched.

"Any questions?" Luc prodded.

She shook her head.

"Good. I'll need this done by my dinner tomorrow night."

She stayed silent, but the revulsion and contempt in her eyes was exactly what he wanted to see.

So much for being professional. Snapping at her about the plates yesterday had been legitimate frustration at her oversight, but this? Davin was trying to push her buttons, wasting her time on the thinnest of pretenses instead of giving her legitimate work.

And she couldn't let him think he was getting to her. She needed this job, and not only for the money. Being an assistant hadn't exactly been the plan, but at least she was back to working in finance. Considering the wide berth everyone had given her after Keres, this was her last chance at a toehold in her chosen field. Quitting in her first week would mean no one would take her seriously ever again. Davin's shenanigans would *not* send her back to the fast food world.

Decades, he'd said, so there had to be hundreds of magazines, but that was fine. Shoshi's problems with the objectification of women didn't make her incapable of touching a magazine and looking at the date on the cover. And she could probably find a list of the centerfold models by hair color, by name, by whatever other criterion he could throw her way. Thanks to the internet, information like that had to be one judicial search away. He'd meant to shock her, and he'd succeeded—briefly. But even if Davin was determined to beat her down, there was no way she'd give in, or give up. Ultimately, these were just magazines.

Unless they'd been *used.*

Shoshi shuddered. The ultra-wealthy may sometimes be eccentric, but no one would want to preserve magazines like that. Right?

Chapter 10

"YOU KNOW HE'S MESSING WITH YOU," NAT COMMENTED that night as they waited for their rescheduled drinks.

"Of course he is. But what's the point? He doesn't really benefit if I quit."

One of Nat's perfect eyebrows crooked up. With her stylish cobalt top and clingy black slacks, not to mention slickly styled hair and gorgeous dangling earrings, she looked better suited for Griffith & Moore than Shoshi did. Just add a work jacket.

"Who are you kidding?" Nat said. "You can't afford to quit."

"You know that, and I obviously know that…"

"He knows it too, *chica*. He knew it when you agreed to take the job." Nat still didn't know all the details, but apparently Davin's offer didn't need context to be transparent. *Desperate.* But if he didn't want Shoshi there, why hire her in the first place?

"Really, with the Spanish, already?" she muttered, softening the comment with a smile. "You haven't even had a drink yet."

"It's circumstantial, not alcohol-induced," Nat shot back. She claimed she didn't "really" speak Spanish, but sometimes she still sprinkled her thoughts with phrases picked up through her parents. It had been one of the primary selling points to her current boss as she fought through his prejudice against women dealing with cars—he spoke some Italian, but not always enough Spanish to communicate with the other guys. Nat might not be able to write a dissertation, but she had no problems getting her coworkers to understand her.

Then again, that may not be her Spanish skills. She had a way of getting through to people. What would she think if she knew everything about how Shoshi had gotten her new job? Nothing good.

"What's the point, then?" Shoshi asked. "If he's not trying to make me quit."

Nat shrugged in that perfectly feminine way Shoshi had never learned. Maybe it was something passed on through a mother. Shoshi's dad definitely hadn't been able to teach her tricks like that, even if he'd done just about everything else.

"Torturing you," Nat said.

It took Shoshi a moment to remember what she'd asked. Still, she thanked the server who dropped off their drinks then let a taste of her martini wet her mouth rather than respond.

"Think about it," Nat continued. "He knows you don't have a decent way out, so maybe he's just a miserable, sadistic asshole who enjoys tormenting you."

"And that pleasure is worth my salary?"

Nat lifted her fancy dark beer, which had a nice, solid layer of foam. "He's not the one paying," she pointed out before taking a sip.

Shoshi gaped at her friend. "That's despicable."

Nat chuckled. "Yeah, you're right. Sounds nothing like him. What was I thinking?"

Shoshi sighed. The twelve-dollar martini was a luxury, and the only drink she was allowing herself tonight, or else she would have downed the rest of it right then. "So what do I do?"

"Don't let him see it bothers you. Maybe he'll get bored."

"And fire me?" Although then he'd technically have to pay off her loans, not that Nat knew that. Shoshi could barely believe it herself. If she saved everything she could for however long she kept the job, getting fired early might not even be the worst-case scenario. Except for the part where she'd probably have to move to the middle of nowhere to get a job even remotely related to her degree. But that was getting way ahead of herself.

"And meanwhile," Nat said, ignoring the comment, "you get to enjoy the salary and your first night out in ages."

"Yeah," Shoshi said with a little headshake. "You're right." She took another small sip as a chatting group in office wear passed by their little table. It seemed so foreign, being surrounded by people who were supposedly her peers—working professionals unwinding after their day. Lately, she'd spent more time serving up their drunk desires in the form of burgers or Frosty shakes than she had socializing with them. No wonder she didn't fit in with her new coworkers.

"What's up?" Nat asked, following her gaze.

"No, nothing. I'm sick of talking about my work. What's going on with you? How's Gerardo doing?"

"He's fine, good," Nat said with another little shrug. They'd moved in together about a year ago, though Nat still joked he was more her roommate than boyfriend. She fingered one of her earrings. "How's your car?"

"It's great, so much better, thank you. I guess at least he did that, right?" Shoshi never could have afforded all of those repairs. Between that and the signing bonus, she'd definitely come out ahead so far. She would just have to keep reminding herself of that any time she was near Davin. "What about you, things okay at work?"

"Yeah, everything's the same." Nat exhaled roughly, dropping her hand to drum her fingers on the tabletop. "Let's face it. Your work crap is the most interesting thing we have to talk about, so lay it on me."

Shoshi half laughed, half sighed. "I don't fit in there, you know? I'm not even sure that's a bad thing, but technically, that's the world I'm supposed to be working in—finance—and I can't connect with anyone there. It's like, working behind the counter turned off my 'office' vibe, and I can't get it back."

Nat's nose scrunched. "You've been there less than a week."

"Ugh, I know. I told you, it's stupid. I'm probably reading too much into things."

"What things?"

"Stares, double takes, that whole up-and-down examination. Davin made a big deal about my clothes, too. Everyone seems surprised he hired me, and apparently there's a company pool going, about how long I'll last." *Screw it.* Shoshi gulped half of her remaining drink.

Nat paused in perusing the tabletop appetizer menu to look over Shoshi's pale-blue blouse, then down to her hands resting on the table. Why was it that having a perfect manicure was considered a requirement for professional women?

"You don't look bad, Shosh," Nat said, "but maybe it's worth it to upgrade your wardrobe. Buy some new nail polish, some hair gel. Play the game."

"Says the woman who gets to wear tee shirts to work."

"You got to dress down at Wendy's, too," Nat pointed out.

"Okay, true. But I adhere to the dress code."

"Look." Nat moved aside her beer and leaned forward, bracing her forearms on the table. "You want to know why I wear overalls and not just jeans? Or why my nails can't be done?"

Shoshi nodded, though the nail thing was obvious. The polish would chip in five seconds of working on a car.

"Can you imagine what any of the guys would say if they saw me with my nails painted, tinkering away under the hood? Or the customers? I have to strip away any obvious femininity to get an ounce of respect, because that's the deal where I work. Wearing overalls means the guys don't spend all day staring at my ass. Would I rather wear jeans sometimes? Or have my nails done for longer than a weekend? Sure. But I have to adapt to my environment, and so do you." After a pause, she added, "Tell me this: if you *had* gotten the job you originally interviewed for, would you dress differently?"

Would she? Shoshi'd probably get her nails done, at least. Maybe do something with her hair other than pulling it into a ponytail every day, or at least smooth it down with the hairspray she'd picked up last week. She might not have bought new office clothes quite yet, but they'd definitely be a bigger priority. "Okay, maybe I would," she admitted.

"That's what you've been missing. Assistant or no, you're back in that world. You're going to the same office you would be otherwise."

"You're right." Laid out like that, it seemed so obvious. And regardless of Davin's little games, it was Shoshi's job to be the best assistant possible. She raised her glass to clink it with Nat's. "What would I do without you?"

Nat's lips twisted wryly. "Freeze to death in parking lots."

Shoshi's purse buzzed as she got into her car after saying good night to Nat. She dug out her cell, but there were no missed calls or messages. *Weird.* She started the car and began pulling out of her spot before she figured it out. *Damn it.*

Sure enough, the iPhone had a text from Davin, demanding she bring food for him back to the office.

        And no sandwiches

Well sure, because sandwiches would have been her first thought for him.

And what was he doing in the office, anyway? He'd left before she had, and there hadn't been a meeting of any kind on his schedule. Had he gone home only to go back to work later? That made no sense, even if he had warned her about the "untraditional" hours.

Shoshi made it to one of the Davin-approved restaurants only ten minutes before they closed, but a generous tip hopefully ensured the employees' forgiveness for the late order. Since she hadn't eaten with Nat, and this little detour meant she wouldn't get home until at least eleven, Shoshi added an order of chicken fried rice for herself. She held her breath as the server swiped her card. Somehow she didn't think Davin would have accepted her overextended credit limit as an excuse if she failed to provide him with dinner. Thankfully the machine chirped its acceptance on the first try.

Most of the lights in the office suite were off, but the glow from Davin's unusually open door was enough for Shoshi to make it to her desk. She took out the carton of rice then brought the rest of the food to Davin along with a non-plastic fork. This late at night, he could do without the china.

"Thanks," he muttered without looking at her.

Shoshi bit her lip to keep her shock silent. It was the first time he'd thanked her for anything. Had he even noticed? Weird how he was more polite when he wasn't paying attention. She waited until he reached for the bag—already distracted from whatever he was doing. "Mr. Davin?"

"Yes?" He opened the steaming plastic plate of spicy beef.

"I wanted to speak with you about an expense card." Tonight seemed as good a time as any.

His hands paused, and he focused on her for the first time since she'd come in.

"For purchases such as this," she elaborated, "to avoid a slew of expense reports." And the complex calculations of balancing reimbursement schedules with her own expenses every time he had her pay for something.

"Talk to Priscilla," he dismissed with a small shake of his head.

That was easy. Whatever he was working on had him either in a good mood or too preoccupied to mess with her. Shoshi wasn't going to question it. "All right. Thank you."

"And Shana," he called as she reached the door. "Since you're already here, you might as well get moving on your project. Or have you finished already?"

Shoshi closed her eyes and exhaled, counting down from seven. "Of course." Was sleep deprivation one of his torture methods, then? At least she'd ensured she wouldn't starve. But maybe she should start keeping a spare outfit and toothbrush in her desk.

Chapter 11

THE BLARING OF HER ALARM BLASTED AWAY ALL OF SHOSHI'S resolve to work on appearing more professional. The best she could do was pull her hair into a half bun, shoving in the few pins she found in an old makeup bag and praying they and a generous dose of hairspray would hold the unruly mass. Alone in the elevator on the ride up, she smacked her cheeks to get some color, then resettled a couple of hairpins using the somewhat reflective surface of the walls in lieu of a mirror.

Before starting in on the daily tasks like checking messages and confirming schedule changes, she gulped down a cup of coffee, then made herself another one. Thank goodness Priscilla kept the company kitchen well stocked. Davin wasn't in—probably still sleeping, since there wasn't a meeting on his schedule until lunch—so Shoshi took advantage of his absence to finish going through his filing system, even though what she really wanted was a nap.

When she couldn't find any more reason to put it off, she collected more transparent sleeves and resumed sorting the magazines. She only had a couple more piles to alphabetize.

Still, stuffing each magazine into its own sleeve had turned out to be time-consuming, if also mindless. She worked with the door to the conference room open, in case someone actually needed something from her, but took the risk of streaming music quietly. A small touch, but as long as she had the music to distract her, she didn't have to think too hard about what she was doing.

Still, after a couple hours Shoshi broke up the monotony by talking to Priscilla about the credit card.

The office manager pursed her glossed lips before resettling them into a vacant smile. "Of course. It should take about a week."

"Thank you." Shoshi waited a moment, but Priscilla didn't say anything more. Seriously, what had she done to piss the woman off so badly? Unless this was nothing more than blind loyalty to Davin. Maybe Shoshi could sway the woman to her side, or at least ease the tension. "I'm heading over to the break room," she said. "Could I get you a coffee or anything?"

Priscilla blinked twice before saying, "No, thank you." Even the fake smile had disappeared.

Shoshi still walked to the break room so her offer wouldn't seem like a lie. She grabbed a bottle of water—the three coffees she'd already had were probably enough for one morning—and returned to the magazines. Sleek black binders now containing much of the collection waited to be labeled.

When Davin arrived, greeted cheerfully by Priscilla, he glanced at Shoshi in the conference room but entered his office without a word. She switched off the music and checked the time. After one. The sandwich she'd brought—in part because of last night's jab—still waited unconsumed. She should have taken a break before Davin's return threatened to interrupt her lunch, but better late than never. First, of course, Shoshi detoured to scrub her hands clean, even though none of the magazines had featured any questionable stains, thank G-d. On the plus side, her bun was still in place, and most of her usual frizz was under control. She ran dampened palms over her hair to smooth the rest then laid a fingertip over the hamsa.

She'd mostly stopped wearing it the last couple years, not wanting the precious charm to be ruined by the same gross film that had clung to her after every shift. She hadn't exactly meant to start wearing it daily now, either. But there was something comforting about the little hand with the blue stones. Would her dad have been proud of her for making the most out of a bad situation? Of course if he'd been alive to tell her, she might have had other options.

Shaking off the morose thought, Shoshi made her way back to her desk, waking up her computer as she sat down. As she ate, she read through some light research on the companies in which Davin's funds invested. He may treat her like crap, but he had an astounding track record getting returns on the investments he directed. Steady builds, big exits. Maybe she could find his original discovery documents for some insight on how he made his decisions.

The thought was interrupted by the phone ringing. Shoshi swallowed quickly, rinsing her mouth with a sip of water before picking up. "Luc Davin's office."

"Oh, uh. Hello," a woman's tentative voice responded.

Almost everyone who called was startled by Shoshi's presence. Apparently Davin had either screened all his calls or—

perish the thought—picked up on his own before. "How may I help you?" she asked.

"Oh, yes, well. This is Lucas's mother…" She trailed off before adding, "Is Lucas available?"

"Of course, Mrs. Davin. Let me transfer you. I'm going to put you on hold for just a moment, all right?"

"Yes. Thank you." She sounded distant, as if they had a bad connection, though nowadays, what were the chances of that? Shoshi hit the Hold button and stood. Where were his parents from? In the bit of research she'd done, there'd been no mention of Davin's family, or much on his background at all. Like he'd intentionally scrubbed his past from the internet.

Stepping into his office, Shoshi said, "Mr. Davin? Your mother is calling on line one."

He went stock-still. The moment stretched until the very air felt ready to snap.

Then he simply resumed typing. "I thought I was clear about my calls." There was no emotion in his voice, as if she'd said a man he'd once passed on the street was calling rather than his mom.

Shoshi shut her mouth when she realized it had dropped open. How callous was he? "Of course," she forced out. A tightness started growing in her chest. Shoshi had to try twice to swallow past it. "If you could get me that list, then, of approved names, since for most people immediate relatives would be a no-brainer."

Davin pushed back from his computer and fixed her with a stony stare. "You aren't paid for your opinion."

"An added bonus for you."

Shoshi didn't wait for him to dismiss her, striding out. She gave herself a few beats before taking a measured breath and picking up the phone. "Mrs. Davin, I'm so sorry." Well at least that was true. "I hadn't noticed he was actually pulled into a meeting. Can I take a message for you?"

Silence greeted the statement as Shoshi's heart beat against her ribcage. "No, that's all right, dear," Davin's mother finally said. She sounded crushed. Her voice faltered as she added, "Thank you," before hanging up.

Shoshi dropped the handset into its cradle and trudged to the break room. More coffee was the only way to get through this day. Too bad she couldn't have it spiked.

Luc grit his teeth and helped himself to a generous pour from the sideboard. Drinking alone in the office wasn't the best look, but really, who was going to stop him? Only a week in, and it was already a tossup which one of them was hating this little arrangement more.

Shoshana had plowed through Alistair's collection with a resolute determination that belied her initial shock at the assignment. Luc had a sneaking suspicion she would have reacted similarly if he'd told her to go scrub the toilets with a toothbrush, stoically handling the task. Perhaps he'd underestimated her desperation after all. He'd definitely underestimated how her blend of righteousness and disenchantment would stab at him. The calls he took were his own damn business.

He slammed the tumbler back down on the sideboard, his knuckles turning white before he managed to pry his fingers off the crystal. Luc spun away, striding to the large windows showcasing the city below.

For too long, work had been his only true escape, albeit one he'd never deserved. But damn it, now he wanted it back. If crushing Shoshana was the only way to reclaim that sliver of peace, so be it. He'd simply have to find her breaking point faster than planned.

Shoshi didn't say a word when she finished assembling the binders for whoever it was—if there was in fact some investor who cared about preserving his *Playboy* collection. What were the chances they were actually Davin's? He paused at her desk on his way out, instructing her to have a messenger pick up the boxes and send them to a Manchester address. He didn't provide a name, "for the sake of privacy."

Shoshi kept his gaze evenly until he added, "My coat." She got that without a word, too. She didn't trust herself to speak. What kind of person ignored a phone call from his mother?

Davin, of course, was entirely unperturbed by her silence. But hours later, despite her exhaustion, Shoshi tossed and turned, fuming.

Entitled, ungrateful people who didn't appreciate what they had—that was who.

Huddled in her father's old sweater, alone except for the memories, Shoshi couldn't help the surge of grief. She'd work at a dead-end service job the rest of her life if it meant having one more conversation with her father, even on the phone. Or with her mother, even if Shoshi wouldn't recognize her voice.

Curling her knees up, Shoshi wrapped her hands around her waist, holding herself since there was no one else to do it.

Chapter 12

A MECHANICAL CHIME CUT THROUGH THE AIR. AND again. Shoshi rubbed the gritty feeling from her eyes as she reached for the iPhone charging on the floor. The steady hum of her new space heater filled the apartment, making her smile. She'd earmarked forty dollars from her first paycheck for a fluffy new comforter, but the little heater already meant she fell asleep without shuddering from the cold and didn't have to wear a thousand layers inside. Such a small but infinitely important change, even if dealing with Davin was the price.

She glanced at the time before reading his email. *7 am? Really?* The unsurprisingly curt message "requested" she bring files from the office to his place ASAP.

Shoshi let her hand drop into the warm stream from the heater as a faint hint of early-morning sunlight trickled in through her window. What were the chances that was all he wanted and she'd at least have the rest of her Saturday free? She slowly drew in a full breath, then sighed all the air out at once as she sat up. At least she could justify wearing business casual since it was the weekend.

Half an hour later Shoshi sat in her car, headed into the city. She dipped her hand into the small container of Krave she'd brought with her for breakfast. Sure, she could afford some other options now, but the cereal was addictive and easily portable. Plus, if he was going to make her go in, she could grab a yogurt at the office.

Somehow the silence in the Griffith & Moore suite felt different on a Saturday, less hostile. In Davin's office, she pulled out the iPhone to double-check the list of files he wanted. *That's weird.* Many of them were recent. Davin seemed to prefer keeping at least basic information and some of his own notes on paper, but most of the information for these would be stored virtually. The files themselves were quite thin, supporting the theory that everything he wanted was probably easily accessible to him from home. What was his obsession with wasting her time?

Shoshi grabbed the stack of folders and dropped them on her desk beside her purse. She pulled out her trusty travel mug, its Bentley logo long scraped away, and headed to the break room, which was rapidly becoming her favorite place in the office. Davin would at least have to wait for her to make herself some decent coffee.

A grinding noise halted Rico by the reception desk of Griffith & Moore. Was someone there this early on a Saturday, or was something wrong? Neither was a great option. He liked getting a feel for a company's space before he started working. He hadn't considered the possibility he wouldn't be alone to set up his office and explore.

He crossed the executive half of the office to the door that had not yet been embossed with his name. While he'd been given a temporary pass and keys to enter the main office on the weekend, and security downstairs had taken note of the pass and his ID, the interior offices of Griffith & Moore stood unlocked. Rico had been assured there would be locked file cabinets provided to him before he started, and sure enough, the chrome cabinets had round keyholes.

He set the box he held on the sleek glass-top desk that was now his and stripped off his coat. The computer was off, and he didn't have the information to set up his account, but that could wait until Monday. The office itself was smaller than Luc Davin's, but Rico wouldn't be spending as much time in personal meetings, and the space was well appointed with built-in shelves over a currently empty sideboard.

When he stepped back out into the open space, which now included a desk that hadn't been there during his interview, the grinding noise had stopped. He followed the pouring sound that replaced it to a compact kitchen. At least there wasn't some technical problem he'd have to try to deal with while he was here.

A woman stood before the coffee machine, the messy waves of her dark hair curling around and over the bulky collar of her coat.

"Hello," Rico said.

The woman jerked, spinning around. "Hi," she breathed. A dark-rose sweater peeked out from beneath her black coat, matching the flush that spread under her light-olive skin.

"Sorry, I didn't mean to startle you. Didn't think anyone else would be here." Maybe she wouldn't be staying long. Other employees would likely go in and out as the day went on, but he'd counted on the early hours.

Her dark eyes crinkled with a touch of humor. "Neither did I." She gestured to the machine behind her. "Would you like some coffee…?" She trailed off, eyebrows rising with the unfinished question.

"Rick," he filled in, holding out his hand.

"Shana." Her grip was light but steady.

Rico's hand lingered as he tried to place the name. "Oh," he said with a smile, letting go. "You're the other newbie."

Her expression shuttered as her lips stretched into a tense smile. "So, coffee, Rick?"

"No, thank you." He saved his one cup a day for an afternoon pick-me-up. "How are you liking it here?"

She turned away to fit her mug with its lid. "I'm still settling in. How about you?" she added, facing him again.

"We'll see on Monday, but I'm excited to jump in."

She nodded once, cradling her coffee. "So I suppose I'll be seeing you around, then," she half asked.

"Maybe we could have lunch together Monday." He dropped his voice conspiratorially, adding, "Us newbies ought to stick together."

Shana seemed to relax for the first time since Rico had startled her, and she shot him a more genuine smile that reached her large, expressive eyes. "I would really like that."

Shoshi tapped her fingers to the music flowing through the repaired radio as she drove to Davin's. Rick may be newer than her, but at least he was *nice*. And having someone to take a lunch break with, even if just the one time, would be a welcome change. Plus, he was kind of cute, with his close-cut brown hair that sported a touch of gray, his tawny skin, the crinkles around his eyes, and a kind smile.

He was almost certainly the new finance director, the man for whom Davin had passed her over. But Rick had at least ten years on her, if not more, and Davin had indicated the other candidates had more experience—not that that was an especially high bar. What mattered now was establishing a rapport with Rick, since he had to have connections throughout the finance world. Maybe he'd even help her find a real position if he got to know her a bit.

After a deep breath in and out, Shoshi gathered the files on the passenger seat and got out of the car. She wound her way through the apartment complex then knocked on Davin's door.

No one answered. *Great.* He'd probably left again, because the last thing he actually needed first thing Saturday morning were the files she held. Her lips twisting to the side, Shoshi dug in her purse for the key. She should remember to put it on a keychain so it'd be easier to find.

The door opened and closed silently, and Shoshi stalled inside. She'd parked in the garage this time, so she hadn't gone out onto the slushy street and her boots remained relatively clean. Where would he want the files?

Ahead of her to the left, a lock clicked, and a lithe blonde woman walked out, wrapped in a small towel that revealed bronzed skin despite the season. She looked at Shoshi with passive curiosity as her hand released the clip holding her hair, letting it fall in a perfect curl. "Hello."

"Uh, hi," Shoshi stuttered. "I'm sorry, I'm, uh, just dropping these off for Mr. Davin." She gestured with the files to emphasize the comment.

The blonde shrugged. "Okay." She took a couple steps, disappearing into a door across from the one that presumably led to the bathroom. Did Davin keep such a tight hold on his virtual presence that no one knew he had a wife or girlfriend?

"Shana," his voice called from further inside.

Shoshi stepped slowly down the hallway, passing a compact kitchen to her right. Then again, Davin seemed to have meetings during most meals, so his kitchen probably didn't get much use. The long wall to her left was bare. Davin's office didn't have many personal effects, except his framed degree and a couple discreet work awards, but his home had to have more of a personal touch *somewhere*, right?

A couple more steps revealed Davin seated at a dark wooden table in a dining alcove to her right. His shirt was open at the collar, the sleeves rolled up, and faint stubble covered his unforgiving square jaw. Something tightened low in her stomach, but which of the four Fs her body was leaning toward in that moment was anybody's guess. Well, she could definitely rule out one of them.

Blinking away the odd sensation, Shoshi murmured, "Good morning," and set the files on the corner closest to her.

He didn't acknowledge the stack of folders, or her. Shoshi snuck a glance at his living room ahead and to the left, connected with an open floor plan to the dining area. Sunlight streamed through windows set diagonally on either side of the black leather couch. Matching armchairs sat in front of each window, also angled toward the center of the space. The wall behind the couch was bare, but a bookshelf stood against the outcropping extending from the closer window. On the whole, his place was spacious but smaller than Shoshi'd expected—less lavish.

Heels hitting the wooden floor signaled the blonde's approach, and Shoshi moved a couple steps further into the apartment, out of the other woman's way. She now wore a halter top that draped over her chest and skinny jeans with knee-high stiletto boots. A fur-trimmed coat hung over her arm. Her gaze landed on the stack of files, and she braced beside it on the table, leaning toward Luc. "Guess I should let you get back to work." Somehow, even that phrase had flirty undertones.

Davin nodded. "Goodbye, Stacy."

"Lexi," the blonde corrected, frowning as she straightened. So, not a girlfriend. She glanced at Shoshi before offering an overly friendly, "Bye!" Her heels clacked back down the hallway, and the door closed behind her with a small click.

Only then did Davin stand. Shoshi rolled her eyes but managed not to shake her head.

"Problem?" he asked. Utter nonchalance showed in every line of his face.

"Of course not." Shoshi's sleep-deprived mind wasn't fast enough to stop her from adding, "Why should you have any respect for a woman you obviously spent the night with." She cringed internally at the line she'd crossed, pulling her shoulders back in preparation for his response. Whatever that instinct had been before, now it was definitely *flight*. If only that were an option.

One of those dark eyebrows rose, but then Davin turned away and disappeared into his kitchen. Exhaling, Shoshi ran her hand through the hair she'd left down today, lightly massaging the top of her scalp as she resettled the curls.

"There are clothes in the middle compartment of the right-hand bedroom closet for the dry cleaner," Davin said from inside the kitchen. Liquid sloshed as he spoke.

"Is there anything else you need before I go?" Shoshi asked, matching his expressionless tone despite the tingle of adrenaline in her veins.

"Not at the moment."

So he'd used her as a prop, to usher out his one-night stand. *What a catch.* She walked back down the hall to the door Lexi had ducked into, which opened into Davin's bedroom. A king-sized bed dominated the space, charcoal sheets twisted from his night. Another angled window lit an alcove with a cozy corner chair. At first glance, no personal items stood out here either. At least the air was free from the heavy, musky scent of sex.

Shoshi turned to the closet he'd described—because of course he'd have more than one. A pile of suits and shirts lay haphazardly tangled in the center compartment. A covered wicker hamper stood below, presumably with the rest of his laundry. Thank goodness Shoshi didn't have to deal with that. She gathered the pile into an empty plastic garment bag, one of a few stuffed into the high shelf, and tied off the open end so nothing would spill out.

As she left, a glance back into the main room revealed Davin on the couch with his tablet, eyes narrowed on whatever he saw, bare feet crossed at the ankles. The stack of files was nowhere in sight.

After a quick lunch, Shoshi settled on her bed with her laptop, turning down her music. One of the few luxuries she continued to allow herself was decent Internet access, so she could hunt for a job and have some connection with the world outside of food service. Now, she pulled up her neglected social media accounts and updated her work information, listing Griffith & Moore but leaving the position field blank. It felt sketchy, but technically it was true, and maybe it would catch the attention of some recruiters.

Almost automatically she pulled up the bookmarked pages with her job search, but there were no new prospects, just some reposts of positions to which she'd already applied. Was it silly to look for a new job so soon after starting this one? Then again, the likelihood of finding something anytime soon was slim to none. And despite its drawbacks, at least this job could be considered a step in the right direction.

Since her new salary would be subject to a different income tax bracket, if she lasted there long enough, a new budget was in order. It was going to be a trade-off of sorts, with her student loans. If Davin did fire her, it would make sense to pay off as little as possible now, and to save as much as she could—assuming he actually made good on his promise to cover her loans. But if he didn't, that would mean paying more in interest down the line.

What would her father do? He had always opposed owing anyone money, but then he also hadn't had much in the way of savings to dip into when he was diagnosed. It would be all about finding the right balance. At least Shoshi could pretend doing this was using her education.

With an Avril Lavigne playlist for company, she worked up three different budgets, including a decadent one that left nothing for savings, just for fun. It assumed she'd quickly develop a social life that required expensive dinners, frequent nights out, and even a long weekend away every couple of months. *Yeah, right.*

She decided on the most sensible version, switched the music to a randomized mix, and nudged the laptop aside. A three-dollar bottle of wine beckoned from her kitchen counter, and she did still have a few of her favorite novels for company. Grocery shopping could wait until tomorrow, and despite Nat being right, clothes shopping would wait until her first paycheck. Then she'd get to buy new slippers, that comforter, and some hair products to help her appear more "professional"—because goodness knew untamed frizz meant a woman couldn't be capable or intelligent.

On that note, Shoshi could use the down time to do her nails, but the polish had a better chance of surviving through at least part of the week if she applied it tomorrow night. And that meant…

She pushed off her bed and walked over to the waiting wine. Bending over to peer into the very back, she riffled through her utensil drawer for a corkscrew. When was the last time she'd needed to open a bottle of wine?

She had just worked the cork loose with an utterly satisfying pop when a soft chime sounded. Shoshi twisted to find the source, then shook her head. Davin must be getting to her. She grabbed a juice glass, which seemed more appropriate than a coffee mug, and poured the Riesling into it.

The iPhone chimed again, unmistakable this time. She took a sip anyway, allowing the crisply sweet wine to bathe her tongue for a couple seconds before swallowing. As the song switched to Christina Perri's *Human*, Shoshi crossed to her bed and dug the device out of her bag.

All the latest message had was a time—less than forty-five minutes from then. Shoshi tapped the bubble so she could see what else Davin had written. The message before had a vaguely familiar address. A new one popped up with a *blip*, instructing her to be ready to take notes.

Shoshi glanced between the phone in one hand and the glass in the other, then down at the sweats she'd changed into after getting home. She sighed and pulled up Davin's schedule, in case she'd forgotten something. But no, there was nothing, today or tomorrow. What could he possibly need her for right now?

Still, this *was* what she had signed up for. Untraditional hours. On call at all times. She tossed the phone on her bed and moved back to the kitchen counter. The gurgle of the wine mocked her as she poured it back in the bottle. She jammed the cork back in, stuck the bottle in the fridge, then got ready to venture outside again.

The address Davin sent her turned out to be the Roaring Serpent, the bar where they'd first met. Shoshi pulled the door open with a *whoosh*. The bar was much busier than the last time she'd been inside, a cheerful buzz filling the space. Happy hour offers dominated a chalkboard behind the bartenders. Shoshi was quickly forced further inside by a smiling couple on their way in.

Davin wasn't anywhere she could see, but she'd made it there a whole four minutes early. Should she text him, let him know she was there? There wasn't really a point. Besides, then he'd probably be late specifically to keep her waiting.

She smoothed her hair back as she approached the bar. The same bartender from the other night glanced her way, but he didn't seem to recognize her. Then again, he'd probably seen hundreds of customers in the ten days since. Or maybe she looked slightly less of a mess this time around. A girl could hope.

People moved in on either side, flagging down the bartender. Shoshi set down the portfolio she'd brought and stared at one of the happy hour fliers by her arm, avoiding his gaze. Who knew how long she'd be here? Although if Davin left, she could still stay for a drink, even if that would dip into her new food budget.

"Shana." Davin's deep voice easily cut through the upbeat chatter.

Shoshi resisted the urge to check the time. He'd put on a suit jacket, though the collar of his shirt lay open like it had this morning. So clearly they weren't meeting with anyone work-related.

Without another word, he walked purposefully away. Shoshi grabbed her portfolio to follow him. How a booth sat empty with the bar so filled was a mystery, but Davin slid in, and Shoshi lowered to the edge of the seat across from him. He drew a stack of blue folders from his soft leather briefcase, setting them to his side. They looked like the files she'd brought him that morning, but then again, so did most of the other ones in his office.

Shoshi opened her portfolio and slipped the pen from its attached elastic holder. A waitress paused by their table and Davin ordered a scotch before they both looked at Shoshi expectantly.

When she hesitated, Davin flipped open one of the files and said, "You may as well get something."

Shoshi smiled at the waitress. If this was going to be her evening, wine wasn't going to cut it. "Patrón on the rocks, please."

The waitress nodded and moved on. Davin considered Shoshi a moment, as if weighing her drink order against whatever he thought he knew about her, then launched into a commentary on one of the startups he was evaluating.

She clicked her pen and began scribbling notes. She may be a bit out of practice, but her professors had definitely prepared her for jotting down fast-paced lectures.

What felt like hours in to Davin's stream of dictation, uninterrupted even by the waitress's smooth refills, a new voice appeared. "Would you help my friend and me settle a bet?"

Shoshi's hand stopped at the arrival of the jean-clad butt now right beside her, and she took the chance to flex her fingers. Davin leaned back against the seat and looked up at the woman, a small curve finding his lips.

"My friend over there," the brunette in a sparkly top continued, gesturing to someone Shoshi couldn't see past the woman's curves, "she says you're drinking bourbon." She leaned toward Davin, bracing her hand on the table almost like Lexi had that morning, which brought her butt even closer to Shoshi, who shifted away. "But I say, you're a scotch kind of guy."

Seriously? The women were welcome to Davin—not like Shoshi wanted him—but what was she, invisible? Wasn't there some kind of code that prevented them from hitting on someone with—even if clearly not *with*—another woman?

Shoshi lifted her untouched second tequila to her lips as Davin and the brunette chatted. She flipped to the start of her notes, going through the comments on startups' weaknesses, suggestions for their further development, and general sketches of personnel suggestions. She'd taken it all down without taking it in. The amount of information Davin kept in his head was astounding.

When the woman walked away, Shoshi followed her path to a striking South Asian woman smiling at Davin. His glass landing on the table drew Shoshi's attention back to her boss.

"You can go," he dismissed.

Resentment crawled along the back of Shoshi's neck. Apparently these notes weren't so urgent after all.

"And take the files and my briefcase," Davin added as the two women came back up to the table.

"This is my friend, Esha," the first woman said.

Shoshi gathered everything up and slid out of the booth. Neither of the women seemed to notice her. But it didn't matter. Shoshi should just be glad they had distracted Davin, giving her the gift of freedom for the rest of the night. With Davin as the only reward for their good deed, the other women were definitely getting the raw end of this deal.

Chapter 13

SUNDAY PASSED WITHOUT A WORD FROM DAVIN. MAYBE he was in church, atoning for his sins. Or maybe the two women from the bar had worn him out. Either way, Shoshi had time to take care of some errands, do her nails, and prep some food for the week in case Davin had her running around, which seemed pretty damn likely.

Monday morning she pulled her hair back in a secure bun—with the help of some new hairpins and argan oil—and even lined her eyes, then slipped her favorite blazer on over an emerald tank top. Besides being the first person at the office to be genuinely nice to her with no ulterior motive in sight, Rick would be an invaluable connection in the finance world. Maybe he could become a reference for her, eventually. The first impression she'd made may not have been the best, but her second had to be. Shoshi even suffered through the biting cold of wearing a skirt and hose in January.

After checking Davin's messages and her email—to which his non-private account now redirected—she took the oh-so-urgent files from this weekend and knocked on Davin's slightly open door to go through a rundown of his schedule for the day.

His eyes zeroed in on her as soon as she came in, skimming her outfit top to bottom, then back up before reaching her face. "I see you've decided to put in some effort," he commented, already looking back at his computer.

Shoshi wasn't going to rise to the bait. She could be professional, even if he wouldn't. "You have a lunch meeting today at twelve thirty with the cofounders of that integrated ad company." The gesture of faith on Davin's part was intriguing, given the tiny size of the company. Even the associates had seemed surprised, from the bits of conversation Shoshi'd picked up on her trips to the break room. What did he see in this company's potential that the rest of them didn't? "And you'd requested a general rundown at four o'clock with the associates. Oh, and a conference call at eight thirty with the partners in New York."

"Move tomorrow's dinner," Davin responded, "I'm getting tired of Mistral. Get me Thai for lunch, by eleven fifteen, and be ready to leave at noon."

Damn it. Would Rick mind an early lunch—or a late one? And what was the point of Davin eating lunch before his *lunch* meeting? Apparently she'd find out. "Did you need me for anything this evening, Mr. Davin?" Shoshi asked. Maybe he'd deign to give her some warning.

Davin fixed those amused pale eyes on her face before letting them trail down and up again, more slowly this time. "Are you offering something, Shana?"

Shoshi's mind stuttered, her cheeks heating as embarrassment coiled in her gut. She swallowed, then strode as purposefully as she could to the cabinets to replace the files. "The curious friends from the bar didn't wear you out?" she retorted with her back to him. She could practically feel his eyes on her, suddenly hyperaware this skirt remained a touch too tight. Though after ten days of healthier eating, she actually had dropped a little of the bloating the crap food had caused.

But she refused to get flustered by his pointed examination. Davin had no sexual interest in her; he just strove to make her as uncomfortable as possible, knowing she wouldn't call him out. It wasn't like she could go to HR and complain about him staring when she couldn't even confirm he was doing it.

"Don't forget to type up and file those notes," Davin added as she slid the drawer closed. "I suppose it's too much to hope for that you already have those done?"

"Right away." Shoshi left without looking at him. She plopped into her chair, head rolling back as she blew out her breath, then reached up to smooth her hair. Sure, she'd dressed mostly for her now cancelled lunch with Rick, but it had also felt nice, like she really had transitioned back to office life.

Until Davin's perusal had made the armor of professionalism feel indecent. Or worse, like she was a fraud who didn't belong in these offices, who would never measure up—and everyone there knew it. Now she felt more like a kid playing dress up. And it wasn't even 8 AM.

"Good morning, Shana," Rick said as he walked in a while later.

"Good morning, Rick." Shoshi ignored the disapproving look Priscilla sent at her casual use of his first name. The office manager had greeted him as "Mr. Mora."

He paused by Shoshi's desk. "Are we still on for today? Oh come on," he added, reading the answer on her face.

A touch of delight spread through her at his faint disappointment. "Mr. Davin needs me at noon for a meeting."

"Ah." Rick slipped his hands into his pockets and nodded. "I have my own meeting before lunch, but I hope we can reschedule." He paused. "You look very nice, by the way."

"As opposed to casual Saturday?" she said with a light chuckle, and immediately kicked herself mentally. She'd never been great at accepting compliments, and his had caught her off guard.

"If I recall, you looked nice then too." Rick's lips tugged into a slanted smile. "So, tomorrow? If Luc's schedule allows."

"I'll let you know as soon as I do."

"Great." His warm brown eyes lingered on her a moment before he continued on to his office.

Shoshi held back a smile, watching over the top of her computer as he disappeared. At least when Rick looked at her, he saw the polished professional she was trying to be.

Just before four, Shoshi trailed Davin to one of the open conference rooms in the main portion of the office suite. Every spot at the main table was filled with employees whose names she hadn't quite pinned down. Sebastian wasn't among them.

Davin took the last remaining seat at the table, at its head of course, and Shoshi dropped into a chair set off diagonally behind him to take notes. He didn't speak much as the others reported to him on their funds' statuses, on potential investments, on companies they thought were worthwhile for his funds as well as some of the smaller ones. Shoshi zoned out as she wrote on autopilot. Each of the associates had almost certainly uploaded all this information to the company's online system. She probably wouldn't even need to type up the notes.

It wasn't until almost an hour in that a name resonated with her mind more actively than note-taking required. As the woman kept pitching SynPro, something tickled the back of Shoshi's memory. She'd heard the name before, or read it before. And something else.

She'd read so many discovery files in the last eight days, not to mention taking in Davin's various comments and notes. To be fair, it didn't really matter. He had probably caught whatever it was her mind was trying to puzzle out, or he would soon. He'd been doing this successfully for years before Shoshi ever entered the picture.

Only when the associate repeated the partners' names did the pieces click. Shoshi waited for Davin to shoot down the woman's proposal. She should have done her research better.

"Sounds good," he said instead. "Start negotiating terms for your fund, for the first round, and we'll see where the idea may fit with some of the others."

"Okay, great." The woman leaned back with a satisfied smile.

"Mr. Davin?" Shoshi ventured as he asked, "What's next?"

The room stilled, over a dozen pairs of eyes training on her before exchanging glances with each other. Davin didn't turn toward her.

"Yes?" The syllable was more than terse, but his decision made no sense, unless he didn't realize…

"I wanted to be sure you knew Brant Carter has headed multiple failed startups in the last few years." The silence grew until it pressed like a weight. Shoshi swallowed but kept going, her eyes trained on the back of Davin's head. "Two Griffith & Moore funds have invested in companies he's been largely involved with in the past, and he's approached you for several of his other ideas, which is possibly why Paul Hyland is being listed as the founder of this—"

Davin's head snapped toward her, and Shoshi shut up. He glared at her a moment then turned back to the other employees. The woman who'd pitched SynPro was scrambling through her notes.

"Why wasn't this in your discovery?" Davin asked.

"Mr. Davin, I—I'm not sure where your assistant is getting this information, and Paul Hyland was involved in the development of two great companies, one of which is poised for a solid buyout in the next month, I assure you—"

"Stop. Hold off and do your research. Vet the rest of the team as well."

The woman nodded stiffly, her glare skewering Shoshi.

"Next," Davin said coolly as the others exchanged a mix of sympathetic and anxious glances, avoiding his gaze—and hers. So much for trying to make friends with her coworkers.

"Look who's making a name for herself." Sebastian headed to the drink rack, smirking at Shoshi as the coffee machine gurgled out her afternoon dose of caffeine. "Angela, for one," he added, "had many names for you yesterday."

Shoshi winced. "I couldn't not say anything."

"Oh, don't worry. I like you better with a backbone."

She chuckled lightly. "Thanks?" She plucked a chocolate from the shared office bowl, unwrapped it, and dropped it into her fresh coffee. It would have been even better with a shot of something, but Shoshi could make do.

Sebastian wandered closer as she stirred. "Want my advice?" he asked smugly. Today's dark-lilac shirt seemed to bring out both his dark skin and his bright smile. Damn, he dressed way better than her.

She fixed him with a mock-stern look, leaning against the counter as she stirred. "How do I know today's not your day in the pool and you won't just sabotage me?"

His smile widened to a grin. "Tell you what, I'll tell you what day I bet on, if you agree to quit that day. Otherwise, you'll just have to risk it."

Shoshi rolled her eyes. "Oh, come on. The pool can't be that big."

"Couple thousand," he said nonchalantly, shrugging.

"Wow, can I get in on that?"

His grin flashed again. "Unfair advantage."

"And it isn't unfair if you and I make a deal?"

One shoulder lifted, and his head tilted to the side as his eyes widened with mock innocence. "Just playing the game. So what'll it be?"

Shoshi made a show of tasting her makeshift mocha, as if there was really something to consider. "Seems to me I should be talking to her, not you."

"No, you should really give her a day or two," commented

another of the associates from yesterday's meeting, joining them in the break room. "If you're talking about Angela, that is."

"Oh, we are," Sebastian confirmed.

The newcomer chose a mug from the cabinet and set the coffee machine going. Turning back to face them, she resettled the pendant that hung tastefully a couple inches below her collarbone, then folded her arms over her ribcage. She wore a navy skirt suit, and her dark hair lay in perfectly styled waves—not even one hair out of place. *Face it, Shosh. Everyone here is better dressed than you.* Even compared to the extra care she'd taken with yesterday's outfit. Filling out her office wardrobe notched a little higher on Shoshi's To Do List.

"Angela will realize you did her a favor," the woman said. "Things would've been much worse if she'd missed the connection and lost money." One shoulder shrugged delicately. "That doesn't mean she isn't pissed."

"Right," Shoshi breathed.

Sebastian and the woman whose name Shoshi still didn't know—could she ask?—exchanged a look. "Listen," he told Shoshi, "a few of us are going for drinks tonight, around seven. You should join us."

The woman dropped her arms to pick up her cappuccino. "Yeah, and hey, if Angela comes, buying her a drink couldn't hurt." She smiled kindly.

"Okay, yeah. That sounds great." Shoshi smiled back. Then reality caught up with her, and she sighed. "Unless Mr. Davin decides he needs me for something," she amended.

"Wouldn't want you to get fired," Sebastian said, the smirk reappearing. "Not today, anyway."

Their coworker shot him a mildly reproachful look but didn't contradict him. "Well, if it works out," she said, heading back to the cubicles.

"Yeah, sure," Shoshi called after her.

Sebastian tipped his vitamin water in lieu of a goodbye and followed the woman out. Shoshi lifted her mug to her lips, taking a moment. Davin might prevent her from going tonight, but she'd been invited, and that was progress. Maybe, despite yesterday's awkwardness, she was starting to fit in.

Chapter 14

R EADY FOR LUNCH, HOTSHOT?”

It took a second to register Rick's smile, Shoshi's mind still on the email she was finishing up, and another second to replay what he'd said. "Hotshot?" she asked.

"I heard you made quite the catch Monday."

"Oh." She shook off the comment. "I got lucky. And I need just a second to finish this, then I'm all yours."

His eyes rounded a bit at her choice of words, and she flushed. But backtracking would only make it worse. Instead Shoshi scanned the email, added a signature, and sent it off.

They'd had to reschedule until Wednesday—Davin had "requested" she work through lunch yesterday, and predictably, he'd also kept her busy late enough that she hadn't been able to join the others for drinks. But today his lunch plans thankfully didn't include her.

A mix of professional and personal anticipation swirled through Shoshi as she stood. Rick was kind, obviously success-ful and intelligent, and he hadn't forgotten about his invitation.

He could have easily brushed her off when she'd had to post-pone—twice. After all, she was just another employee, and it wasn't like she was his only option for company in the office. Still he'd remembered, insisted. Even refilled her coffee mug for her when he passed on his way to the break room. Was he being professional and courteous, or was there something more?

"So how's week one treating you?" Shoshi asked as the elevator descended.

"It's a well-run operation Luc's got here. I'm still getting a feel for it, before I truly dive in or consider any changes."

"Makes sense," Shoshi murmured.

"What about you?" Rick asked, pausing for her to exit into the lobby. "Is it everything you hoped?"

"Hardly," Shoshi scoffed, then froze. Her mouth dropped open, her jaw fighting the command to snap shut. "What I mean is," she redirected haltingly, "this is hopefully going to allow me to transition to something more in line with my education. But nowadays, it's great to have steady work, and I look forward to learning from this position."

Amusement softened the lines of Rick's face as they continued toward the main entryway. "This isn't an interview, you know. Or wait." He stopped. "Did you…?"

"No," Shoshi assured quickly. She knew very well Griffith & Moore didn't have any new openings. "Maybe we should pick a topic besides work," she suggested.

"All right, then." He resumed walking, and Shoshi moved in beside him. "Where are you from?"

"Philadelphia, originally. I moved out here for school, then stuck around." Shoshi murmured a thank you when he held the door for her at a nearby upscale diner. "And you?"

"Chicago, though New York before that for a short while, when I was little, and Spain quite briefly before that."

"What brought you to Boston?"

"The weather," Rick said without a hint of sarcasm.

The start of a laugh sputtered out on Shoshi's lips.

"No, really." He paused as they got settled at a table. "Boston winters have nothing on Chicago's wind chill. And at the time, it was a good promotion. I wasn't tied to staying in Chicago, so here we are."

"Here we are," Shoshi echoed. Something about how he looked at her definitely didn't feel professional, spreading warmth through her. Or maybe she was thawing out from their brief walk outside, since she'd once again worn her skirt. Boston weather might be less bitter than Chicago's—she'd have to take his word for it—but it was still cold.

A waiter came up, and Shoshi skimmed the one-page lunch menu. Rick ordered without hesitation, so she chose the first dish that seemed good and wouldn't be too messy to eat in a semi-professional setting. The waiter repeated their order back at them then disappeared.

"So, what do you enjoy outside of work?" Rick asked, lifting his water glass.

Right, because normal people had hobbies aside from hunting for jobs. Shoshi'd played soccer for a couple years as a kid, and she and Nat had checked out a stand-up/improv festival last summer, but neither one seemed like the kind of answer he was looking for. "You know, Mr. Davin keeps me pretty busy, actually. So did my work before that. I think the only hobby I have left is reading."

"That's a good one to hang on to. It is tough, carving out time while you're still building your career. Important not to forget, though."

"I'll take that under advisement," she said politely.

Laugh lines appeared at the outside edges of his eyes and lips. "Start demanding Luc goes home early for the sake of your social life."

"That'll go over perfectly. I'm sure my social life is his main concern." Shoshi even managed to keep most of the sarcasm out of her voice, so it sounded more like a joke than bitterness.

"Well. Lucky for me we work together, then."

"Why's that?"

A hint of confusion appeared between his eyebrows, but soon smoothed out. "Because you definitely seem worth getting to know."

"Oh, goodness," Shoshi brushed off, unfolding her napkin for an excuse to break eye contact for a moment. "However did I give you that impression?"

Rick watched her without commenting as the waiter set a breadbasket on the table.

Shoshi shot the man a quick "thanks" before he stepped away. "So, what about your family, then?" she asked Rick to revive the conversation. "Are they back in Chicago?"

Work or circumstance kept Rick and Shoshi from crossing paths for the rest of the week, with the exception of his daily "good morning." That, or he was avoiding her after their lunch. Maybe it was that Davin kept her busy, requiring her to go over discovery documents and process negotiated deals or proposed changes. The workload had gone from a measly crawl to a pace that would rival Usain Bolt's, as if Davin was trying to punish her for speaking up Monday. *Joke's on him.* This was precisely the kind of work that could make her new job a real learning opportunity, even if she also had to handle his schedule, and dry cleaning, and at one point grocery shopping—goodness knew why since he never ate at home.

But by Friday, Shoshi had almost survived two whole weeks, and that was worth celebrating. Although Nat hadn't responded to her invitation to go get drinks yet, and Shoshi hadn't seen much of Sebastian for the last few days, either. Maybe he'd lost the pool after all, though the idea that her new coworkers didn't think she'd last even this long rankled.

Of course, since she wasn't going to be paid for at least another week, having no one to go out with might not be the worst thing. On the plus side, she had received her company charge card, so Davin's random demands would no longer push the limits on her credit cards' available balance. And maybe it was wishful thinking, but Priscilla seemed to have stopped sending dagger-filled glares Shoshi's way. Pretty significant progress, considering.

When the phone rang Friday afternoon, Shoshi didn't even look away from her computer as she picked up. "Luc Davin's office."

"Hello."

The soft voice jerked Shoshi's attention away from the screen. She shut her eyes, shaking her head against what she was about to do.

"This is Lucas's mother. Is Lucas available today?"

Shoshi glanced at the time, though she already knew Davin was right in the office behind her and not on any calls. Two in the afternoon. Wasn't that right around when his mom had called last week? "I'm so sorry, Mrs. Davin." Still true. Shoshi swallowed then forced out the rest. "He's in a meeting with our new finance director." What did Rick have to do with the lie? Nothing, but specifics should make it more believable, less hurtful, right? "Can I pass on a message for you?"

"No." The older woman paused before adding, "Thank you, dear."

Shoshi's shoulders dropped at the little click on the line. She set the phone back in the cradle, rubbing the hamsa she'd worn again between her fingers.

The spreadsheet Shoshi'd been working on blurred as she blinked away the memory of Mrs. Davin's disheartened voice in an attempt to focus, only to be drawn back into a roiling mix of fury at Davin and heartache for his mother. The poor woman. Didn't he understand how precious parents were?

Of course not. He didn't seem to appreciate anything at all.

Luc scanned the report that had finally arrived in his private inbox.

No criminal activity, of course, but then the company background check would have caught that. Emancipated at seventeen when her father died, with no close relatives on the radar. *Interesting.*

He skimmed down for the details on the mother— abandoned? Unfit? Addict? Criminal?

Dead. Complications during childbirth. No wonder indignation had burned in Shoshana's eyes and colored her cheeks last week. Luc flicked the nugget of guilt aside onto the gargantuan heap he was used to ignoring.

Her father's death had been slower, following almost a year of illness and expensive treatments. As a high school senior, Shoshana had become an orphan, and absolutely nothing remarkable had followed except her steady academic performance, her focus remaining on her studies and eventually her jobs. She probably hadn't even done the normal overindulging most college kids did, or if she had, never in a way that landed her on anyone's radar. She did maintain a storage unit in Philadelphia, keeping up with payments even when her bank balance dipped precariously low.

The only bad decision even Luc's PI had found was the job she'd taken at Keres Financial, which no one on the outside had predicted imploding.

Still, what was this ridiculous naïveté mixed with righteousness in her?

It wasn't like she'd been sheltered from life's ugliness; she simply clung to the fallacy that everyone deserved the benefit of the doubt. Every moment of disgust, of disappointment, stemmed from expecting better—from him, from everyone. Well, knowing Luc would soon disabuse her of that.

Chapter 15

A LITTLE AFTER SIX, THE INTERCOM LIGHT BLINKED ON Shoshi's office phone. She picked up the handset and jabbed at the button. "Yes, Mr. Davin?"

"Dinner with Aldrich Fuller at seven thirty in Peabody."

Shoshi paused. How was it none of these "extra" dinners ever showed up on his digital calendar? "Did you need me to call a car for you?"

"Have you decided to quit?" came the flat reply.

"Of course not." Apparently it was a good thing Nat wasn't available.

"Be ready to leave in twenty."

He hung up, and Shoshi let the handset fall back into the cradle. Aldrich Fuller wasn't one of the bigger accounts, so she hadn't focused on him. Now she had barely any time to brush up on his history with the firm and the status of the companies in which he'd been investing through them. But at only five million dollars, it didn't make much sense for his account to deserve Davin's personal attention like this. A hundred thousand in annual fees was nothing to sneer at, but it barely registered compared to some of the bigger endowments and portfolios Davin oversaw.

Twenty minutes later, Shoshi knew as much as she could manage. When Davin opened his door, she stood outside it with his coat, ready to go. His gaze skimmed over her in familiar disinterested assessment as he slipped the coat on, then he moved to the elevators. Shoshi rolled her eyes at his back but stepped in behind him.

As usual, they didn't speak while Shoshi drove, though this time Davin stared out the window more than at his tablet. By seven twenty-five, Shoshi pulled into a dark parking lot beside a brick building with no noticeable signs. Was he planning to put her out of her misery with some kind of ritual sacrifice?

She followed him up a few steps to a wooden door embossed with a silver logo. It swung out, revealing a large man in a black tee shirt who looked them over. Davin didn't say a word, but the bouncer or security guy soon stepped back, allowing them to pass into an entryway sectioned off with rich brocaded cloth.

A petite woman in a black outfit that was more straps than dress greeted them.

Oh, no. Davin wouldn't… There hadn't been any tacky neon signs of nude silhouettes outside, but if this place was intended for a wealthy clientele, it would presumably be discreet.

The woman wound past semi-private areas, distinguished by the placement of couches and tables, which were clustered around individual performers or facing the main stage with its three poles—currently unused—and led them up another half flight of stairs to a private room with one other occupant.

"Luc!" The older man didn't get up, leaning back against the burgundy couch, arms spread along its top. His collar was thrown open over a light-blue vest, and if he'd worn a jacket, he'd already discarded it. Hints of silver lay almost like deliberate highlights in the gentle wave of his blond hair. Shoshi's palms itched with the urge to smooth her own hair back, and she hugged her portfolio closer.

"Aldrich," Davin responded. As the hostess hung up their coats, he rounded the table set a fair distance from the couch and lowered to a spot about half a seat away from the other man.

Shoshi dropped to the edge of the angled couch, silently praying that this "gentleman's club" had dedicated rooms for anything involving bodily fluids—and that this wasn't one of them. As Davin and Mr. Fuller exchanged their version of pleasantries, Shoshi dragged her eyes away from the pole on the far end of the table, and the second one on the small private stage in the corner.

Three new women entered. Two wore similar designs made of black straps and carried trays of food and drinks they set out on the table. The third, dressed in a collection of scarves in a rainbow of tones with golden cords wrapped around her breasts, waist, and thighs, walked over to the stage. Bronze skin and black hair enhanced the Middle Eastern look in the low lights, though she could have been tanned and made up to play the part. A light melody with a strong beat flowed through hidden speakers, and the woman began belly dancing on the stage.

Neither man paid any attention. Shoshi offered the dancer a small smile. Despite the unease eating away at her insides, the other woman didn't deserve to be ignored.

"Relax! Come on," Mr. Fuller said, pouring three clear drinks from a mystery carafe. "You both look like you're still at work."

Davin shrugged out of his jacket and undid his tie, leaving the ends trailing over his torso. His eyebrow arched when he caught Shoshi watching him. What was he expecting her to do? She *was* still at work.

"Have a drink." Mr. Fuller reached one of the ceramic cups toward her. "Loosen up."

Shoshi accepted the cup but didn't bring it to her lips.

"You don't need to convince me." Davin picked up the third cup and knocked it back, then cut his eyes at Shoshi.

Hypnotic music filled the air as both men watched her. Shoshi lifted the drink toward them as if making a toast, plastered on her customer service smile, then took a small sip that nevertheless burned its way down. She reached forward to place the cup back on the table, and Fuller's eyes dipped to her bust. Her bra was still in good enough shape that nothing slipped out, but gravity tugged on her top, likely giving him an eyeful. She hadn't exactly been expecting this after-hours "meeting" when she'd gotten dressed this morning. At least she'd slipped her necklace into a secure pocket in her purse, so it hadn't been swinging free like some kind of justification—or neon arrow— for his ogling.

Davin reached out to choose among the finger foods the black-clad women had brought in, his arm coincidentally blocking Fuller's view. Thank G-d for small favors. Stuffing her discomfort into a compact ball in her gut, Shoshi managed to sit up before Davin made his selection. Her fingertips drummed on the well-used portfolio with its fresh notepad.

Fuller's eyes strayed to follow the dancer's undulations. He smushed two of the appetizers into his mouth and knocked back a second drink before asking, "So how's my money doing, Luc?"

"Do you doubt me?"

The man laughed. "No. No, but this is the first time you've brought one of your associates to distract me from your news." His eyes raked over Shoshi again, stilling on her crossed hands. "Does nothing here entice you?" He leaned toward her, all solicitous, and yet his attention slithered like gunk down Shoshi's spine. "The chef here can create anything you like. What's your pleasure?"

Davin leaned back into the couch, tracking Shoshi's reaction but not intervening.

"You know," she said with another forced smile, "I was just so mesmerized by the performance, I hadn't paid any attention to the food."

The satisfied smirk that appeared on Davin's face was the first indication she'd said something wrong.

Fuller gestured, and the dancer made her way from the stage, still jerking her hips rhythmically. Her hand pulled a scarf from one hip, baring evenly tanned skin. She looped it around the closer pole, arching backward before waving her torso up then throwing the scarf in Shoshi's direction. It floated to the floor.

The men laughed at something one of them had said as embarrassment pounded through Shoshi, whooshing in her ears. Who did business like this? Exploiting women, throwing away money, wasting everyone's time...

But wishing "boy's clubs" like this would finally be relegated to a shameful corner of the past where they belonged wouldn't get her anywhere. Shoshi had to survive in *this* reality.

"And that mobile app?" Fuller asked, stuffing another finger food–sized concoction—this one seemed to have tentacles—in between his lips. "The whatchamacallit."

Shoshi flipped open the portfolio and picked up her pen. He was talking about a new version of those drunk-protect apps. This one not only asked you three basic questions to ensure your mind was still working, it then asked you one preset personal question to make sure the person accessing the phone actually was the owner—and if you got it wrong, it took a series of flash-less pictures at one-minute intervals and sent them to a friend until someone with allowed access unlocked the phone or the battery ran out. Of course it let users choose a few contacts to exempt from the lock and an emergency contact for safety.

"Not too bad," Davin replied. "They'll be scaling up soon. We're on track so far." His fingers snatched a mint scarf out of the air.

The dancer was down to a few strategically wrapped bits of fabric. Shoshi's eyes darted from the half-empty plates of food, to the carafe of mystery alcohol, to the nearly blank page of notes. Davin dropped the scarf between them. Challenge sparked in his eyes as he kept talking, as if daring her to walk out.

A freckled redhead in emerald bands brought in a fresh tray with three shallow bowls—of what, Shoshi couldn't make out—and another carafe of alcohol. The pale yellow of the liq-uid suggested this one was wine. A second woman, curvier and with magenta streaks in her hair, laid out napkins, silverware, and the glasses that confirmed Shoshi's suspicion about the wine.

She tried to focus on Davin's rundown of the man's invest-ments, but she'd read these superficial stats before they left the office.

"Ladies first," Fuller interrupted. "Some say Rae's cooking is better than sex. I say they're not having the right kind of sex." His wink was followed by a wheezing guffaw.

Disgust crawled up her throat, and Shoshi barely suppressed a shudder. She set the portfolio aside and accepted a serving of ravioli with red-tinted flecks in the sauce that were probably lobster. TV shows joked that strip clubs offered pretty great food, so their clients would have no need to go anywhere else—like in casinos. Apparently gentlemen's clubs attempted to raise the level on all fronts, to please their wealthier clientele.

With the change of courses came a new dancer as well, this one dressed in booty shorts, a sparkly bra, and a tied-up button-down shirt, all in jewel tones that emphasized her rich brown skin. The music became less melodic, with a harder beat and overtones of guitar. The new dancer swung directly up onto the pole, inverting into an upside-down split. *Damn.* The athleticism was undeniably impressive.

But when the dancer began humping the air, Shoshi stared down at the bowl balanced in her lap. Davin's attention on her was palpable, though the instant she glanced at him, he looked to the dancer, tipping his head back. Shoshi slipped a creamy forkful into her mouth. Whatever else she could say about him, at least Davin kept her well fed.

Shoshi didn't make it home until well after midnight, but even so, the first thing she did was toss her clothes in the hamper—which had lasted pretty well since college, aside from one hole in a side panel—and get into a hot shower. She scrubbed her entire body with soap three times before getting out.

It wasn't that the dancers weren't skilled, they obviously were. And the food had truly been good, if the setting could be ignored. But Fuller had insisted on the men getting side-by-side lap dances for dessert. At least neither had objected to Shoshi excusing herself to the restroom. She'd spent most of the night hoping she would become invisible to Fuller if not to Davin himself, who had clearly brought her only to make her squirm. Otherwise, he could have ordered a car, like he had for Fuller, who'd been well and truly sloshed by the end of the night.

Then again Davin, who'd remained remarkably clear-headed, may have only ordered the car so Shoshi would hear the Manchester address. But it was almost reassuring that this was the same man with the *Playboy* collection—that Davin didn't necessarily have a slew of clients so obsessed with female nudity.

Still, what was he trying to prove? That he could be more despicable than Shoshi could handle? He was underestimating how much she needed this job. And on Monday she'd shown she was better at it than he expected. Why was he so intent on torturing her? He didn't seem to treat other employees this way, and he hadn't had a personal assistant to kick around before.

Maybe that was it—he thought this mistreatment was what assistants were for. It might have nothing to do with her at all. She should try not to take it so personally, even if the way he looked at her—that combination of challenge and defiance and amusement—implied personal was all it was.

Huddling under her covers as she waited for the electric heater to warm her little studio, Shoshi tried to think of anything other than Davin's games.

Next week, she should get her first paycheck, which meant technically she could go shopping tomorrow and charge a new comforter to her card, since the statement closing date would be after the direct deposit went through. Replacing things like a dresser and nightstands could wait. Her system of cardboard boxes worked, and the rack that served as her closet had enough space for the new business clothes she was supposed to buy. Maybe with her new budget, shopping might even be fun.

Chapter 16

HONEST-TO-GOODNESS SUNLIGHT SHONE THROUGH THE window, and Shoshi stretched under the covers, each muscle luxuriating in the comfort of warmth and peace. For once, there was nowhere to rush.

She took a deep breath before picking her phone up from the floor. No missed calls or messages, of course. No one she knew would contact her in the middle of the night. She checked the iPhone also, just in case, but Davin was probably still sleeping off the indulgences of the night before.

After a decadent breakfast of a bagel—a real one from Bruegger's, not a Hannaford multipack—with a fried egg and some turkey bacon, Shoshi sorted her laundry into two loads, layered them back into her hamper, and headed to the laundromat. There was something calming about doing a normal chore on her own behalf, continuing to tidy up her life. Now she had a salary, benefits, a stocked fridge, a totally livable budget, and an employer she wasn't embarrassed to list places like Facebook and LinkedIn. Maybe her superficial connections with Sebastian and Rick counted more as tentative seedlings than solid networking, but it was a start. Now she just had to ensure these steps in the right direction would last. Finding some new wardrobe staples was nearing the top of Shoshi's list, but clean underwear mattered more. And time waiting for her clothes was also time she could spend reading. It was almost leisurely.

When the iPhone buzzed in her hoodie pocket, Shoshi startled, then sighed. At least her clothes were already in the dryer. Whatever Davin wanted, it was going to have to wait until her laundry was done. She kept her thumb in her book to mark the page and pulled out the phone. No new text message showed on the screen.

Shoshi unlocked the device anyway, but the only notification was for new messages in her work email. She must not have noticed the vibrating alert before. How did it turn off? Davin had proven he wouldn't be emailing when he wanted something from her.

Both the dryers with her clothes were still going, so Shoshi tapped the little email envelope. She searched the screen for something like a settings icon, but one of the senders' names jumped out at her. *Rick Mora.* It was probably a work message—to schedule a meeting with Davin, maybe—but she opened it anyway.

Her lips twisted to hide her grin as she skimmed the message. He started with a joke about hoping she was a workaholic since he didn't have another way to reach her and ended with an invitation for drinks. He'd specifically included his cell number. Almost definitely personal.

Shoshi pulled her own phone out of her pocket and typed in a message. She hit END to clear it, then typed in a new one. Definitely better.

Drinks sound great, she sent to the number he'd given her. If he knew who sent the message, that would mean his invitation to her had been unique. The first of the dryers beeped, so Shoshi put both phones and her book away and started folding. Before she'd finished with the first load, her phone buzzed against her hip.

Wonderful. Any chance you're free tonight?

Rico checked his watch and flipped the collar of his coat up against the wind. As people flowed in and out of the bar entrance offset behind him, gusts of warmth puffed against him. He tapped his foot to keep his blood flowing, until he caught sight of Shana coming down the street.

Her hair was down today, simply pinned on one side, unlike how she kept it pulled back at the office. She smiled when she saw him, and Rico's lips curved as well. He stepped toward her, stopping beside the door and opening it as she joined him.

"Thank you," she mouthed, or maybe said, it was a bit too loud to tell.

Shana hovered inside the door, and Rico paused as well until he spotted a half-empty alcove with a free couch. He led the way over then waited for Shana to slip out of her coat and sit down before doing the same.

"It's nice to see you again," he said. "More than just in passing, I mean."

"Likewise." Her smile was more hesitant now, less genuine, like she kept switching between being professional and friendly. Or maybe she was nervous.

He angled his body toward her on the couch. She didn't lean away. "Can I get you a drink?" he offered.

"White wine. Thank you."

"Be right back," Rico murmured and made his way over to the bar. As the bartender poured, he turned to watch Shana. She looked great in jeans and a teal sweater that clung to her curves. Her shoulders slouched a bit as she glanced around the room, her eyes not stopping anywhere. One hand's fingers played with the tips of the others. There was something intriguing yet indecipherable beneath her professional veneer, in addition to her obviously sharp mind. Not many would have caught and remembered the pattern she had in that meeting, not after so little time with the company's files. And of course, she was pretty.

Rico nodded to the bartender as he picked up their drinks then wove around the tables, back to Shana.

A soft smile accompanied her acceptance of the glass. "So how was the rest of your week?"

"Not bad. It's a busy firm, so there's a fair amount of paperwork to process. But the team seems competent."

Her eyes widened a fraction before she glanced away briefly. "Good," she said with a tense smile.

"We're talking about work again," Rico pointed out. "Let's not. You said you moved here for school?"

She hummed in confirmation as she sipped her wine.

"What did you study?" He tasted the cognac he held. It wasn't bad.

Her lips parted before she exhaled and they resettled into another small smile. Each one was slightly different from the last. "Finance." She paused. "I have a master's from Bentley."

Surprise rocked his torso back. No wonder he couldn't reconcile her personality with her position. She didn't have the mannerisms of an executive assistant, of someone who could put anyone at ease, was the consummate professional yet able to fade into the background at the same time as they kept everything running smoothly. Shana didn't fade, and she struggled to suppress her natural reactions for the sake of work. An assertive edge always felt right below the surface. "How did you end up working for Luc?" Rico asked.

"Desperation." She softened the comment with a new, self-deprecating smile. "It's a difficult economy for recent graduates. Davin offered me a steady salary, and the work is at least tangentially related to finance. Plus, he has an impeccable reputation in the industry, and I'm sure anyone interested in venture capitalism could learn a lot from working with him."

The answer was nearly interview-acceptable. "So you're not planning to be at the company for long."

"It would be nice to find a job that actually uses my education," she admitted. "And doesn't require handling someone else's dry cleaning."

He chuckled. "Hang in there."

She tilted her glass in his direction then took a long sip.

"Luc does have a solid reputation, and a superior network. Working with him should definitely help open some doors for you." Rico could help with some introductions, but the personal and professional of their situation was already so muddled. The whole point of tonight was for it to swing more toward personal.

Shana's large, unguarded eyes held his a moment, but not long enough for him to decipher her thoughts. Then she shook her head and set her glass down on a nearby little end table. "We're talking about work again."

He almost contradicted her, but she was right. "So we are. What should we discuss instead?"

She looked blindly away from him as she thought, and a hand brushed the top of her head, resettling the loose curls of her hair. Rico's smile deepened when she refocused on him. "What kinds of books do you like?" she asked.

"I read quite a bit of nonfiction. Biographies, historical analysis, ethics, some philosophy, things like that."

"Oh, have you read *Conversations with RBG*? I've heard it's captivating."

"Not yet." Though perhaps he should add it to his list. "Have you?"

"No, I haven't had a chance. It's in my library queue, though." Her lips pressed together in a disappointed slant. "Lately, I've been reading so sporadically that I've stuck to re-reading old favorites, so I don't have to start from scratch every time."

"I almost feel bad for monopolizing your evening, then."

"No, please." A hint of warmth touched this smile. "Monopolize away."

Rico forced his gaze up from her lips. Their eye contact held, building into a pleasant undertone of awareness. A repeating chime made her turn away, one hand patting her coat before she drew her purse out from beneath it. Rico let the cognac wash away the lingering taste of desire.

She glanced back at him to say, "Sorry. The glamorous life of an executive assistant." Her eyebrows drew together as she read the screen, then her shoulders dropped with her exhale. She slid the phone back in her purse. "I really am sorry, but I have to go."

Rico set his drink aside and stood with her. "Luc needs you on a Saturday night?"

"Davin needs me whenever he feels like it." She shrugged into her coat and her mouth opened as if to say something, but she reconsidered.

"Another time, then." Rico could work around the demands of her job. He might not need to worry much about proving himself, but she was young enough that prioritizing her boss's happiness made sense.

The tension Luc's text had brought on seeped away as Shana tilted her face up to meet Rico's gaze. "I would really like that."

"Good." He reached for his own coat. "Let me walk you out."

Shoshi knocked on Davin's door, but of course there was no answer. She brought out his key—a stray ribbon from the office making it easier to find—and let herself in. The hallway was dark, but light shone from the left corner of his living room. Davin wasn't in view, so Shoshi called out for him.

"Don't forget to take your shoes off," he said from somewhere further in his apartment.

Shoshi rolled her eyes. She'd already been there enough times not to need the reminder. She set her purse and the bag of takeout on the floor so she could pull off her boots, then grabbed the food and walked down the hall.

Davin barely glanced up at her from his spot in the far armchair. She put the bag on his dining table and waited for further instructions. Was this all he needed? Even if he'd already ruined her date—it *had* been a date, right?—she'd rather have the rest of her night free if possible.

"Mr. Davin?"

"Silverware and plates in the kitchen," he said, still focused on his notepad.

Shoshi walked around the wall to the kitchen entrance and pulled open cabinets and drawers until she found silverware and a stack of pale-blue ceramic dinner plates with a darker blue band around the edges. He hadn't said anything about a drink, probably because a decanter and filled tumbler already stood on the coffee table near him.

She brought the place setting to the dining table and took the containers out of their bag like she would have at the office.

"Over here," Davin said when she'd almost finished.

Of course. Shoshi took two trips to carry the dishes and dinner over to the smaller table. At least this time it was early enough that she hadn't had to beg the restaurant to make the order.

When all the food was set out—and it was actually a *lot* of food—Shoshi counted silently to five then said, "Mr. Davin, if you don't need me here, I'd really appreciate having the evening to myself." Could she try to salvage the rest of the night with Rick? Or maybe with a book.

"Not your best move," Davin commented, "reminding me how dispensable you are."

Shoshi clasped her hands together. When he didn't say more, she asked, "Is there something else I can help you with, Mr. Davin?" The question was starting to sound sarcastic to her, but he didn't react to the tone.

He continued writing for a few heartbeats then set the notepad and pen on the end table between his chair and the couch. His eyes found first her then the dinner he'd requested—a mix of sashimi, sushi rolls, and a baked roll slathered in a pale-orange sauce. One of the containers crinkled under his fingers and offered a light pop when he opened it.

"What's going on with the Haward development?" he asked.

Haward? Too bad the iPhone with its access to the company files was safely in her purse in his entryway.

"Might as well sit down," Davin added before she could figure out a way to answer him. "We're going to be here awhile."

Chapter 17

AVIN HADN'T EXAGGERATED. ONCE AGAIN, SHOSHI HAD gotten home after midnight. Most of the time, he had simply been talking through things out loud again, and she could have been replaced by a voice recorder. But once in a while, he'd asked questions about the pieces, how the people fit together, or how the overlap in who was set on which board could be tweaked. He'd mostly ignored her suggestions, but he'd asked. That counted as progress, right?

Better yet, Rick had texted her in the morning and even agreed to come out to Watertown for lunch, which halved her commute. Shoshi beat him to the restaurant, but he soon pulled up in a rideshare. He smiled as he walked toward her, a dark sweater and gray slacks showing underneath his coat.

When he reached her, his hand grazed her arm and he bent down. Shoshi caught up to his air kiss a fraction of a second later, but he lingered for a moment after their greeting. A light scent of vanilla blended with something vaguely foresty clung to him.

"So what are the chances Luc can spare you for the duration of an entire meal?" he teased with a half smile.

"Who knows," Shoshi murmured as they broke apart to head inside. "You should just enjoy me for however long you have me." *Moron.* What a dumb line.

But Rick laughed. "Invaluable advice."

Shoshi covered a yawn as she pulled her chair back from the wooden table. "Sorry."

"Late night?"

She raised her eyebrows and nodded, holding back another yawn.

"Luc do that often?" Rick asked more seriously.

"I've only been there two weeks," Shoshi reminded. Though all told, she'd probably worked close to 150 hours already.

"So far?"

"Yeah. Fairly often." Unless he was busy with better company than work.

They both smiled up at the waitress who brought their menus and poured Shoshi a coffee. Rick ordered some orange juice instead.

"Do you want me to talk to him?" Rick asked when the waitress walked away.

"About what?" The coffee wasn't amazing, but Shoshi gulped down half of it anyway to try and kick-start her brain.

"The way he treats you." Rick rested his forearms on the table, leaning forward.

Shoshi set down the coffee cup. Something about his steady concern hit her harder than it should have, and her inhale stuttered. They were barely acquaintances at this point, yet he cared more about her wellbeing than just about anyone she knew, except for Nat.

"You shouldn't have to be at his beck and call at all times," he continued, "living your life according to his whims."

Shaking off the weird feeling, Shoshi quipped, "That's the job description."

Rick's eyebrows dipped.

"Please, you don't need to say anything," she added more seriously. The situation with Davin was unconventional, to say the least. But there was no need for a third party to get involved—not unless he wrongfully fired her, and then that was a problem for their branch's HR representative. If Rick intervened, Davin could claim he fired her for having an inappropriate relationship with a senior staff member, even if they hadn't actually crossed any lines.

"It wouldn't be a problem," Rick assured.

"No, it would." Shoshi sighed. Rick was trying to be nice, but Davin was *her* problem. "Look, we're already pushing boundaries here. Professionally, you would have no reason to know or care about when Davin needs me."

"And personally?"

Shoshi's lips tugged into a little smile at his confirmation that there was something here, even if only the potential for friendship. "Personally we should keep out of the office. Okay?"

Rick watched her for a prolonged moment but finally nodded. "All right. No more work talk, even if it kills us."

"To shitty bosses everywhere," Nat said a few days later, lifting her margarita in a toast, "giving us not only reasons to drink, but the money to do it."

Laughing, they all clinked their glasses together. Besides Nat and her boyfriend, their small group included Gerardo's coworker Nikesh and his boyfriend, Walt, and Nat's friend Tanisha, whom Shoshi'd met in passing before. Tanisha's boss had apparently been caught snooping through her email account, which had set off a quick round of other terrible boss stories. Shoshi had judiciously stayed quiet. And besides, the whole point of tonight for her was to get away from work. She dipped a chip into the milder of the two salsas on the table and eased the bite of spice with a sip of her own margarita. They'd ordered a pitcher, which was already nearly empty, though Walt and Gerardo had gone for beers instead.

"So, I'm an extrovert, which is my way of saying nosy," Walt joked, leaning forward to reach the spicier salsa. Before he dipped it, his chip waggled between Shoshi and Tanisha. "Are you two seeing anyone?"

"Who has the time?" Tanisha said.

"Uh, kids who are still in college, for one," Walt shot back.

"I'm working on my PhD in neuroendocrinology, thank you very much," Tanisha corrected, though she leaned back with her margarita, not seeming all that offended. She flicked a tight dark curl off the maroon frame of her glasses.

Nat elbowed Shoshi. "You're blushing." She twisted to peer at Shoshi. "Wait, *are* you seeing someone?"

"I… Just the twice," Shoshi said for Nat's ears only, but the rest of their group had fallen quiet to listen in. "It was pretty casual, maybe just a friendly thing."

"The protesting doesn't help," Nikesh teased.

"Yeah, so tell us more," Walt added, resting his chin on his hand.

"There isn't really more to tell." Rick hadn't liked it when a message from Davin interrupted their lunch, but true to his word, he hadn't said anything else about it. He'd pulled her in for a hug as they said goodbye, and she could have sworn his gaze had dropped to her lips. But he hadn't made a move. Now every time he walked past her desk, Shoshi's mind went to his woodsy, fresh-earth scent.

Unfortunately, passing greetings were as close as they'd come that week, Davin requiring her presence at every lunch meeting and late into the night. Somehow he was managing without her tonight, but Rick had his own dinner meeting. Still, Shoshi would be getting her first paycheck tomorrow, so rather than drive herself crazy wondering whether she'd read Rick wrong after all, she was determined to enjoy a night out with Nat and the others.

"Oh, crap," Nat muttered under her breath, setting down her empty glass. She leaned closer to Shoshi. "I forgot to warn you," she said, wincing, "Connor said he might stop by."

There went that plan.

"Hello, all," he said, sauntering up to the table, setting off a round of greetings. He looked exactly the same as she remembered, like the poster child for old money and WASP privilege.

"Here." Nat jumped up. "Babe, give him your chair, and I'll just sit in your lap."

Gerardo spread his arms, emphasizing his empty lap. "Just come sit here."

"Yeah, we're all friends here, right?" Connor stepped in to take Nat's seat. "Shana. Good to see you out and about," he said as if she was infirm, out on a day pass from the hospital. "It's been a while." Connor had been at Bentley with Shoshi, and he'd actually introduced her and Nat in the first place. He'd also been jealous she'd beat him out for the job at Keres—then oh so smug when everything had fallen apart. "Have you found anything yet?" he asked, lips spreading in a false smile that might have seemed concerned if not for the obvious underlying satisfaction.

Behind him, Nat frowned, mouthing, "Sorry." But Shoshi didn't blame her. Connor was a good friend to have, when he thought you were worth befriending. At least the others were distracted by a discussion on the nuances of identity politics in a social media world.

"I'm actually at Griffith & Moore now," Shoshi said, letting him make his own conclusions about her position there.

Connor's expression sobered, and damn, it felt good. Almost even worth the last three weeks of dealing with Davin.

It didn't take long for Connor's features to rearrange into a smile she would have once called genuine. Charm had always come easy to him, and only experience revealed it to be hollow now. "Always knew you'd land on your feet. We should have lunch sometime. Catch up."

With a noncommittal hum, Shoshi stole a few seconds by sipping her drink. She'd bet anything "lunch" with Connor would go pretty much like Davin's lunch meetings: water and barely touched salads. Good thing Shoshi was accustomed to a weird eating schedule. Figuring out which meetings required early lunches delivered to the office was a challenge, but it was getting easier to brush off Davin's frustrated glares. What truly pained her was all that uneaten food being ordered and plated only to be thrown away. But doggie bags were universally considered gauche, and apparently meeting over coffee—or actually *eating* lunch—never crossed anyone's mind.

But none of that was the point right now. "Sure, sounds good," she said. Networking wasn't about liking people, anyway.

"And hey, I could try and introduce you to Luc Davin," Connor said, that smugness filtering back in. "Good to have an in with the higher-ups."

"I didn't realize you knew him." Had they met at a condescending, self-important men's support group?

"Oh." A transparent shrug accompanied the syllable. "We've crossed paths a couple times." Meaning they'd been in the same room once or twice.

Shoshi hadn't asked for this moment, but she also wasn't going to pass it up. "I'll be sure to tell him you said hello." Of course, she'd be doing no such thing.

Catching the thread of their conversation, Walt asked, "Is that the one you went out with?"

A short laugh burst from her lips. "Bite your tongue." There was plenty of tension between them, but none of it was sexual. At least him making a pass at her was one thing she didn't have to worry about. "I just work with him."

"In the same company," Connor corrected. When the table hushed, no one quite calling him out on it—no one ever did— he added, "It's never good to exaggerate."

"You don't say," Shoshi murmured.

"Should we get some nibbles and another round?" Nikesh redirected.

"Good call," Gerardo said. "Let's grab another chair, too."

"Here, take mine," Shoshi offered. She laid some cash on the table to cover her drink and stood. "This was great, but I have an early morning." It was true, but not wasting any more of her time on Connor was an upside. At least Davin paid for the pleasure of patronizing her.

Restlessness skittered under Luc's skin as he scrolled through his email, hardly reading the subject lines. All of it could wait until morning. But it didn't have to. Sipping from the tumbler of amber liquor he'd grabbed before settling in the armchair illuminated by his bedroom window, he thumbed open a message at random. Less than halfway through, he let the phone drop.

He could call Shoshana, invent some ridiculous errand for her with an equally ridiculous deadline. Forward some of these emails and have her deal with them. Contradict himself and insist she did it with his supervision since she lacked the necessary context. Not that that would stop her from powering through. Still, he could disrupt her night, force her to his side for the perverse pleasure that flickered through him with her every resentful or reproachful look.

The shadowed slopes of the woman in Luc's bed stirred, emitting a soft, contented moan. As her eyes found him, she stretched with a knowing smile, arching her back enough to lift her ass and displace the sheet covering her. An exposed nipple pebbled under his gaze. Luc tilted the scotch to his lips.

Indignation sparked deep in her eyes, and she pressed up into a half-seated position, letting the sheet pool at her waist. A hand rose ostensibly to resettle her hair, but mostly to showcase the fullness of her breasts.

Primal satisfaction filled her face as Luc set aside the emptied tumbler and stood. Perhaps a second round would prove more distracting than the first.

Chapter 18

"AND THAT'S WHEN I KNEW SPORTS WEREN'T FOR ME," RICK finished saying with a self-deprecating grin.

Shoshi laughed at the mental picture of him as a child, sliding right past a soccer ball on a muddy field—and into the net.

Rick's hand landed on hers, warm and solid. "This is nice. Thank you for coming with me." They'd spent a few hours Saturday wandering around the MFA before grabbing a late lunch.

Shoshi's laugh faded away into a small smile as her cheeks warmed. "My pleasure," she told him, meaning it. Walking around the museum had been both engaging and leisurely. Rick was funny, sweet, courteous, intelligent, handsome—other than their work situation, he was basically perfect.

A server came by to collect their empty lunch plates, and Rick withdrew his hand, leaning back in his chair. The burgundy sweater he wore brought out the rich undertones in his skin despite the gray outside. "Should we get some coffee?" he asked.

"I thought you didn't drink coffee?" Every time he'd poured some for her at work, he had also picked up a water bottle or juice for himself. Never coffee.

"One cup a day. In the afternoon, usually."

"Oh well, if you're tired…" Shoshi trailed off with a smirk.

"That's it, exactly," he said wryly. "Can't keep up with you without a caffeine boost."

"It's my fault. I shouldn't forget the age difference."

"Oh yeah." Rick's hand came to the left side of his chest. "My poor, aging heart can't take all this excitement." His laugh underscored Shoshi's own chuckle.

But so did the iPhone's chime. She glanced toward the purse hung on her chair. Her ancient cell had well and truly died, so she'd paused her service. She could have replaced the battery, assuming that was the problem again and the poor thing hadn't merely given up. But for now she could use the company smart phone, cutting the monthly bill. She hadn't yet assigned distinct sounds to the three people most likely to contact her, so it could theoretically be Nat texting. But if it was Davin…

"I'm sorry," she told Rick before pulling out the device.

"It's fine," he said, calmly understanding. Then again, he knew Davin.

And sure enough, the big, successful venture capitalist, who had somehow functioned without an assistant just three weeks ago, desperately needed her. To arrange a dinner party? The text was vague, but the message was clear: meet him, now.

"It seems I have to pass on that coffee," Shoshi said.

"Emergency, huh?" Rick commented. His disapproval was evident in the tightening of his lips, but he didn't bring up Davin's overstepping again.

"Thank you, though. This has been fun." Maybe she could pretend she hadn't seen the message and stay for a bit longer?

"Let me walk you out." Rick stood and pulled out his wallet to set some cash on the table.

"Thanks." He'd even refused to let her pay for her ticket to the museum. It might be old-fashioned, or un-feminist, or whatever, but it was also sweet.

They walked to her car in silence, the easy mood of minutes before ruined. Shoshi yelped as she slid on a patch of ice, muscles wrenching to try to keep her upright. Rick's strong grip caught her elbow, saving her from an embarrassing—and painful—fall. Her other hand landed on the front of his shoulder.

"You all right?" he asked as she caught her breath.

She nodded, looking up at his slightly amused expression. "Not funny." But her lips found a mirroring smile.

"Of course not," he said with mock solemnity.

As their humor melted into a softer awareness, Rick bent his head to brush their lips together. The light touch didn't last long. He leaned away, warmth filling his eyes, and Shoshi tilted her chin up. He hesitated the briefest moment before kissing her again, their lips slipping together chastely. Safe, and soft, and nice.

When they pulled back, Rick murmured, "I'm told you have to get to work."

Shoshi sighed, stepping away. She patted her pocket, verifying the iPhone hadn't fallen, and turned back toward her car.

Rick slipped an arm around her shoulders as they walked. "Just in case," he teased, pulling her snugly to his side.

Davin might have first dibs on her time, but he couldn't prevent Shoshi from savoring these little moments.

"You're late," Davin said when Shoshi found him at a booth in the Roaring Serpent. He set down his silverware and nudged away what looked like a half-eaten appetizer combo platter, then tossed his napkin on top.

"Haven't mastered teleportation yet, but I'll work on it," she said, stuffing her sarcasm beneath a thick layer of saccharine deference.

Davin speared her with a look. "Are you going to keep hovering?"

Shoshi shrugged out of her coat and slid into the booth, staying close to the edge of the seat, diagonally offset from him.

"The Something Ventured dinner needs to be salvaged," he said as a waitress switched out his leftovers for a fresh drink. "Priscilla should have emailed you details."

"Oh." Shoshi fished the iPhone out of her pocket. She refreshed the inbox, tuning out his annoyance. "I haven't received anything, but I can call her and get up to speed."

"No." The sharp syllable snapped Shoshi's attention back to him. "Don't call her."

"Uhm… Is everything all right?"

"Didn't realize you were here to gossip," he said tightly.

"I was expressing concern, actually." *Something human beings feel.*

Davin's eyebrow arched in response.

Shoshi stifled a sigh and opened the portfolio she'd thankfully left in her car last night. "What are we aiming for with the Something Ventured dinner?" she asked, using one of the phrases she'd found in a list of tips on dealing with a difficult boss.

Davin remained unimpressed. "You're *aiming* to keep me moderately content with your performance so you can keep your job." He scrolled through something on his phone, reclining against the corner between the bench and the wall.

How did he expect her to do anything when she didn't know what plans had been put in place, who would be attending the dinner, or even what the point of it was? Winning over new investors? Celebrating a milestone of some kind? Arranging introductions? What were the chances he was looking up something helpful on his phone?

Shoshi's fingers brushed skin before she realized she hadn't worn the hamsa today. She'd gone months without it before, but lately she'd had it on more often than not, especially around Davin. She could handle him without it—not like the little hand actually warded off malevolence—but there was something comforting about having this tangible reminder of her father, of his encouragement and support.

Her hand dropped as the waitress paused by their table. "Get you something?" she asked. Her open, helpful expression shone a blinding spotlight on how just minutes around Davin had decimated Shoshi's earlier good mood, replacing it with a strained tension.

"Lemonade, please," she murmured, slumping against the back of the bench to give her wrenched muscles a moment of relief before pulling herself together.

"And a menu," Davin added, despite the perfectly good food that had been cleared away minutes earlier. At least he'd eaten some of it, unlike all those untouched lunch meeting salads. Besides, he was far from alone in the thoughtless waste of food, and if Shoshi said anything, he'd probably start throwing away more just because he could.

She stilled the pen tapping on her notepad and forced herself to meet Davin's gaze. "So this dinner, it's for investors?"

"Some, and some of the entrepreneurs we've worked with." He frowned and picked up his phone again. With a small wave to the menu that landed beside Shoshi, he added, "Order something."

"I'm fine, thank you."

This look was half-reproachful, half-patronizing. "It's rude to take up a table without ordering."

She held the extra-long plastic-coated menu page out to him, but he made no move to take it, so she angled it up between them, rolling her eyes while he couldn't see her. This wasn't worth the fight. And anyway, if he was going to force her to order something, she could get it packed up later to take home. It wasn't like Davin could think any less of her.

After ordering a veggie pasta dish that should still be fine when reheated, Shoshi turned her attention back to the task at hand. "Do you know how far along Priscilla is in planning?"

"She hasn't been shirking her responsibilities," he retorted as if Shoshi'd accused the office manager of something.

"I didn't mean to imply she had," she corrected dutifully. Davin clearly liked the woman, and he was so prickly today, maybe something was truly wrong. Or maybe he enjoyed Shoshi's company as much as she did his. Since she wasn't going to get any answers from him, she pulled up his calendar to search for the dinner. Which was taking place during Davin's trip—in *New York*. Shoshi wouldn't have to go with him, would she?

"Distracted already?"

Her fingers tensed around the phone. "Maybe if we moved to the office, I could find what's been planned."

"Plan's been scrapped."

"What about a guest list? Or at least a head count?"

He ignored her. If the curtness hadn't been his default mode, she might have thought he was actually stressed.

Scrolling through some options online, Shoshi suggested, "A custom trivia event? Or an escape room?"

Davin's disdain spoke for itself. He set his phone aside and downed the rest of his drink.

"A cooking class? Standup comedy?"

"What's next, a magician?" he bit out. "Can you at least pretend to be useful?"

Sure, because whatever was happening was her fault. "Maybe if you gave me *some* information—"

"I don't have time for this," Davin muttered, sliding out of the booth. "Let's go."

Shoshi and the waitress who set down the pasta she'd never wanted both gaped at his retreating back. The waitress collected herself first, offering a bemused, "D'you want your check, then?"

Shoshi sighed. "And a box, please." At least the gooey pasta looked pretty good. She handed her expense card to the waitress, wincing as her muscles pulled. Davin was barely in view on the sidewalk, impatience radiating off him. All she had to do was plan an event with an unknown budget for an unknown number of guests she'd never met to enjoy in a city she'd never been to. And even if she pulled it off, it still wouldn't make the man literally tapping his foot outside happy. Too bad keeping him happy was basically her entire job.

Davin made some final swipes on the third draft of the guest list they had managed to pull together from company files and his memory and passed the sheets to Shoshi. He traded the pen for a fork and chose among the cartons of Chinese food he'd had her order.

Now that she finally had an approximate head count, with some helpful notes on dietary restrictions in the company files, she could get back to figuring out how to entertain them all. "Dinner theater?"

"We aren't actually a hundred," Davin commented, but as the hours had ticked by, the rancor of earlier had ebbed. The slanting grooves above the bridge of his nose hasn't exactly disappeared, but they'd smoothed enough to lose that menacing edge. "Is there a Rangers game that night?"

"Er…" Shoshi did a quick search for the team's schedule. She was getting better at typing on the smart phone. "No. There's a concert, but…" She brought up the VIP details. "It doesn't matter. The suites are too small." She double-checked the guest list, but at least half would have to decline to make renting a suite an option. Splitting a networking event in two didn't seem like a great call. "German beer hall?" she suggested next.

He didn't answer right away, but this silence felt contemplative rather than dismissive.

"Fourteen beers on tap, some appetizer platters, wine options," she read from the description page. "Oh, or you could go without their package deal, and then there's a full menu available."

Davin watched her as if trying to find something to shoot down. His gaze lingered on the hair she hadn't bothered to put up after leaving Rick. But then his chin dipped once, and he said, "Fine. Make it happen. Once it's confirmed, send updated invitations ASAP. Actually, do a mock-up now so I can make sure you don't mess it up."

A thread of satisfaction wound through her relief. There was plenty left to do, but at least she had a clear plan now. "It'll be faster on the computer."

He was already back to tapping on his tablet, so she gathered her notes and went to boot up her desktop. Should she go make some coffee? Or maybe warm up the pasta she'd left in the office fridge? Or there were like eight barely touched cartons back in the conference room with Davin. It wasn't worth going back in there now, but since he'd likely leave the food for her to clean up, maybe Shoshi could pack it up and save a bit on groceries.

Mostly she wanted to get these mock-ups done so she could go home. And take a painkiller. She twisted gently to try and loosen the muscles that had stiffened over the hours of sitting. Keeping an eye on the conference room door, she braced her palms on her desk and bent for a deeper stretch, blowing out her breath to stifle her groan as her muscles protested.

Just as she was settling in to create the digital invitations, a woman strode into the darkened offices, the sharp *clack* of her heels echoing. Shoshi started to stand, but Davin passed by her desk, meeting the woman partway.

He tucked his hand around her waist. "Let's have a drink here first."

His date smiled up at him as if "drink" was code for something even less appropriate. "Wow. Is this *really* your office?" she purred as Davin led her inside.

"Name on the door and everything," he said. The woman's giggle turned into an unambiguous moan.

Shoshi shuddered as she firmly shut his door. When that didn't quite help—or was she imagining things?—she turned on some music. Davin could make her stay to do work she could just as easily have done at home, but he couldn't make her care about his little tryst. And he sure as hell couldn't make her listen.

Chapter 19

*I*T WAS ASTOUNDING HOW LITTLE TIME IT TOOK TO GROW accustomed to a new normal, no matter how exhausting. By the middle of her fourth week, the early mornings and late nights, constantly reshuffling schedules and running errands— it had all become nothing more than Shoshi's everyday reality. Even the utter unpredictability of Davin's demands had somehow gained a sense of stability. And despite his efforts, Davin's loose morality was also starting to fade into the background, like a constant low hum rather than the shocks it used to be.

What did it say about her that she'd become desensitized so quickly?

That she needed this job. Davin goading her didn't change that, though having met Rick did help make it all more tolerable. Her brand new cheery yellow comforter—almost too upbeat to belong in the faded, bare apartment—and the undercurrents of warmth developing between her and Rick were the two bright spots in Shoshi's days. But two was good. Infinitely better than zero.

She opened her middle desk drawer and brought out the pastry she'd saved for herself from this morning's leftovers. The rest had of course gone into the break room, but this was the last raspberry Danish. Sure, cutting out the Dunkin Donuts and Wendy's meals was one of the perks of this job, but that didn't mean she couldn't indulge occasionally. She lifted off the top plate and leaned back with her coffee. Davin was on a conference call, so as long as the light by the used line stayed lit, she should actually have time for a little break.

"You're not listening to me!" a young woman cried at Priscilla, and Shoshi set her mug back down.

"Please, lower your voice," Priscilla said, a warning edge to her tone.

The girl—young enough to still be a teenager—turned, exposing a very pregnant belly. "Luc told me, see?" She waved something in her left hand. "Come see him, any time. I need to talk to him!"

"Mr. Davin is—"

"Unavailable," the girl finished, mocking the office manager's excuse. "He said you'd say that, and he said don't listen. I ain't going nowhere 'til I see Luc." She crossed her arms over her baby bump.

Shoshi nudged aside her untouched pastry and rushed over as Priscilla threatened, "I would rather not have to call security."

"What's going on here?" Shoshi asked.

"You don't scare me!" the teen not-quite-yelled, her intricately braided hair flying as she spun on Shoshi. "I'm here to see Luc, and ain't nobody's gonna stop me. And when he hears—"

Shoshi lifted her hands in a surrendering gesture. "I'm Mr. Davin's assistant. Why don't you come with me?"

Priscilla's expression pinched in disapproval. She'd taken the last couple days off but seemed even surlier today than normal, a hint of purple under her eyes. Shoshi's concern had been coldly rebuffed.

"I ain't going nowhere but to see Luc, and I don't believe none of that 'unavailable' crap."

Shoshi gestured toward Davin's office. "That's my desk over there. It's right outside Mr. Davin's door, but"—Shoshi's hand landed gently on the girl's elbow when she started toward the office—"Ms. Klein was right, he truly is in a meeting. You're more than welcome to wait at my desk until that's done. I promise, you'll be the next person he speaks to."

The girl's eyes flicked over Shoshi's face, her breath huffing out as she weighed the truth in what she was told. A light pink underlay the dark copper of her skin, enhancing the vivid lines of her cheekbones and the pretty turquoise lining her eyes. She was definitely beautiful enough to be Davin's type. And hopefully legal, though she looked awfully young. Whether Davin wanted to or not, he *would* be speaking to her.

"What's your name?" Shoshi asked.

"Kayla," the girl said, resettling the strap of her backpack on her shoulder.

"Why don't you come with me, Kayla." Shoshi walked with her across the executive half of the suite. "Can I get you anything? Some tea, or water, or we have some pastries and snacks in the break room. Or if you're hungry, I can order you something."

Kayla shook her head. Shoshi gestured to her desk chair. The girl dropped her backpack and lowered onto the seat, bracing her weight on her hands first as she navigated her baby bump between the armrests. "No, thanks," she said once seated. "Maybe some water. You sure he's in there?" She twisted the chair around and eyed Davin's closed door.

"Unless he decided to climb out the window, he's in there. Look." Shoshi pointed to the light shining by the button for Line 2. "That light means he's still on his conference call. When that shuts off, I'll make sure he sees you."

Kayla's eyes trained on the desk phone. "Okay." Her fingers played with whatever she had shown Priscilla. It looked like a business card, the edges ragged from being handled.

"You sit tight. I'll go get you that water."

Priscilla glared, muttering something under her breath as Shoshi walked to the break room. She pulled out a couple bottles of water and some string cheese, then set a few pastries on a plate for good measure. Kayla seemed really worked up—anxious. But if Davin was the father of her child, and he'd been avoiding her…

Just when Shoshi thought she'd grown a thick enough skin to deal with his complete disregard for the parade of women she occasionally had to usher out of his apartment, he sunk to new lows.

Shoshi set the plate and bottles in front of the girl, then leaned against her desk, gripping the edge because she couldn't very well go into Davin's office and interrupt this call.

Kayla twisted open a water bottle and drank half of it in one go.

"Are you feeling all right?" Shoshi asked.

"I just need to talk to Luc." Her gaze flicked back to the phone. Despite the cold, she wore ripped jeans, though some tights peeked through, and a tee shirt that looked way too thin.

At least her coat was nice and thick. Could Shoshi ask about the girl's life? There had to be some kind of local nonprofit that offered support for young mothers.

Kayla put the bottle back on the desk, then craned her neck toward the floor. Her breath puffed out as she stopped straining and leaned back in the chair. "I need my backpack."

"Oh, of course." Shoshi bent to scoop it up.

The girl managed to balance the bag on her lap and pulled out some manila folders. Was she serving Davin with some kind of legal papers for child support? Good for her, not letting him off the hook. But that poor baby, if it was stuck with Davin for a father.

Kayla held the folders to her chest and let the backpack drop with a thunk.

"You sure you don't want a pastry? They're really good," Shoshi coaxed.

For the first time, Kayla's lips tugged up into a small smile. "You're hungry, huh?"

"A little," Shoshi admitted. "But I'm fine."

Kayla considered the plate Shoshi'd brought, hugging the folders close. She licked her lips, but then her eyes narrowed. "The light."

Shoshi glanced at the office phone then bent down to pick up Kayla's backpack again. The girl lifted from the chair and slung the bag over one shoulder. Shoshi knocked on Davin's door and cracked it open to verify his call had ended. The room was silent, so she stepped in.

"Mr. Davin, there's someone here to see you."

"If they're not on the schedule, Shana, didn't we cover this? I'm—"

"That's not possible this time, Mr. Davin." Shoshi stepped further into the office so Kayla could follow her.

Davin glanced up from his desk and instantly stood. "Kayla."

"Luc, I kept telling them—"

Davin held one hand up, cutting the girl off. "Hold my calls," he instructed briskly.

Well that was easier than expected. "Of course," Shoshi murmured. "Let me know if you need anything," she added to Kayla before backing out of the room.

Back at her desk, she gulped her cold coffee. The raspberry Danish stared up at her, but the blend of distaste for Davin's behavior and worry for Kayla's welfare gnawed at Shoshi's gut, replacing her hunger. As she moved the chair to its normal position, something caught under the wheel. She pulled a blue plastic band printed with BRIGHTER PROMISE from the floor. It had to have fallen out of Kayla's backpack. Shoshi put it by the phone then downed the rest of her coffee.

Davin had a meeting scheduled with a couple associates in twenty minutes. Would it be presumptuous to push it back? Did it matter? He could be as mad as he wanted, but whatever Kayla needed from him mattered more than a rescheduled meeting. He'd just have to deal. Shoshi shot off a quick message then glanced at the closed office door. Neither Kayla's nor Davin's voice could be heard, which had to be a good sign. Still Shoshi's eyes kept being drawn to the door, as if it would suddenly become transparent.

Had Davin really gotten the girl pregnant and then turned his back? Would he at least be kind to her, or would she face the same predatory derision he so often turned on Shoshi?

Were there other little Davins running around somewhere? Were court-mandated child support payments the reason for his relatively modest one-bedroom apartment?

Shoshi groaned and dropped her head into her hands, fingertips circling over her temples. She had to pull herself together, to stem the torrent of her curiosity, to steel herself against Davin's heartlessness. She couldn't keep getting invested like this only to end up thrown by some new revelation. She was here for the paycheck, the résumé boost, and firsthand experience with venture capital funds—and that was all. From now on, she would keep her emotions out of it.

Luc followed Kayla out of his office, his hand on her back. "The car?" he asked Shoshana, who'd stood when his door opened.

"It's waiting for you downstairs." There was something different about how she looked at him. The disdain, disgust, self-righteous judgment had all disappeared into a blankness, hidden behind a wall. He hadn't expected it to happen this quickly. Who did she think Kayla was?

Not that it mattered, not right now. "Good," he said. "My coat, and cancel the rest of my day."

Shoshana's eyes paused on Kayla, who had calmed down considerably. "Good luck with everything," she told the girl kindly, handing over his coat.

Kayla nodded shyly, shifting the strap of her backpack with one hand as the other curved protectively over her child.

"Let's go," Davin said and led her to the elevator. Kayla's smile dropped, but she didn't argue. She'd come to him for a plan, and now they had to put it into motion. Her baby deserved no less.

Chapter 20

"GOOD AFTERNOON, MRS. DAVIN," SHOSHI SAID AT 2 PM that Friday.

"Hello, dear. Is Lucas available today?" There was no hope in the rote question.

Shoshi understood it now—the depth of Davin's apathy for others left her drained, and she'd only known him a month. His mother… "I'm sorry, Mrs. Davin. He's unavailable. Could I take a message for you?" Shoshi shut her eyes against the already automatic response. Both the people on the line knew it was all a lie.

"Please," Mrs. Davin said for the first time, and Shoshi's eyes snapped open. She picked up a pen. "Tell him Lacey really loved his gift. Used it to make herself a skirt for her party, showed it off to all her friends." A smile had worked itself into the woman's voice. "She's quite the talented little girl."

Little girl? "Of course, Mrs. Davin. I'll be sure to tell him."

"Thank you, dear."

Shoshi let the phone drop softly into its cradle. Who was Lacey, that Davin bought her gift himself? Of course, he might have ordered something for her before Shoshi had started here, or maybe Priscilla had. He'd had Shoshi buy and send some gifts—to certain investors, to their wives, to board presidents. Never anything personal, but she'd thought that was because he had no contact with anyone personal. Nothing but the weekly calls he didn't take.

Did Davin already have a child he'd left behind, absolving himself of the responsibility in any but the most perfunctory way? No wonder he couldn't bring himself to talk to his mother. How could he live with himself?

Oh, look. Anger. So he hadn't completely wiped out her ability to feel, just any expectation of decency on his part. Maybe that was for the best. She would keep her head down and do her job. His personal life, from degenerate debauchery to interpersonal drama, wasn't hers to deal with, despite the pleasure he seemed to get from parading it all in front of her. Shoshi was there to keep his work life running smoothly, and for the sake of her sanity, that had to be it. No matter how often she had to remind herself of that.

A small plate of heart-shaped cookies appeared, hovering above Shoshi's desk. "Rough phone call?"

"What?" She followed the arm holding the pink cookies up until she reached Rick's face. "What are those?"

"Acknowledging holidays is good for company morale," he said with a cheesy smile. "And you look like you could use a morale boost," he added more seriously.

"Gee, thanks." But she smiled anyway and took a cookie. *Hearts.* Valentine's Day was this weekend. She and Rick barely knew each other. What was the protocol here? Ignoring it would have been her play, but that didn't seem like an option now. Or was she reading too much into some cookies? She needed to find time to get Nat's take. "So how are these doing at boosting company morale?"

"Not too bad, though I don't think it's the cookies, necessarily. You'd hope an office full of professionals wouldn't get too worked up over store-bought sugar cookies."

"True. We should really have more to live for." Like men who could make you smile out of nowhere.

"Like these." He lifted his other hand into view. "Homemade double-chocolate brownies," he clarified.

Shoshi sat up a little straighter. "Oh, so the cookies are a decoy, so you don't have to share."

"I can be persuaded. In my office?" His head tilted toward his door.

Shoshi was about to agree when her gaze landed on her top sticky note. "I have to give Davin a message. But I'll be by in a couple minutes?"

"Don't wait too long. No guarantee there'll be any left."

Shoshi shook the smile from her face as he walked off. She got up, grimaced at the gold lettering of Davin's name, and forced a couple deep breaths before knocking.

"What," he said when she stepped in.

"Your mother called."

Predictably, he didn't acknowledge the statement.

"She asked me to tell you that—"

"I don't want to hear it. Anything else?"

"Lacey really enjoyed her gift," Shoshi recited anyway. The least she could do for his mother was pass along the message as promised.

Davin's eyes found her, laser-focused but with a touch of something else. Curiosity? About her, not the message. Like he was weighing her in his mind.

"She made a skirt that was a big hit with her friends."

His square jaw clenched, accentuating the stark, symmetrical angles.

"Who's Lacey?" Shoshi asked in his continued silence.

He simply turned back to his work. "That's none of your concern."

It was exactly what she'd tried to tell herself. Still she couldn't force herself to match his detachment.

"You're dismissed," Luc said coldly, startling Shoshi into motion.

The note crinkled in her fist as she turned her back on his indifference.

When Rico opened the door to her knock, Shana looked even more tense than she had at her desk. "Are you all right?" he asked, shutting the door behind her.

"Davin's getting to me a bit," she said with a small shake of her head. Her hair would have bounced if she hadn't had it slicked back, like she usually did for work.

Rico went to his desk and picked up the plate of brownies Jordyn had set aside for him. "Then I guess you need these more than I do," he joked.

She froze for a second, then chuckled, her shoulders dropping a good inch as she relaxed. "Chocolate solves everything, huh?"

"Try it and see."

Her fingers pinched one of the gooey squares, her other hand cupping to catch the crumbs as she brought the brownie to her mouth. The humor edging her eyes disappeared into a widened surprise. "Wow." She nodded, swallowing. "These are pretty good. Have you tried them?"

"Not yet." Rico smiled, bringing his thumb to the outside edge of her mouth, where a chocolate crumb lingered. Her lips parted as he brushed it away.

"We're at work," she murmured when he cupped her jaw.

With a harsh exhale, Rico nodded and backed away. The rest of the brownie she'd taken stayed cradled in her hands. He set the plate with the others back on his desk. "So I was thinking…"

"Uh-oh." She smiled, then tore off a piece of the brownie and popped it in her mouth.

"How about an early dinner Sunday? At my place," he added. "Restaurants tend to be a mess on the fourteenth." Overpriced *prix fixe* menus, endless clapping at couples getting engaged, and of course the tiny issue of it being impossible to get a reservation anywhere decent at this point.

"That depends. Would one of us be cooking? Because, my kitchen skills are pretty rusty lately."

"I thought more along the lines of ordering in. We could watch a movie, relax." *Get to know each other a bit more intimately.*

A light blush filled her cheeks. "I suppose I could be convinced."

"Here," Rico said, picking up the plate again. "Have another brownie."

She laughed but stepped closer, emitting a sound of protest when he tugged the plate away from her hand. He took advantage of her proximity, bending down to kiss her. Her outstretched hand dropped to his waist as she leaned into him, smiling against his lips.

Shoshi yawned as she searched for a parking spot Sunday. Davin had kept her up until four the night before, claiming they had to make up for time lost during the week. Of course when Shoshi had asked about Kayla, he'd ignored her, as if the words never left her mouth. The hours of taking repetitive notes, acting like a mute sounding board, seemed like he was looking for a way to punish her for overstepping—and he didn't mind wasting his own time to do it.

She had to stop this. It was bad enough she had to spend all those extra hours with Davin outside the office, but he'd started dominating her thoughts other times, too. She had to find a way to disconnect whenever she could.

Once she'd shut off the engine, Shoshi flipped down the sun visor so she could fix her lip gloss. The brush stopped in the middle of her lip when the iPhone chimed. *Relax. It's probably Rick.* She really had to figure out a separate notification sound for Davin.

Shoshi finished painting her lips before finding the phone in her purse.

> Reservation for 2 at Abe & Louie's, 6pm

Right, of course. Because why shouldn't she be able to get reservations an *hour* in advance on Valentine's Day. She sighed, bringing one hand to her eyes before remembering her makeup. *Damn it.* At least she'd only touched the bridge of her nose. Blowing her breath out, Shoshi pulled up the restaurant's site and clicked the reservation link.

What were the chances she could avoid a call altogether?

None. It wasn't exactly a surprise that no tables were available through the online system, but a girl could hope. And now, she could pray as she called.

"Abe and Louie's," a smooth voice answered. The muted bustle of a busy restaurant sounded behind the hostess.

"Hello, I would like to make a reservation for two."

"When would you like to come in?"

"Tonight, at six."

Silence met the statement, not that Shoshi had expected it to be that easy. "Excuse me?" the hostess asked after a moment.

"I know, it sounds absolutely crazy—"

"We are all booked for tonight, and we don't accept reservations on such short notice. I'd be happy to help you with a reservation for…the twenty-eighth?"

"Unfortunately, that doesn't work. I—"

"May I suggest you plan ahead in the future." With that, the line went dead.

Before Shoshi could hit redial, a message from Rick popped up on the screen. Should she go up and continue calling from his place? But then Davin would be intruding on their plans, and she was nervous enough about spending the evening at Rick's and everything that might mean. She would just have to try calling again.

"Abe and Louie's," the voice answered with the exact same inflection.

Shoshi injected extra perkiness into her tone. "Hi. How are you doing?"

"How can I help you?" the hostess asked, the words already threaded with a touch of impatience.

"Have you ever had an unreasonable boss? Because I am having a bit of a situation with mine, and I was really hoping you could—"

The line clicked.

Shoshi's sentence ended as a plea to the air. "Help me out."

She swallowed and shook off her failed attempts, dialing again. This time she aimed for an imperturbable calm. *Fake it 'til you make it.* "Yes, I'm calling on behalf of Luc Davin to confirm a table for two at six."

"Uh…I'm sorry, what was the name?"

"Luc Davin. He'd like his usual table." Shoshi winced at the cheesy line. The restaurant was close enough to his place that him going there regularly wasn't *too* big of a stretch.

The hostess cleared her throat, then whispered something Shoshi couldn't hear. *Come on.* This was what personal assistants did, wasn't it? Dropping names for effect. Her next call may have to include figuring out which celebrity Davin could impersonate.

"Right," the hostess said loudly enough that Shoshi could hear, though it wasn't directed to her. "Ma'am?"

"Yes?"

"We'll have a table for Mr. Davin at six. You said for two?"

Unbelievable. If Davin's name was all it took, why hadn't he called himself? "That's right. Thank you." This time Shoshi hung up without waiting for a reply. Done, she texted to Davin. Enjoy your evening. And leave her out of it.

Hopefully now she could focus on Rick. Dinner, a movie, maybe some cuddling… Maybe more. She hadn't slept with anyone since before Keres Financial had imploded, first because she'd been so busy, then because socializing hadn't really been the priority. It hadn't helped that all the fast food had made her feel gross, and look a little sickly. Overall, she hadn't exactly been in the mood.

But it had been about a month since she started at Griffith & Moore and begun eating healthier. The late nights weren't doing her any favors, but her reflection still looked way better now. More like herself, though that might have something to do with not being surrounded by grill and fryer grease for hours on end. Tonight could be good.

Rick met her at the building's door with a small bouquet of roses. Shoshi's apology for being delayed by Davin died on her lips. "Thank you," she said instead, leaning in for a small hug.

Rick kept his arm around her as he led her to his condo, only letting go to unlock the door. The nearly sterile white hallway of the building opened into a dark entryway, with a stairwell to her right, a closed door in front, and an intricate coat tree in the corner.

"Can I take your coat?" he asked decorously.

Shoshi stripped it off, revealing the asymmetrical surplice top she'd splurged on when buying a few new pieces for work. Rick's eyes dipped for the briefest moment to the cleavage the deep neckline revealed. Underneath, she wore only a basic black bra—she didn't have anything more exciting—but if they got that far, hopefully he wouldn't care about the lingerie.

"After you." Rick gestured up the stairs.

Shoshi went up ahead of him. Was he watching her butt as she climbed? The stairs ended in a parquet floor, opening out into a beautiful space, dining and living areas delineated only with furniture so as not to obstruct the view of the navy yard outside his windows.

Past a simple yet functional corner kitchen to her right stood a dining table, with two settings at an angle to each other. Rick held out one of the chairs for her, and Shoshi murmured her thanks as she lowered into it, sniffing her bouquet one more time before laying it on the table. To be fair, the whole room smelled pretty fantastic from the dinner waiting in covered dishes in his kitchen. At least he'd stuck to his word and ordered in—the white bags pushed to the back of the counters proved that—or else he'd definitely be too good to be true.

"I have something for you," Rick said, slipping an envelope from beside the other place setting.

"Oh, no. You really didn't have to get me anything. I mean, this dinner—"

"It's for both of us," he assured. "And it's more like a job perk. Open the envelope."

Shoshi swallowed her protests and did as he said. Inside were two tickets to the ballet for the following Thursday. Her lips parted in a little *oh*. Could she make plans she might not be able to keep?

"I saw Davin will be in New York," Rick explained, "and the company has box seats for the season." A soft smile touched his lips and brightened his eyes, the sunset's colors caressing the warmth of his skin. "Would you like to go?"

"Yeah, uh, I." Shoshi pressed her lips together against the stammering, counting to five to gather herself. "I would love to."

She'd never actually been to the ballet, but it seemed right up Rick's alley. A sophisticated evening of culture. "I feel bad I didn't bring you a stapler or something," she half joked, setting the tickets aside. Finding him a belated gift slotted into her running To Do list.

"Your company is more than enough," Rick assured politely. "So. You hungry?"

Chapter 21

S HE'S STILL HERE!" A NOW FAMILIAR VOICE PROCLAIMED AS Shoshi refilled her coffee mug.

She turned to face Sebastian's teasing smirk. "And you can tell whoever bet on the next couple days that they're out of luck, since Davin's out of town." His trip to New York could not have come at a better time. A couple of Davin-free days would be unbelievably restorative, even if he did still make her deal with the hotel concierge rather than talking to them himself. Or if, goodness forbid, something went wrong with the Something Ventured event, though she'd handed that off to one of the local executive assistants. But either way, a few phone calls were a small price to pay for three whole evenings she could count on having off.

"You look far too happy for it to be just that," Sebastian commented, pulling something out of the fridge.

Shoshi shrugged. "The rest is not exactly safe for work."

She laughed as his eyebrows shot up. The fridge door stalled, open in his hand. Rather than elaborate, she grabbed a Coke from the drink rack.

When she turned around, Sebastian grimaced. "Death by soda?"

"Don't tell me you're worried for my health." It was almost touching.

He let the fridge door drift shut. "You know they use that stuff to unclog pipes and clean blood off asphalt."

"Don't tell anyone, but that's actually why I grabbed it."

His confusion deepened. "Planning an elaborate murder?"

"What? No, I'm going to pour it down my kitchen sink and hope it does the trick." The bottle was going straight into her bag before she forgot it.

Sebastian nudged a chair back under its table as he crossed to grab his own drink. "So you're just misappropriating work resources for your own benefit."

"Living life on the edge," she said as they left the break room.

"Well maybe with Luc gone, you can finally make it out for happy hour with the rest of us. Unless you're a teetotaler and he's your go-to excuse."

Shoshi grinned. With Davin dominating her time, the associates hadn't bothered to invite her out again before now. Maybe she could finally start getting to know them. "That sounds great. I'll even buy you a drink."

He swung a couple fingers in her direction. "Deal."

"See ya, Sebastian."

Shoshi nodded at Priscilla as she headed back to Davin's office. With him gone, she had time to explore his files more thoroughly, add in the recent notes, maybe streamline his system if necessary. First up, though, was dealing with his desk. Davin usually kept it clear when he left for the day, but he'd either been in a rush or hadn't felt like taking care of it before heading to the train station.

She straightened the papers he'd left, separating out a few envelopes with addresses attached on sticky notes. Normally, he would drop those on her desk so she could mail them, but apparently he'd decided that was too much effort today. Under the papers, he'd left a company checkbook and ledger open. Shoshi started to flip it closed, but a carbon copy of a recent check didn't look quite right.

It was written out for forty grand, but the recipient line was blank. There was a chance he just hadn't pressed hard enough, or maybe he'd filled in the recipient later. Shoshi flipped to the account pages, but there were no more details listed, just *XX* and the amount. And the blankness repeated several times. *Not again.*

But there it was: forty thousand dollars of the company's money, made out to an unknown recipient, about once a month. Everything she could have said about Davin, but she'd never doubted his ethics when it came to his job. Pandering to investors by blurring moral lines, sure, but stealing from the company? Was that an inevitability for anyone who rose to the top in the financial world, or was Shoshi just that lucky in the jobs she was offered? Or just that oblivious.

Should she be giving Davin the benefit of the doubt, or quitting? He didn't seem to have a personal moral compass, but could he really be siphoning off this much money with no one noticing? Surely his expenses were accountable to someone, if only for tax purposes.

Idiot. If anyone would know what these checks were for, whether they were legitimate, it would be Rick. But could that be what happened to the last finance director—had they gotten fired before they could discover this misuse of company funds? Would Rick know about these payments yet, even if they were legitimate? It took time to go through a company's records. Plus, he'd be relying on his subordinates, who might be getting kick-backs to hide the discrepancies.

Stop it, Shoshi. Even if Davin was doing something fishy, that didn't mean any of her other coworkers were involved. And if he was embezzling funds…

Then he wouldn't have been so careless. Every action of his was meticulous, intentional. Manipulative and despicable, sure, but in control.

Shoshi uncurled her fingers and tried to rub away the gouged nail marks in her palm. She wiped away the touch of perspiration from her upper lip then scrubbed her palms on her slacks before shutting the ledger and slipping it into Davin's desk drawer.

She filed the papers from his desk, nearly crumpling them in the process. She was so jittery, the last thing she needed was coffee, but still she picked up her mug and took a bracing sip. Could she ask Rick about this? If he didn't know already, he could look into it, maybe check with senior company partners in New York.

The same senior partners Davin was meeting with now. If this was about siphoning off company money, and it went higher than Davin…

Then at least Shoshi had advance warning this time. If she could figure out what was really going on, maybe she could avoid the worst of the fallout. She wouldn't let Davin destroy what was left of her future.

Heart still pounding in an unsteady rapid beat, Shoshi strode out of his office and over to Rick's. There was no response to her knock.

She waited a moment and tried again. Silence. All the questions roiling in her gut would have to wait.

Shoshi met Rick for a late dinner as planned, exchanging air kisses with him before she sat down. A waiter appeared almost instantly, asking what she would like to drink. Fingers tapping out her jitteriness on her thigh, she ordered then turned to Rick. "How was your day?"

"It was good, productive. Still a lot to comb through, but it looks like company records are pretty accurate, well kept."

"Good." She forced a smile.

"Better now, of course. Ending the day with you, and with no unforeseen interruptions." He sat back, relaxing in the chair.

"That's sweet," she said. And it was. Rick was expecting a Davin-free evening, which was what she wanted, too. They'd agreed not to discuss work things during their time together, and that was what she should try to do despite the apprehensive dread that had only coiled tighter over the last few hours. "So everything's on the up and up?" she prodded. It was close enough to what they had been talking about.

The waiter reappearing with her drink prevented Rick from answering. "Are you ready to order?" the man asked.

Rick looked to her, and Shoshi nodded. "Go ahead," she said, quickly flipping open the maroon folder that held the menu. She skimmed the list of entrées and settled on veggie lasagna. As the waiter moved on, she tasted her pomegranate martini, but even that didn't help her relax. "So, good week so far," she repeated.

"Yes, it is. How was your day? Luc get off okay?"

She hummed in the affirmative. "He should be occupied with a dinner meeting for most of the night." He was with the other execs, so he shouldn't need her for anything. Though he was still stuck in her head. So much for a Davin-free night.

"Good," Rick said, nodding. After a pause, he added, "So I picked up that Ginsburg book."

"Oh, yeah? How is it?" Their conversation was stilted, but it was her fault. She tried to focus in on what Rick was saying, but her mind kept slipping back to what she'd seen, and she had to replay his last words to come up with decent replies.

"Are you all right?" he asked eventually, seeing through her lackluster responses.

An affirmation died on her lips and Shoshi sighed. It wouldn't be fair to drag him into whatever she'd found, but it was probably worse to lie, right? "I found out something, about Davin."

Rick's silverware clinked against the edge of his plate as he set it down. "I thought you didn't want me getting involved."

"I don't," she said quickly, also putting down her fork. "But it's about company finances, and I don't know who else to discuss this with."

"Why not talk to Davin?"

"Because accusing your boss of embezzlement isn't a great career move." The words rushed out far ahead of her brain, and Shoshi winced. *Embezzlement* wasn't a word to toss around in the finance world.

Rick's expression soured and he straightened in his seat, the authority of his position radiating off him. "What exactly did you find?"

"Are you sure you want to know?"

"At this point, I don't think either of us has much choice." He didn't look happy about it.

Shoshi took a big sip of her martini, then replaced the glass carefully on the table. Was she making a mistake, confiding in Rick? Given what she'd found, *was* there any real choice?

"Shana," Rick said firmly.

The little stones in the hamsa pressed into the pad of her fingertip before she registered she was clutching the charm. Shoshi forced her hand back into her lap. "I was putting away his company ledger, he'd left it open on his desk." She paused, swallowing, but Rick watched her steadily. "Every month, there's a recipient-less check for forty grand, from a company account. And I just need to know he's not doing anything illegal."

"Illegal?" All the severity dropped from Rick's posture. "Shana, those checks are for charity."

Shoshi shook her head as the word registered. He couldn't possibly have said what she thought she'd heard. "Charity?"

"Yes. Luc personally oversees our office's charitable giving. Maybe I shouldn't be telling you this, but some of the staff are convinced the account actually comes from Luc's salary, or rather, that he negotiated a minimum amount for the fund in exchange for a reduced salary." Rick sat back as humor edged his expression. "That would be smart, really, saving the company a bit on employment taxes. The charities would end up receiving a bit more, too. And since the donation is officially made by the firm, it would be another tax break for them. But regardless, that's nothing more than a rumor."

"Nearly half a million dollars annually in a charity fund at his discretion," Shoshi repeated, trying to sort through the information.

"Around that. I haven't finished going through this year's return." Entirely unperturbed, Rick resumed eating. He seemed so relaxed now that the payments had been explained, but the whole thing made no sense.

"And people think it's Davin's salary, that he's earning so much he would give that amount away?"

"Their theory is that half comes from his compensation and the rest is a company match, part of the overall charitable giving plan. But Shana, it's nothing more than office gossip."

Even if half were to be Griffith & Moore's contribution, that meant people believed Davin was personally donating something like two hundred and forty thousand a year. Had he encouraged the rumor—or even started it—so people would admire his philanthropy? Even so, why would he put in the work of overseeing the donations? "Which charity?" Shoshi asked. Was it a bizarrely elaborate scheme to line his own pockets through the front of a false nonprofit?

"Charities," Rick corrected, washing his veal down with a sip of wine. "There are many, most focused on helping at-risk teens." He caught sight of Shoshi's confusion and set down the glass. "Look, I know he hasn't been the best boss. He's demanding, and fairly unreasonable in how he treats you, no question. But those checks aren't anything inappropriate. Those payments are entirely sanctioned."

"Okay. Good." Shoshi shot him the best smile she could manage and downed the rest of her drink.

"This really got to you." A more personal concern filled his eyes—not about his job or the company, but about her.

The sucking pit of anxiety that had been growing in Shoshi's stomach since she'd seen the checkbook let up a bit. "My first job after grad school was at Keres Financial," she explained.

Surprise blended with understanding to replace Rick's concern. Everyone in the finance world knew what happened there.

"I guess I'm just on edge." Shoshi slid another forkful of lasagna into her mouth. Maybe she really had overreacted. Davin encouraging a rumor to feed his ego wasn't exactly illegal. Perhaps overseeing the charitable giving of the Boston office would have been a part of his job in any case.

Shoshi counted as she took a calming breath, then another. She should have been enjoying her rare evening off, and being here with Rick. Instead, Davin spiraled through her thoughts, perplexing and aggravating. Unsettling. Which had to be exactly what he'd wanted when he'd left the ledger in the open—to throw her off even in his absence.

But that was the important part: Davin *wasn't* here. He and his demands would be back all too soon, and Shoshi should be taking advantage of the break while she could. Everything Davin-related would have to wait.

Chapter 22

IT DIDN'T WAIT LONG. THE FIRST THING SHOSHI DID WHEN she got back to work in the morning was search for any record of charities acknowledging donations from Davin or from Griffith & Moore. There were a few sizeable donations, including to the Boston ballet, the New York Philharmonic, some more in L.A. and Chicago. The company apparently sponsored the arts in each of its cities. But absolutely nothing linked either Davin or the company to any group supporting underprivileged youth.

It didn't make sense. Sure, plenty of donors were lumped together under "Anonymous," but wouldn't Davin *want* the public image boost? Maybe Rick was wrong, and the money actually went to the arts. But he'd have access to the receipts.

Receipts can be faked. Shoshi shrugged off the niggling doubt. Between his salary and a portion of carried interest, Davin's annual compensation had to be pretty significant. But lavish luxury didn't seem to be his style, based on his apartment. Sure, it was nice—really nice—but even Rick's was bigger, with two more bedrooms, and it had to be more expensive as a penthouse, not to mention his rooftop access. Davin could hypothetically be hoarding the money somewhere, but there was no evidence of anything like that. There was no real reason to assume he was stealing.

No real reason to believe the rumor, either. Why would anyone give up so much of their salary for that kind of arrangement? Sure, as Rick said, that meant the charities would get something like twenty thousand more—and the company would be easy to convince, with the extra tax break such an arrangement would provide on money they'd be spending anyway. But there was no such benefit for Davin. So what, people thought he just didn't want the money?

Somehow that would make his abandonment of Lacey—and maybe Kayla and her child?—even worse. Though he hadn't *entirely* abandoned Lacey, if he still sent her birthday gifts. And he had spoken with Kayla. The whole thing could be a trick to lower his child support obligations, maybe. If the rumor were true.

Shoshi sighed and opened her desk's top drawer. All the questions kept spinning around her mind in an endless, inescapable cycle to nowhere. Meanwhile, she still had work to do. As she took out the file she was supposed to be dealing with, something snagged on her fingers. She pulled out a blue rubber bracelet with BRIGHTER PROMISE printed on it. Shoshi had forgotten to return it to Kayla when Davin rushed the girl out of the office.

A local charity's website was the first search result, its home page a menu over a slideshow of photos. Best-case scenario, Kayla worked at the nonprofit, and Davin had donated to them on behalf of the company. It couldn't be that he used the charity fund to meet and take advantage of underprivileged and under-age girls. Everything bad that could be said about him, but he wasn't *that* depraved. He couldn't be.

Still, the knot in Shoshi's stomach tangled in an expanding mass as her mind flip-flopped between suspicion and logic. Was she being naïve, believing there were lines Davin wouldn't cross?

The photo on-screen switched to one of Kayla before she was showing, with a group of other teens, then to a shot of some playing basketball on a court with brightly painted lines and solid backboards.

Maybe she could call the charity, ask about donations from Griffith & Moore. Shoshi moved the cursor to the Contact link as the photo shifted again. To Davin, holding a basketball and surrounded by sweaty teens. He was even smiling—genuinely smiling, not in that predatory, calculatingly amused way of his. This smile transformed him into someone kind and approachable. Captivating. Shoshi would have kept staring, but the photo moved on, back to the first shot.

She clicked to find the phone number, then dialed on her office phone.

"Brighter Promise, how may I help you?"

"Hello. I'm"—What? What was she doing?—"calling on behalf of Mr. Luc Davin."

"Oh, is this about Sunday? I hope he can still make it, the kids are really looking forward to it."

Was this what he did on Sundays, then? "He just wanted me to confirm the details," Shoshi lied. "Address, time, you know."

"Sure. Uh, of course." The woman on the other end of the line sounded wary, but that didn't stop her from adding, "The location is the same as last week, our new center, and the kids will be there starting at ten, though of course no one expects Luc to be there the entire day. The artists will be directing the mural's progress, and there will be plenty to keep everyone busy. But, between us?"

"Of course," Shoshi murmured.

"There's a surprise planned, to thank Luc for everything he's done. The older kids have been planning it for weeks now. He will be able to make it, won't he?"

Shoshi's bemused reflection stared back at her from the computer screen that had gone black as they talked. "I'm sure he wouldn't miss it," she said, entirely unsure of any such thing. They were talking about the same person, right?

"Are you sure you don't want to come to my place for a nightcap?" Rico asked Thursday night as they rose from their seats after the lights came up.

Shana looked beautiful tonight, in a simple floor-length dress, and she'd been riveted by the performance, her eyes glued to the stage. They'd have to take advantage of the company seats again.

"It's getting late," she said, regret obvious on her face.

"More reason to come with me. My place is closer to work." And it was nice having her around, even if she had been oddly distracted the last few days. Though the ballet seemed to shake her out of it.

"Davin's back tomorrow, and I can't exactly show up to work in this." She gestured from her bust down to the floor, and Rico's gaze followed, tracing her curves in the navy gown.

"True." He looped his hands at her waist, pulling her closer as the seats around them emptied. "You should leave some things at my place, so we can avoid this problem."

Her eyes widened, and she leaned back slightly. They hadn't known each other for long, but he had the space, and having her stay once in a while would be nice. He wasn't suggesting she move in or anything that drastic, but there was also no point in waiting, playing the dating game.

"That's quite the offer," she said after a moment, hands resting lightly on his upper arms.

"It will be tough to find space in my closets," Rico teased, and she smiled. He bent down for a soft kiss, then asked, "Would you like me to take you home?"

"I'm the one with the car," she reminded.

"True." It was odd that she never invited him over, but maybe she felt uncomfortable about the likely disparity in their apartments. Silly, since unlike him she was at the very beginning of her career, but understandable. Or maybe she had roommates who would mind. "Guess I'll have to settle for walking you to your car."

She chuckled, stepping away. "Back to work?" They had walked to dinner and to the ballet, so her car was still in the garage.

"We just can't get away from it." He followed her to the coat check line.

"Work treated us pretty well tonight, don't you think?" she asked over her shoulder, the flirty heat in her eyes going right to his gut.

Shame they wouldn't be spending the rest of the night together, but Rico nodded. "Definitely can't complain."

Chapter 23

SOMETHING HAD CHANGED WHILE LUC WAS IN NEW YORK. The impassive composure that had signified Shoshana's overwhelming disgust with him had eroded, but not merely into her earlier censure. Something else filled her eyes now when she looked at him. The exact opposite of why he'd hired her.

She still couldn't prevent a reaction when she disapproved of something, lips tightening, shoulders stiffening, the furling and unfurling of a fist. But it was different now. Like a schoolteacher with a promising if unruly pupil. Like she saw potential for better and expected more, not in general anymore, but specifically from *him*.

Where had that come from?

He'd thought she had finally come to see him for who he truly was, no more of that bullshit of searching for redeeming qualities, of remaining convinced there had to be more to him. But that was how she looked at him now, like she'd been shown proof of something that definitely wasn't there.

Luc was irredeemable.

$\diamond \quad \diamond \quad \diamond$

Was Davin different, or was she just seeing him differently? He'd always gotten a perverse pleasure from baiting her, but ever since he'd returned from New York, he seemed to try even harder. Changing his mind four times in one day about the location for a dinner meeting; exaggerated indifference toward the endless parade of young, beautiful women in his bed; and enough take-out food to feed a family despite the groceries he insisted she keep stocked in his fridge. She still hadn't learned who Lacey was, and he still hadn't spoken to his mother. When Shoshi asked how Kayla was doing, he'd once again implied she was more interested in gossip than in her work.

But something about his behavior now seemed almost desperate for her disapproval. Had that always been the case?

Of course, there was no guarantee it was the case now. She could be reading into it, trying to reconcile the man who gave countless hours of his time to charity—and possibly hundreds of thousands of dollars, crazy as that sounded—with the one whose demands and derision dominated her days. Was one nothing more than an act? And which one?

She hadn't brought Davin up with Rick again, though he hadn't been thrilled when Davin summoned her in the middle of the night—from Rick's bed. Shoshi herself hadn't been thrilled to chauffeur two tipsy women from his apartment to their own, with a stop for milkshakes and fries, of course. But it all seemed a bit for show. Not that Davin didn't enjoy it just as much, probably, either way.

At least he'd started to ask for her interpretation of discovery documents and sometimes even her assessment of the companies he was considering. And otherwise she tried to fade into the background, like a good executive assistant was supposed to.

When Davin requested last-minute reservations again on Wednesday night, Shoshi breathed a quiet sigh of relief. If he was busy with a dinner date—even if she had to deal with the morning-after cleanup of his one-night stand—that meant she should be free to enjoy Nat's birthday party. *Enjoy* might be pushing it, of course, since the only people she'd really know there were Nat and her boyfriend, and maybe Tanisha and Nikesh, who both seemed nice enough.

And Rick would be there. It wasn't clear how he'd feel about being surrounded by twenty-somethings drinking and dancing the night away, but he'd said he wanted to go.

At seven, Shoshi poked her head in to remind Davin of his waiting reservation. The restaurant wasn't far, maybe a ten-minute walk, but even if he wanted her to drive him, she would have plenty of time to get back, change, and meet Rick before heading to Nat's. The present she'd picked up and wrapped—how *nice* was it to be able to afford a real gift for someone?—waited in her trunk.

Davin nodded. His last meeting had been at lunch, so he sat with his tie and jacket off, his collar unbuttoned. She'd seen him like this many times, but usually at his apartment. Somehow the look was more striking in the confines of his office. Even his hair was a tad mussed. Not that he looked *bad*, just a touch more disheveled than usual. Had something gone wrong?

Worse, was she starting to feel sorry for him—the man who, no matter how good he might be to other people, unquestionably derived pleasure from torturing her?

"You're too nice for your own good," Shoshi's father had chided sometimes. She did have a bad habit of putting other people's needs first, like spending hours helping a friend with a complex diorama for class then pulling an all-nighter to get her own work done. "Being kind is a great strength," her dad had said, gripping her hand from his hospital bed. "But don't let others walk all over you when I'm not there to stop them."

"Lose your favorite pen?" Davin asked when he came out of his office a few minutes later.

Shoshi swallowed, blinking away the faint moisture in her eyes, and forced the pain of the memory from her expression. "Did you need anything else tonight, Mr. Davin?" she asked as she went to get his coat. He had of course smoothed his hair and replaced the jacket and tie, once again flawless in his suit in a way Shoshi still never quite managed with her own clothes. His pale eyes skimming her head to toe seemed to echo the sentiment.

"Taylor Barker and Annemarie Oberto are coming in tomorrow morning. Make sure you have—"

"Two mochas and a latte," Shoshi finished for him, nodding. She'd asked Annemarie's assistant, so she could be prepared.

Davin crooked one eyebrow, a corner of his lips curving up almost imperceptibly. Something inscrutable filtered into his eyes—respect, maybe?—but then he blinked and turned away, not finding anything worth his interest. Then again, the less interesting he found Shoshi, the better.

Rico smiled as Shana approached him with two bottles of beer. He'd found a discreet spot on a couch at her friend's place, staying out of most of the revelry. Usually he forgot how much younger Shana was, not that it was a problem. Having young company kept you young, and it wasn't like she couldn't keep up with him when they talked.

"You're bored, aren't you," she not-quite-asked, lowering beside him.

He accepted one of the beers—a nice local ale—and took a sip. Per Shana's recommendation, he'd left his tie, vest, and jacket in the car, but he still stood out among her friends, most of whom wore jeans or even leggings. Even Shana had changed. "Are you having a good time?" he asked instead of answering her question.

She shrugged, leaning back against the couch. Rico put an arm around her shoulders, pulling her close. She instantly brushed her hair to the other side, away from his face. "It's a little odd, seeing some people from my past. Otherwise I don't really know anyone here besides you and Nat."

"Are you saying we should get out of here?"

Her chuckle rubbed against his torso, inaudible with the music pulsing through the air. "We have to wait for the cake, at least." She looked up at him. "Unless you really want to leave?"

"No, it's fine. You should have fun with your friends." It was one night, and Rico didn't mind just relaxing.

"I want you to have fun too," Shana was saying as her friend came up and tugged on her hand.

"Let's dance," half yelled the woman in a mini skirt with a "birthday girl" sash across her chest.

Shana looked back at him but let Natalia pull her away into a group of women bobbing along to the beat of the music. Her movements were smaller, more restrained than her friends', as if she was just humoring them, and she kept glancing his way. For better or worse, she didn't belong there any more than Rico did.

Sure enough, she broke away after a few minutes, her laugh fading into a small smile as she joined him back on the couch.

"Are *you* having fun?" he asked again.

"It's Nat's birthday. It's about how I expected." She tipped her head back, tilting the beer to her lips, exposing the smooth line of her neck. "What?" she asked when she caught him watching her. She started to laugh, but then her eyebrows drew together.

"You okay?" Rico asked.

She nodded but pulled her bag from behind her, digging through it. Her lips pursed when she slipped out her phone. "Looks like you get to leave after all," she tried to joke.

Luc? Really? Even excluding standard work hours, the man spent more time with Shana than even Rico did. "What would happen if you didn't go?" he asked. "If you hadn't checked your phone?"

"He would have a valid reason for firing me."

This was getting ridiculous. Unfortunately, Rico had agreed to stay out of it. He understood paying your dues, and Luc didn't seem unreasonable in anything other than his treatment of Shana. But she went running whenever he called. It might be good for her to keep him waiting for once. "What about the cake?" Rico asked.

Her cheeks tensed, but she didn't rise to the bait. "I have to go find Nat. Do you want a ride into the city, or are you having just too much fun to leave?"

"I can pull myself away," he assured.

She leaned in for a quick kiss before getting up to say her goodbyes. Rico rose too and wound his way amid clusters of bodies toward the door.

"Are you kidding, Shosh?" a woman's voice asked from the dining room side of the entryway.

"I'm sorry, Nat," Shana answered. "It's work. I don't have a choice."

"It's always work, lately. Whatever. Guess I should be glad you unchained yourself from your boss long enough to be here at all. However does he manage when you're not there to kiss his ass?"

"Happy birthday, Nat," Shana said, calm despite the resentment in her friend's voice.

Did Luc realize he was jeopardizing her relationships?

Rico waited by the door for Shana to join him. She shot him a wan smile, then led the way back to her car.

"So, you've been hiding something from me," Rico said to lighten the mood.

She shot him an alarmed glance.

"Your nickname." Whatever her friend had called her.

"Oh." Shana shook her head, looking back to the street. "My full name is Shoshana. I shorten it, for work, since we have to deal with people from all over. This way they're not..." She paused, searching for the words. "Taken aback, by how Jewish it is."

"You're Jewish?" Should he have known that? He hadn't thought about it much, but he'd mostly assumed she was some flavor of Christian. With her dark features and wavy hair, she could even pass for Hispanic, at first glance.

She nodded, pausing to look at him. "Why?"

Rico stopped on the sidewalk beside her. "No, I... You know, I do the same thing?" he redirected. "My full name is Ricardo." But a whitewashed name had seemed easier for everyone to trust, not to mention spell and pronounce, back since grade school.

Her breath puffed into the freezing air as she chuckled. "Really? So what do your friends call you?"

"Rico." Though really, only his family called him that. "Rick's fine too. I'm used to it."

She hummed her acknowledgment. "I wonder what else we have in common."

Rico laced their fingers together, their gloves making it a bit more awkward. "A fondness for spending time together, I hope." She smiled, squeezing his hand, and he bent down for a slow kiss that turned the air around them foggy.

When they pulled back, he asked, "Are you sure you have to go?"

Her reddened lips parted, and she sighed, looking away with a nod. "Yeah. The boss man awaits."

Chapter 24

OUTSIDE DAVIN'S APARTMENT, SHOSHI TRANSFERRED THE takeout he'd demanded—hadn't he *just* been at dinner?—to her other hand to pull out the key. She opened the door, set the food down, and bent to unzip her boots.

"Oh," came a surprised woman's voice, followed by a little giggle.

Shoshi straightened, leaving her boots partially undone.

Dressed only in an oversized tee shirt that drooped off one shoulder, and hopefully underwear, the redhead stumbled a little, catching the hallway wall not to fall. "I thought Luc was kidding." She giggled again.

Davin came out from his bedroom, smirking at Shoshi. His shirt was unbuttoned, but he wore his slacks—thank G-d. Still…

"Why am I here, Mr. Davin?" Shoshi asked. At least he usually had the pretext of work, thin as it sometimes was.

"Raine's doesn't deliver." He said it flippantly, as if his desire for specifically their food was reason enough to pull her away from the scraps of a life she was trying to fit together around his demands.

Shoshi picked up the takeout and, without taking off her boots, walked it to the kitchen. It would probably go straight into the fridge anyway, since he *had* just had dinner. Although the redhead looked like she could use something to soak up the alcohol clearly dominating her body. Some small, naïve part of Shoshi hoped that was why he'd asked for the food—to sober her up.

"You know," Shoshi said, trying to keep the irritation out of her voice as she came back into the hallway, "there are several efficient food delivery apps nowadays, so individual restaurants don't have to have their own delivery service. I'd be happy to help you set up an account."

"Why pay them and their drivers when I have you?" He didn't even look at her as he said it. The redhead giggled again.

Shoshi's hands balled into fists. "I'll get out of your way," she said, walking past the couple. "Enjoy your evening."

"Shana," Davin called.

Gritting her teeth, Shoshi turned back to him. *This* was the man who volunteered every Sunday with kids? Teens who apparently looked up to him, wanted to honor him? What he did on his own time was his business, of course—or it would be, if he stopped dragging Shoshi into it—but how could he be so caring and also so callous?

He held her gaze until the redhead twisted, slumping against the wall. "Luc, come on," she whined, poking at his chest. "No threesomes. I don't want to share you." That giggle sounded again.

Shoshi's eyes grew wide, but she couldn't stop them. She spun away, Davin's startled expression echoing in her mind. He seemed as taken aback by the suggestion as she was. Or at least surprised. Threesomes were definitely par for the course for him, so it had to be the idea of sleeping with Shoshi that he found as perturbing as she did. *Common ground*, she thought bitterly, not even pausing to zip up her boots as she rushed through the deserted hallways to the safety of her car.

That Friday at 1:59 PM, Shoshi walked into Davin's office without knocking. She'd switched all calls to redirect automatically from her desk phone, and as always, precisely at 2 PM, the phone rang. But this time it rang in his office, like it must have before she'd shown up.

Davin turned his head to glare at her. Shoshi hit the Speakerphone button, holding his gaze. He never spoke to his mother, but he also *never* had any meetings scheduled for Fridays at two. He'd even insisted on an early-morning train for last week's return from New York, and the only reason had to be not missing this call. For whatever reason, he wanted to know the woman *did* call, every time.

"Mr. Davin's office," Shoshi said.

"Oh, hello, dear," Davin's mom answered.

His jaw clenched and his eyes narrowed on Shoshi, promising retribution.

"Is Lucas available today?"

Shoshi took a deep breath, staring down Davin's ferocity. After Wednesday night, she needed a way to push back. And she couldn't tolerate these weekly hopeless calls much longer, anyway. "You know, he's actually right here."

Perfect silence greeted her statement, neither of the Davins responding to her claim for several moments.

"Lucas?" Mrs. Davin breathed eventually on the other end of the call.

Davin's hand instantly reached for the phone, lifting the handset just long enough to let it drop and cut off the call. "Get out," he growled, his fury nearly palpable.

Shoshi hesitated only a second before obeying. At least he hadn't fired her. It wasn't entirely clear whose side an HR rep would take. But why wouldn't he just speak to his mother? He'd seemed almost pained at hearing her voice. How hard could it be to say hello?

Davin didn't say much of anything for the rest of the day. It wasn't until almost seven that the intercom light on her desk phone lit up, his silent signal for her to come to his office.

"Young company, looking to scale," he said when she opened his door. He fixed her with a look she couldn't quite read, though thankfully it lacked his earlier rage. "Time to go."

"Of course," Shoshi murmured. Something felt off, but the request was no different than plenty of its predecessors. She texted Rico as she got the coats. Even a late dinner with him seemed unlikely.

Come by after? he sent back.

"Something funny?" Davin asked from a couple steps behind her, and Shoshi's smile dropped.

She slipped the iPhone away and handed him his coat. "Where are we going?"

A burlesque club, she realized when they stepped into Sinfernal Fare. The main room had lush velvet curtains and wallpaper, simple wooden tables and chairs, a bar lining one of the walls, with a sort of old-world polish and charm, and velvet half-circle settees around the edges. Well, at least it wasn't a strip club. Burlesque was supposed to be a performance art, right?

"Mr. Davin," a man wearing only slacks and suspenders greeted. His pale torso sparkled in the low light. "We're really glad you could make it. Please," he added and led them to a table by the raised stage. This one had a red-and-gold tablecloth draped over it, and a votive tree in the center. Other than the three of them and a couple other staff members working on the periphery, the club was empty. "Can I offer you something to drink?" the bare-chested man asked.

"Scotch," Davin answered curtly, stripping off his coat. The man—club owner?—took it then looked at Shoshi. His smile slipped into a more passive, curious version.

She shrugged out of her own coat, murmuring a "thank you" as the man took it and walked away. Davin didn't say anything, so Shoshi lowered into a chair beside him and flipped open her portfolio. It didn't seem like him, not mentioning what happened earlier, not retaliating in some way for her pushing the issue. What did he have planned?

"So we have two main girls right now," the club's representative said, setting down a bottle of Glenlivet Archive scotch and two tumblers. He flipped around the third chair at their table and straddled it. "Ideally, we'd want to go up to ten, and throw in ten more background dancers, men and women. Bigger productions, special performances, a wider range of talents and of body types, of course. We have a stellar chef waiting in the wings,"—he filled the tumblers and nudged them toward Davin and Shoshi—"and we'd also want to hire our seamstress full-time. You'll see, she's really talented." He paused, looking to Davin for some kind of acknowledgment.

Davin merely picked up his tumbler and sipped.

The other man's eyes flicked to Shoshi.

"What are the numbers?" she asked. "How much are you looking to raise?"

"Oh, Francie handles all of that. She has a report all done up for you, but she's backstage right now. We'd also do classes during the day on weekends, there's a studio upstairs, and bachelorette events, things like that."

Shoshi nodded, jotting down notes. Davin still didn't speak. "Have you opened to the public?" Shoshi asked. She should have known this—Davin undoubtedly did, and she would have if she'd had any idea they were coming here. How new was his interest in this club?

"Uh, yeah. We've been open awhile now." The man glanced uneasily between Shoshi and Davin then tried to wipe his expression into polite engagement. Purple and green lined his dark eyes, standing out against the almost shocking paleness of his skin. "Later on, we won't close for private events on Friday or Saturday nights, ideally, but today of course, we wanted to give you full access, Mr. Davin."

Davin nodded. "When will Francie join us?"

"She's part of the show, Mr. Davin. They'll be starting any minute. Is there anything else I can get you in the meanwhile?"

"Floor plans," came the curt reply.

"Of course." The man shot up, smoothly turning his chair back around before striding away.

Since Davin was busy stewing, or mulling, or whatever he was doing, Shoshi glanced around the modest club. The light was kept low, shadowy silhouettes of unlit candleholders marking each bare table. The fanciest part seemed to be the bar at the far end of the room, the bottles illuminated proudly against the mirrored wall. As if to confirm the quality, Davin downed the rest of his scotch, barely wincing as he swallowed.

"Are you considering this for the alternative arts fund?" Shoshi asked when the silence dragged on. *Alternative arts* was a way of saying *all those things Puritanical sensibilities would find distasteful.*

"And some others." The lights dimmed further and faint music began playing. Amusement replaced the previous calculated blankness in Davin's eyes. He tipped the bottle and scotch gurgled into his tumbler. "Enjoy the show, Shana."

Five women filed onstage in fur coats—presumably faux?—lit by two white spots from opposite corners of the raised stage. "Big Spender" played through their speakers, and the women split off into staggered rows, their heads down. They danced on the edge of the stage and down onto the extended platform beside her and Davin's table. It wasn't clear if they had anything on under the coats, but if they did, it wasn't much. Davin's eyes were set dispassionately on the performance.

At the end of the first chorus, the fur popped open, revealing differently colored lace corsets and a fringe of miniskirts. Shoshi switched to reading her notes.

Davin's hand snaked out to lift his scotch. "How do you expect to have informed opinions if you don't evaluate the product," he said more than asked.

Shoshi looked up at his profile, the angles of his jaw sharply defined even while relaxed, the clean line of his nose, the dark hair that had barely started to brush the back of his collar. In the dim light, with his attention occupied elsewhere, she could almost understand what all those women saw in him. Almost.

"Were you interested in my opinion?" she asked.

Up on the stage, the torsos of the corsets had disappeared, leaving lace bra cups and the little skirts. Four of the women turned as one, bending over and showing off their thongs. The one in the center rolled and thrust her hips. All very rhythmically.

There was something familiar about that center dancer. Shoshi reached for the second tumbler. Hints of chocolate and some kind of fruit filled her mouth with the scotch. The featured dancer moved down the center platform, toward them. Her black hair was pinned up into a half twist with wisps of purple curling out of it. She winked at Davin. When all five dancers unpinned the skirts, swinging them around, the center one tossed hers at their table, then spun away and dropped into a bouncing crouch. Had Shoshi met her before?

The last time she'd seen purple stripes in black hair had been spread on Davin's pillow—one of the many morning-after scenes she'd had the misfortune of seeing. The woman had refused to get dressed until Shoshi brought over a McDonald's breakfast sandwich and milkshake. Fun morning.

Did Davin invest in all of his one-night stands' endeavors? He couldn't, not with his track record.

The song ended and the women trailed off the stage, snapping. His head turned slightly, enough to make eye contact with Shoshi, and the corner of his lips tugged up. Had he been expecting his hookup's presence to shock her? Either he was grasping at straws or everything he'd put her through thus far had made sure she was inured. Nepotism and an undertone of objectification didn't really rank up there with drunken side-by-side lap dances. Or abandoning a child. Or even his total disregard for Shoshi's time.

"Here we are." The club representative—co-owner?—slid a stack of papers onto the table. "They're really something, huh? Moira's working on a traditional fan dance, but it's not quite ready to show you. We're also planning on getting more lights, props, variety, you know. And backdrops for the stage."

Davin leafed through the papers. A new song started, and two women in new negligee shuffled onstage with a couple chairs. Shoshi let herself relax into her seat, sipping the scotch. This was a performance like any other—dancers demonstrating their skills—and it really seemed like a labor of love for them, even if it was a little rough around the edges. Davin seemed more bored than anything, which was strangely satisfying.

"Oh, and I brought this for you." The man who still hadn't introduced himself slid a colorful postcard offering a free beginner burlesque class in front of Shoshi. "It's great for building confidence."

Davin's gaze snapped to her, suddenly far more alert. Was he looking for an excuse to chastise her again? Worried she'd somehow offend the other man? If there was one thing she was learning from this job, it was how to remain outwardly unflappable.

"Thank you," she told the club's representative, tucking the card into her portfolio even though she had no plans to use it. The polite response only seemed to irritate Davin further. He scowled and finished off his scotch, immediately filling the tumbler once more.

"Do you have many repeat students?" Shoshi asked, gathering the papers Davin had barely looked at. At least one of them could stay professional.

✧ ✧ ✧

"So will you be considering them further?" Shoshi asked when they finally walked into the chill night over an hour later.

"We'll see." It sounded like a *no*.

They didn't speak again until Shoshi offered a "good night" as he got out of her car in front of his building. She passed a hand over her face then unbuttoned her suit jacket, sighing as the tension in the fabric eased.

Just dropped Davin off, she texted Rico.

The phone rang moments later. "Hi," she said.

"Productive evening?" Rico asked.

Shoshi's sarcastic chuckle came out more like an exhale. "If only." Davin had done this to waste time. He'd already made it clear he didn't mind wasting his own to get under her skin. But if this was the worst fallout from that afternoon's call, she would shrug it off. Tomorrow.

"You want to come over?"

Should she? "It's late." And Rico didn't want to hear about Davin, so curling up with her laptop might be more relaxing.

"If you're still in the city, my place is closer. And you do have that change of clothes now."

And maybe curling up with a warm body would help take her mind off the ridiculousness of her boss. "If you're sure," Shoshi said.

She could almost see Rico's satisfied smile on the other end. "Quite sure."

Chapter 25

SATURDAY MORNING CAME TOO SOON, WITH THE ALL-TOO-familiar chime of Davin needing something. All he sent was an address and a time. Squinting at the screen, Shoshi typed a response, asking if she should pick him up.

"What's wrong?" Rico muttered beside her.

Shoshi's hands flew to her hair, smoothing it back as much as possible before swiping her fingers under her eyes to catch stray makeup. "Nothing," she whispered. "Go back to sleep." She slipped out of bed and made her way downstairs to the main level of his condo, holding on to the rail as her eyes struggled to stay open. Rico's bed was on a half level that led to his private part of the rooftop, allowing him to enjoy the sunset, sunrise, midnight cityscape—everything, all from bed. The luxury was pretty incredible.

The phone vibrated and chimed in her hand as Shoshi plopped onto the couch.

> You're on your own. You know what's best, right?

So he wasn't done. Shoshi sighed and checked the previous message. The address was at least an hour away. Quietly as she could, she grabbed her purse and ducked into the bathroom. She'd brought a spare outfit to Rico's after his offer, and a toothbrush but nothing else, so she'd gotten into the habit of carrying around mascara and lip balm, travel-sized deodorant, and hairbands. She'd slept in panties and the tank top that had been layered under her suit jacket. One of the benefits of inexpensive materials: wrinkling them beyond recognition wasn't that big a deal.

When she left the bathroom, the main floor was filled with the aroma of coffee. "You're a lifesaver," Shoshi told Rico, who stood in his boxers.

He turned from the coffeemaker with a mug already in hand. Golden light from beneath the cabinets bathed his torso. "Davin again?"

"Who else." Shoshi moaned a little at the first sip of the rich roast. "For someone who doesn't drink much coffee, you have excellent taste."

His lips twitched up, but his brows were still drawn together in concern.

"Do you remember if I had my necklace on last night?" Shoshi redirected. She didn't remember taking it off before the burlesque club, but it was also possible she'd never put it on yesterday. Now, of course, she couldn't quite remember the last time she'd had it at all. The unsettling possibility she could have lost the little charm had started nibbling uncomfortably at her brain. And pricking at her heart.

"What necklace?"

"The uhm…" He wouldn't understand if she called it a hamsa. "The little hand."

"I don't remember, sorry. If it's here, it'll turn up," Rico said, stepping closer. He bent down for a soft kiss. "What does Davin want?" he murmured above her lips.

Shoshi stepped back, sipping the coffee. "Time and an address. I guess I'll see when I get there." But suddenly not having the hamsa seemed like a bad sign.

She mentally shook the thought away. Much as she liked having the comfort of her father's gift with her, it was ultimately just a necklace. It wasn't like she wore it every day, anyway. Not having it now didn't mean it was gone. She'd probably left it at home.

"Do you want me to go with you?" Rico asked, spurring her back into action.

"No, don't waste your weekend just because I have to," she said, setting aside the coffee and gathering her things. "But thank you."

"Actually, I should probably go to the office. Taxes are due soon."

"Well, see." She faced him and forced her lips into a curve. "This way I'm not here distracting you."

Rico nodded and turned away to rinse the mug she'd used, so Shoshi let the hollow smile drop. "Do you want some breakfast before you go?" he asked.

"No, I'm okay. Thank you." She was too tired to eat. If that changed, there was an emergency box of Krave in her trunk. Being late probably wouldn't make whatever Davin had in store any more pleasant.

A little over an hour later, Shoshi pulled into an unassuming parking lot. She rinsed her mouth with a sip of water, running her tongue over her teeth to catch any lingering specks of cereal. Her hand brushed over the empty spot where the hamsa would have been, but there was nothing she could do about its absence right now, so she flipped down the visor to check her reflection. She'd pinned part of her hair back rather than attempting to smooth it all into a bun, and the frizzy mess poufed around her head. For a Saturday morning, it would have to do.

The plain gray door swung open before Shoshi could knock. A muscle-bound wall stepped out, blocking the space behind him. "Hi, uh." Shoshi hesitated. What was she doing here? "I'm Shana Glass, from Griffith & Moore."

"Spenser," called a female voice from behind the wall. He took a half step back, turning to reveal a woman in a really cute take on a pantsuit, but with a halter top styled to look like a vest and tie. "Hello, hello. Please, come in." The woman gestured smoothly with one red-tipped hand.

Shoshi eased past the security guy.

"May I take your coat?" The woman's tapered eyes turned up slightly at the corners, and her smooth hair fell effortlessly to her ribcage.

Shoshi handed over her coat with a small smile. Was this another club Davin was "considering"? "I'm sorry, Miss, uh…"

"Janine." Her smile was far too genuine for so early in the morning. "Please, come with me." She pushed aside a heavy black curtain, revealing a softly lit room with multicolored clusters of couches and oversized pillows for seating. Low tables cradled drinks that didn't seem to be alcoholic, and the few patrons chatted over music that featured reeds or flutes over-laying soft chimes. Janine led Shoshi to a table with a pitcher of cucumber water. "Would you like some coffee? I know it's early, but I appreciate you working us into your schedule. Braden can make anything you like," Janine said in a soothing tone.

"You know, a mocha would be lovely." And give her something to do as she tried to get her bearings. What kind of club was open Saturday mornings? It was barely nine.

Janine gestured to someone behind Shoshi. "We have three separate floors," she said, flipping two of the glasses set around the pitcher and pouring the water. Not one ice cube or piece of cucumber slid into either glass. "The first, as you see, is mostly a lounge, a place to unwind and relax, indulge the taste buds. The staff circulate, in case they catch someone's eye."

A delicate porcelain cup appeared by Shoshi. To her left the man who held the cup smiled at her, nodding and maintaining eye contact until Shoshi shot him a small smile in return. He didn't straighten until she accepted the cup. The thin layers of paint slid against her fingertips as she tasted the coffee. *Hand-painted.*

The man sat down beside Shoshi, the couch dipping slightly from the pressure. He wore a sleeveless white button-down shirt made from a stiff fabric and simple black pants. His hazel eyes remained trained on Shoshi.

"And the second floor?" she asked.

"Private rooms," Janine said. "Massage tables, recliners for personal treatments, two hot tubs. Everything and anything to tantalize and pleasure. Riley would be happy to provide you with any service, or any of our deluxe additions."

Shoshi took another sip of her mocha—rich and delicious, truly—rather than respond. As she replaced the cup, Riley's hand reached out, brushing some of her hair aside. Shoshi froze. "Please don't."

Riley jerked his hand back, eyes flicking to Janine. For the first time, the woman's mask slipped, and she stared at Shoshi with a startled pout. "I'm sorry, Mr. Davin told us to show you the entire deluxe experience. Riley is one of our best. Unless you'd prefer something a little different?" She waved over a couple of women and another man. "We guarantee absolute discretion." The artificially soothing tone had returned by the time she finished. Another small gesture and Riley stood, lining up with the others.

Shoshi stood too, and the club's employees visibly relaxed—prematurely. "I'm sorry, I believe there's been a misunderstanding. I'm happy to discuss your financial situation, your projected costs and returns. But let's keep the tour hands-off." Whatever the unspoken undertone to their offer, Shoshi didn't want or need their services. And she had a hunch that what they hadn't said would legally be considered prostitution. *Everything and anything.*

Janine stood as well. "I'm afraid I don't understand. Mr. Davin made it clear you wanted experience with our services to make an informed recommendation."

Of course he had. "What's on the third floor?" Shoshi asked, though her *recommendation* was clear. And it wasn't likely Davin had genuinely considered investing in their—what, expansion? Second location? Whatever they had planned. Unless he was starting a "borderline illegal entertainment services" fund.

Janine blinked rapidly, but her lips pulled up at the corners. "Sound-proofed rooms, fully outfitted with a variety of accoutrements to choose from. And strategic skylights or mirrors to enhance the experience. They are for our more particular clients."

They watched one another, both measuring each other up. What were these "particular" services? Better not to know.

"Would you like to see for yourself?" Janine offered. "We cater to all tastes."

Shoshi couldn't even imagine what exactly was being offered, and thank G-d for that. Their clients likely appreciated the judgment-free atmosphere, but she was so not their target audience. "Thank you for the offer and your time," she managed to say. "I'll make sure Mr. Davin follows up with you."

Janine hesitated a moment, then nodded once, almost imperceptibly. "Of course. Let me show you out."

First thing after making it home, Shoshi scoured her apartment for her necklace. When it wasn't in the obvious places like her bed—or under it—or by the bathroom sink, she checked the handful of cabinets and her makeshift dresser. Since she'd already looked through her purse half a dozen times, she turned out every single pocket she owned. She even checked the fridge. Exhaustion could make you do funny things, right?

By the time she was done, her place was a mess. And the hamsa was nowhere to be found. Arms wrapped around her ribs, she spun slowly in the center of the turmoil, the proof of her failure.

Her breath puffed out too loud for the silence of the room. Could she have left it at work somehow? It didn't make sense. If she took it off at her desk, she would have put it straight into her bag. So when was the last time she'd had it? A day ago? Longer?

Overly bright, the yellow comforter disheveled on her bed mocked her. She'd grown too comfortable—careless.

Fighting back the tingle of panic at the base of her skull, Shoshi lunged for the lowest level of cardboard boxes. She pulled everything from the one in the far bottom corner until her hand closed around the velvet box she kept as hidden as possible. Cold hit her butt as she sagged onto the floor, and finally she switched on the little heater.

Even without her opening the gray box, the world seemed to right itself a little, letting her catch her breath. Seeing the pair of rings and the charm inside was always bittersweet, but now tears welled at the visual reminder that she'd lost another piece of her dad. At least she still had these.

So they wouldn't get lost, too, she slipped her parents' wedding rings onto her index finger. Her mother's hamsa was left, resting unperturbed on the white satin. Tiny little diamonds decorated the golden hand, matching the modest stone in her ring. Shoshi's father had made a gift of the charm for their first anniversary. According to him, her mother had never taken it off. Shoshi'd never had the heart to put it on. But bruised as that heart was with the loss of her own hamsa, staring at this frail link to her parents' love always soothed her.

Even now, with her butt growing numb.

Sniffing back the lingering wetness in her eyes, Shoshi replaced the rings and carefully hid the box away again. The chances anyone would break into her place were infinitesimally small, but even that was too much risk to leave her most precious possessions out where they'd be easy for a stranger to find.

Since the effort of standing was too much, Shoshi shuffled on her knees to the bed, then heaved herself up onto it. Tidying up could wait at least a few minutes.

Anger colored the edges of her sadness as Shoshi pounded her fist into the mattress. Logically, she knew losing her necklace wasn't Davin's fault. Not directly, anyway. At most, he'd driven her to a harried fatigue that meant she hadn't noticed the loss immediately, hadn't scooped the charm back up when it fell…wherever it was now. Still, resentment swirled tightly, filling the new cracks in her heart. Whatever Davin wanted to throw at her, however much of her time he wasted with pointless "evaluations" like that morning's, Shoshi would handle it. She was going to get everything she could out of this farce of a job. She had to make this worth it.

But how much more would she have to sacrifice first?

Shoshi startled awake, adrenaline from a bizarre dream still beating through her even as the memory of it dissipated. She'd fallen asleep still wearing the slacks and sweater she'd left at Rick's, her apartment in shambles from her search. There was plenty to do to put it all to rights.

Instead, Shoshi burrowed deeper into the comforter and closed her eyes again, willing herself back to sleep even though what she really should have done was make lunch, clean up, and shower. At least this morning's club seemed to keep their more intimate practices out of their main lounge, so she wouldn't have to scrub her skin raw to feel clean. She wasn't a prude, exactly, or she wouldn't have thought she was before these last weeks with Davin. If everyone was consenting, they could do whatever they wanted—as long as they didn't try to do it to her.

A fresh surge of anger at all the ways Davin had pushed her to the edge was enough to propel Shoshi out of bed. She changed into her sweats, trying to shake the wrinkles out of the slacks before dropping everything in the hamper. Sleeping in work clothes had been sloppy; she needed to keep them as nice as possible for the office. Maybe it was time to go look for a few more new pieces. There was that networking event Monday… Granted, she'd be there primarily as Davin's shadow, but maybe Shoshi could make some connections for herself as well. So shopping would definitely have to happen, but first there was tidying and laundry to do.

And before that, she could use a slightly healthier meal than the morning's cereal. For all the aggravation that went with working for Davin, it was nice, her body feeling less sluggish and her clothes fitting better. Some of her old ones were even a little loose now, in a comfortable sort of way.

Shoshi peered into her fridge, frowning at the mostly empty shelves. At least now the groceries were sparse because she spent so much time eating at work or with Rick, not because she couldn't afford anything. Still, grocery shopping should definitely be added to her To Do list.

For now, she rinsed a cucumber and a couple tomatoes. An all too familiar buzzing followed her shutting off the water. She'd switched the iPhone to vibrate for the meeting, which meant the only way to know who had texted her was to go look. It also meant it could be Davin.

Shoshi sighed when she flipped the phone over. Didn't he have anything better to do?

Thai & report

What exactly did he expect her to report? How good Riley had been at his "specials"? If Davin really wanted to know, he could pay Riley a visit himself.

Her veggies lay waiting on the counter, but apparently they'd have to keep waiting, just like everything else. Hadn't she thought this job would help get her life on track? The current state of her apartment proved better than anything how utterly wrong she'd been.

But the job remained her number one priority, so a little over an hour later, Shoshi pushed open the door to Davin's apartment.

"What took you so long?" he asked from somewhere unseen as she took her shoes off.

"Geography and cooking times," she said, walking down the hall. Given her morning, it was pretty much a miracle that only the slightest hint of annoyance made it into her voice.

Davin sat working at his dining table. His eyes flicked to the unmarked plastic bags she held. "Wrong restaurant."

"This one's better." Since she'd been at home, Shoshi'd picked up food from her favorite place rather than searching for parking by Davin's go-to. If he refused to eat it, she could order delivery, and he'd simply have to wait. She laid out his order then walked to the kitchen to get him a fork. Goodness forbid he use one of the plastic ones the restaurant had included.

"And the rest of that?" he asked as she set the fork beside him.

"Is for me." Shoshi straightened, forcing the frustration out of her expression. A couple more months of practice schooling her face around Davin and she could take up playing poker. "Is there anything else you need?"

Davin's gaze slid down her body, pausing at her jeans. True, they were fraying a bit on the inner thigh, but they hadn't quite worn out, and there was no way he could see that anyway. They weren't at the office, so he couldn't really enforce the dress code. Besides, for once he was wearing a tee shirt himself. He popped the clear lid off the black container, and Shoshi moved back to the other side of the table.

"Next time get the right kind. Attention to detail matters," he said before she could scoop up the bag with her pineapple chicken. "And this morning's meeting?"

Shoshi licked her lips and exhaled a controlled breath, then turned back around to him. "They were unprepared."

Davin's eyebrow crooked as he chewed, that thread of amusement filtering into his expression.

"No financial statements, no detailed plans. They didn't seem to understand that *that* was what I was interested in seeing." Because he'd intentionally led them to expect otherwise. Didn't he care about wasting *their* time, if not hers?

"And their services?"

Shoshi's lips pulled into a false smile even as her feet itched to carry her out of there. "You'll have to try them for yourself. I told them to expect a follow-up from you, since you're so interested in this opportunity."

"You were supposed to evaluate the financial potential, not pass judgment." Satisfaction underlay the censure.

"Janine will be emailing me their current and projected numbers." Thankfully she'd gathered herself enough to ask for the information on the way out. Davin couldn't accuse her of not doing her job, even if that hadn't been the point of this "meeting."

His eyes narrowed, jaw tugging to one side like it did whenever he didn't quite know what to criticize next. In a swift motion, he flicked something onto the table. When no explanation was forthcoming, Shoshi bent to reach the little plastic packet that had landed a smidge too far for anything resembling elegance on her part. It wasn't drugs, was it? The packet was about the size of the ones various shows liked to depict filled with a fine white powder. But a quick glance proved that wasn't the case here.

A fine silver chain lay coiled in the bag that hung from between her fingertips. She looked briefly to Davin, catching only the arch crook in his brow, before flipping the baggie over. Shoshi's heart stuttered as she blinked at the blue stones. The outline of the charm gradually blurred into focus.

When her eyes met his, Davin's expression was indecipherable. "Next time you leave your crap at my place, it goes straight in the dumpster."

The brusque comment barely glanced off the relief flowing through her. "Thank you." She cleared the emotion clogging her throat, then tried again. "Thank you for returning this." Considering his frequent ever-changing guests, how had he even known it was hers? But then, Davin didn't miss details. "It means a lot to me," she added.

"Well maybe if you stopped tugging on it like a security blanket, the chain wouldn't have broken." He held her gaze a moment more before refocusing on the laptop in front of him. "Don't forget my dry cleaning," he dismissed.

Shoshi's fist closed around the charm that anchored the whirl of emotions, too unmanageable and overwhelming to sort through here and now. If not for Davin's implacable presence, she would've torn into the pouch, dropped the hamsa into her palm to verify it was there, and real, and *hers*. She'd reach the privacy of her car soon enough.

Different plastic crinkled as she grabbed her lunch and started back down the hall. Unwilling to part with the little lifeline even to put it in her purse—or risk losing it again by shoving it into a pocket—she tucked the baggie into her bra. The plastic poking her with every breath was oddly soothing. Turned out, the baggie's contents were far more valuable than drugs.

She was almost at his bedroom door when Davin asked, "Did you get the list for Monday?"

The question stopped her in her tracks. "The list?" He didn't answer, so Shoshi walked the few steps back to his table. "Which list?" she repeated.

"The guest list, for the Leap party."

The rational, professional part of her tried to clamber to the surface enough to answer.

Davin set down his fork, frowning. "To know who will be there, who we should be prepared to speak with and connect with one another."

Even before the roller coaster of the day, the thought hadn't crossed her mind. It wasn't their event—just a marketing ploy taking advantage of the leap year to encourage investors to "take the leap" and support some promising Massachusetts startups.

"I'll get in touch with the Leap people and ask for an updated list." And hope they didn't laugh at her.

"By tonight," Davin added, then returned to his meal.

She nodded, not that he was looking. Now that he'd said it, of *course* going over the guest list, developing a strategy, was important. Why hadn't she realized that herself? Shoshi might be getting better at dealing with Davin, but that didn't mean anything if she was failing at the job itself.

At least his generous mood extended to giving her a chance to make it right. And with the twin weights of grief and guilt lifted from her shoulders, she might actually be able to concentrate on pulling this off.

He shouldn't have returned it.

He'd considered it, too. Keeping the thing until Shoshana cracked without its comfort. Or tossing it and taunting her with that fact, a well-timed comment to push her over the edge. Letting the uncertainty of its whereabouts help drive her to that edge in the first place. If she'd had any idea it had fallen in his apartment, landing by the baseboard in his hall… Well, she wouldn't have left it there for him to find.

Luc had meant to drop it on her desk yesterday, to catch a moment when she wasn't there and he wouldn't have to face her relief, or her outsized gratitude. Instead she'd pulled that stunt with his mother's call.

A temporary derailment, nothing more. He'd made his choices long ago.

The necklace had burned in his pocket the rest of the day, a mere echo of the smoldering in his chest. He should have tossed it.

By the time Shoshana stood in his apartment, he'd simply wanted the thing gone. Out of his thoughts.

Now she would read far too much into a meaningless flick of the wrist. And Luc had no choice but to tip the scales back in his favor.

Chapter 26

RICO SET A CUP OF COFFEE DOWN ON SHANA'S DESK, AND her eyes flew open, her head jerking up from the hand that cradled it. She sent him a wan smile. "Thanks." Faint circles showed under her eyes, even though she probably wore makeup to cover the worst of it.

"Why don't you go in my office," he offered quietly. "Lie down for a bit while I meet with Luc."

She started to glance over her shoulder, toward Luc's office, but picked up the coffee instead of finishing the motion. "I'll be fine, thanks."

"You need a break before tonight's event." Half the firm was going, and it was a great networking opportunity for all of them, especially since Shana wanted to find a different position. "You're fixing your hair up later anyway, right? So take half an hour. Luc won't even notice."

"The phone…"

Luc's door opened before Rico could protest. "Where's—" Luc caught sight of him. "Rick."

"Luc. I was just asking your assistant for a small favor. Hope you don't mind."

"I'm sure she was more than willing to help with anything you need." He looked to Shana as he spoke, his expression inscrutable. There was a reason Luc was such a successful negotiator. The man gave nothing away.

"It'll be taken care of," Shana assured woodenly.

"Shall we?" Luc asked.

"Of course." Rico preceded him into the office. He should trust Shana when she said she could handle it, but not interfering was getting harder. Not that he could say anything without exposing their relationship, and that had to be an iffy subject in terms of company policy, even if she wasn't Rico's assistant.

As Luc lowered into his chair, Rico brought his attention to the matter at hand. He was there to discuss tax filings, not Luc's mistreatment of Shana.

Shoshi laid her hairbrush, pins, and hairspray on her desk beside the energy drink she planned to down right before they left for the Leap party. She was going to do everything possible to make a good impression, and that meant stealing a few minutes to pull her hair up. Normally she'd have done it before coming in that morning, but Davin hadn't had any in-person meetings scheduled, and this way she should look less disheveled tonight.

It had taken some faint bribery and promised favors, but she'd managed to get the guest list Saturday. She'd spent hours going over it, then hours more last night with Davin as he did the same. Connor's name had been included, but so had a few others she recognized from school. If she could find a way to reconnect with them at the event, at least she wouldn't be starting from scratch.

"Planning a career change?"

Shoshi jolted out of her seat. She had to be more tired than she'd realized if she hadn't heard him leave his office. Maybe she should have taken Rico up on his offer to lie down. Too late now. "Just want to make sure I look as polished as possible when representing the company tonight." He couldn't argue with that, right? He himself had emphasized the importance of being "well groomed," back when he'd hired her.

Davin swept another unimpressed look over her supplies. "If I were you, I'd worry more about dredging up something resembling a personality."

Shoshi's jaw popped open.

"But by all means, go strip away the last memorable thing about you," he added, shutting himself back in his office.

Numbly, she gathered the supplies. Only when she'd locked the door to the restroom did his comments really hit her. It had to be the exhaustion—why else would her eyes be prickling? That had to explain the block of pressure in her chest, too. What did she care what Davin thought of her? She was too busy trying to survive to worry about having a personality. Besides, executive assistants were *supposed* to blend into the background.

And how *dare* he? He had no idea what it was like, having to strip away her identity to be accepted, to be taken seriously. A woman—with textured hair, no less!—was bad enough. But a Jew, in finance? The antisemitic slurs wrote themselves. There was more than one reason she'd left the hamsa at home today.

Shoshi did what she had to so that when people looked at her, they saw Shana. So that even unconscious bias didn't create extra hurdles in her path, labeling her as either unqualified because of her hair or unethical because of her identity. She couldn't do much about the woman part.

The Leap party was her chance to start rebuilding her network, and she would do everything she could to crack open some doors for herself. Even if it meant jabbing dozens of pins into her hair to get as close to the WASPy ideal as she could manage. Davin might have shown a glimmer of humanity in returning her charm—even more shocking was that he'd included a brand new chain—but he could never understand the need to camouflage pieces of yourself that others deemed objectionable. So what if he found the result boring? At tonight's event, Davin's opinion definitely wasn't the one that mattered.

In the near-dark silence of his apartment, Luc poured himself another drink. He'd done it. Anything positive he'd once glimpsed in Shoshana's eyes had been replaced with a burning anger that bordered on hatred. Which was exactly right.

He downed the liquor and stretched his legs out, letting his head fall back on the couch. Her determination to prove him wrong had transformed her anger into an animated charm whenever she spoke with anyone who wasn't him at tonight's event. Still a little hesitant, unsure. Chattering a little to hide her nerves. But she'd made an impact.

And now Luc could picture that seething scorn she'd turned on him, not the traces of respect or expectant disappointment he'd kept finding before. Or her gratitude from this weekend. Definitely not her perfecting the art of burlesque. Performing just for him…

Damn Ginger for putting the image of Shoshana in bed into his head in the first place.

Luc was already damned for everything else.

Chapter 27

DAVIN'S HEIGHTENED ONSLAUGHT CONTINUED WITHOUT pause. He'd even seemed to stop finding random bed partners so he could turn all his attention to keeping Shoshi from anything resembling a normal sleep schedule. And his mood grew progressively worse.

By the middle of the following week, she was pretty damn sure he was trying to get her to quit. *Tough.* If he wanted to get rid of her, he'd have to fire her and make good on his promise to cover her loans.

Shoshi leaned against the counter in the break room, closing her eyes as the coffee machine gurgled. She hadn't been seeing much of Rico lately, though with corporate taxes due soon, that might still have been true without Davin's interference. His late nights just kept him in the office, rather than running around the city or working at Davin's place, like her.

"You all right, Shana?" Sebastian stalled in the doorway, concerned or maybe scared to get closer.

"It's not today, Sebastian." She'd overheard a few of the others gripe that the original pool had ended without a winner.

The pot had been added to a new one, with new dates. It was more lucrative than ever to root for her to be fired, or quit.

"That's not why I'm asking." He walked further into the break room, gesturing toward one of the tables in a silent question. "You look worn out."

"Always the charmer." Shoshi turned back to the machine and filled her mug.

"Okay, fine."

"Sorry," she corrected. Her exhaustion wasn't his fault.

He nodded, hands slipping into his pockets. "Is this job really worth it?"

She asked herself the same thing almost every day lately, but if she did quit—then what? She had enough now to cover her rent for a couple months, but it wasn't like she'd had time to job hunt lately, even if someone would be willing to overlook this blip on her résumé. Yet another mark against her. And going back to the fast food industry? Not exactly a great alternative. She'd followed up with some of the people from the Leap party, but exchanging emails was a far way off from anything resembling a job prospect.

"Or is it something else?" Sebastian asked in her silence. "You're not involved with Davin, are you?"

A chuckle escaped her. The complete lack of anything sexual between them was probably the one thing she and Davin could absolutely agree on. Besides, if the unthinkable happened and they ever so much as kissed, he'd probably stop to criticize her technique. "Thanks, Sebastian," Shoshi said, walking past him and his confusion. "I needed that laugh."

Her smile faded as she paused to ask Priscilla, "How are things?"

Tensions had eased between the women over the last weeks, the office manager seeming too distracted by her personal life to resent Shoshi's presence at work. She kept all the details out of the office, staunchly protective of her privacy, as was her right. But the purple crescents she hadn't quite been able to hide seemed to have faded finally. "Improving," Priscilla confirmed, holding out her private stash of fun-sized Milky Way bars.

"Glad to hear it," Shoshi said, accepting one.

Priscilla nodded toward Shoshi's desk. Davin's door was cracked open; his meeting was over. Shoshi nodded back, took a big gulp of coffee, then went to trade the mug and candy for her notepad. Davin had gotten in the habit of dictating notes after most of his meetings. Then going over those notes and adding new insights later, often far into the night at his place. For someone who seemed to want her gone, he spent a lot of time keeping her tied to his side.

He barely glanced up as she entered, but his first words were still, "You look tired."

"Can't imagine why," Shoshi muttered, walking to his desk.

"Go home."

That froze her in place. "Excuse me?" Wasn't this the time to go in for the kill—*not* give her a reprieve?

"Take an Uber or something. Can't have you falling asleep at the wheel tomorrow."

They did have a long drive in the morning, out to Connecticut. And he'd been super touchy about vehicular safety ever since she'd met him. Still… "You have a dinner meeting with Ori Lehrer and Amanda Black tonight," Shoshi reminded.

"Believe it or not, I can handle that without you." He fixed her with an unyielding look. "Don't make me repeat myself. And

Shana?" A muscle ticked in his jaw. "If I don't see your car in the garage when I leave, you're fired."

Shoshi's head bobbed. "Careful. Someone might think you actually care if something happens to me."

If possible, his expression grew more austere. She really was exhausted if she'd thought teasing Davin was a good idea. "I care who you'll kill if you pass out behind the wheel."

"Right," she breathed, unable to do more than blink in the face of his severity. It was somehow agonizing but mesmerizing at once.

"Go." He turned away, dismissing her. Or releasing her.

The strange feeling followed Shoshi as she made her way out. Had she hallucinated that conversation? It was more likely that she'd fallen asleep at her desk than that Davin was showing mercy. Still she packed up her things and went to knock on Rico's door.

The second it opened, he asked, "Are you all right?"

Sheesh, did she really look that bad?

"Or does Luc need something," he added, stepping back.

"No." Shoshi shook her head for emphasis, her bun tugging heavily with the motion. "Apparently I have the rest of the day off." She'd need to set up an Uber account. Or should she go with Lyft? Was one generally safer for women?

Rico pushed the door closed, the lines in his face deepening with his concern. His hands came to her upper arms, bracing her. "Why don't you go to my place and get some rest? I have a meeting with the team tonight, but we could grab a late dinner at Pier 6."

"That sounds nice." The waterfront restaurant was a two-minute walk from his place. With their hectic schedules, it had quickly become one of their main go-tos. "But I'm so beat, I think I just want to go home and sleep through to tomorrow."

"You sure?" Rico asked. Something on her face must have answered for her. He frowned but ducked down for a quick kiss. "See you tomorrow, then."

"Good luck with the meeting," she said as he settled back behind his desk.

He nodded, his shoulders dropping with his sigh as he turned to his computer. Had she offended him? A night free from Davin and in Rico's bed definitely sounded more like a dream than her recent reality, but getting to sleep without worrying about anything else—including dinner—sounded even better. There were almost nineteen hours before her morning alarm would go off. Shoshi could use every single one.

Chapter 28

"THIS IS BEYOND RIDICULOUS," RICO MOANED LATE SUNDAY night as Shoshi fumbled to find her ringing phone wherever it had landed on the floor.

"I know. I'm sorry." The ringer shut off just as her fingers found the rectangle. Darkness and stars and streetlights filtered in through Rico's roof access. His breath settled back into a deeper rhythm as he slipped effortlessly back into sleep. *Lucky.*

Shoshi squinted at the phone. Two thirty in the morning? And the number was unknown, but in Boston. *Oh, goodness.* She slipped out of the bed, shivering at the cool air. Too bad Rico didn't have a quilt or anything she could wrap around herself. What were the chances it was a wrong number? The phone lit up again. Shoshi answered the call before the ringing could wake Rico once more. "Hello?" she murmured, gripping the railing to fumble her way downstairs.

"Is this Shoshana Glass?" a male voice asked.

Shoshi's heart stuttered. Something was definitely wrong. "Yes. Who's this?" To this day, other than people in the office, only Nat had this number.

"This is Gabe over at the Roaring Serpent. We, uh." He hesitated. It was too quiet on the other line for a bar, but then it was really friggin' late. "We have a situation."

"A situation?" Shoshi echoed, curling her knees up on the couch. She pulled a pillow over her legs for some barrier against the chill.

"A Luc Davin is here."

Davin? Shoshi's eyes closed as she listened.

"He's pretty soused. Won't leave. He told us to call you. We need you to come pick him up, or—"

"I'll be right there." *Or* didn't sound good. But this made no sense. She'd never seen Davin drunk, no matter how much he indulged. Sure, she'd only known him a couple of months, but he was always in control, even when those around him drifted in and out.

Shoshi padded upstairs to grab her jeans and bra.

"Don't tell me." Rico's sleep-graveled voice froze her in place. "Luc needs something. You need to talk to him."

"Something's wrong," Shoshi explained quietly. "Go back to sleep. I'll see you tomorrow."

"Wrong?" He started to sit up.

"No, I mean, it's Davin. But something's weird. I have to go, I'm sorry."

His eyes opened, frustration mixing with fatigue as he considered Shoshi in the moonlight. "Drive carefully," he said eventually.

Shoshi nodded at his outline and made her way back down the stairs. She didn't take the time to check her appearance in the bathroom, just pulled on the jeans and sweater she'd worn earlier, grabbed her purse and coat, and headed out the door.

She might look like a mess, but apparently Davin would be too drunk to notice.

Rico's place was much closer to Davin's, and the bar nearby, so the drive took almost no time on the deserted, darkened roads. Unsurprisingly, the place was empty when Shoshi pulled open the door. When she caught the bartender's eye, his head inclined toward the booth Davin preferred. She took a deep breath and walked over.

Davin's red-rimmed eyes were only slightly more surprising than his disheveled hair and morose expression. "Shoshananana," he slurred when she approached, then promptly downed the remaining liquor in his glass. "Another!" he called.

"You've had enough, don't you think?" Shoshi asked quietly.

"Never. Not by a long shot. Not…enough." The despair in his voice chilled something deep inside her. Something was seriously wrong.

But given the glare she was getting from the bartender—not that she couldn't understand the man's desire to get home—the *why* would have to wait. She needed to get Davin out of here.

Shoshi walked back to the bar. "Tell me you've stopped serving him."

"Even before I called you," the bartender confirmed. "He said he doesn't drive, so…"

"No, he doesn't." Did he even have a license?

Davin was staring into his empty glass, head dipping then jerking up.

"Is his tab settled?" Shoshi asked.

"Yeah. Gave us a cash tip to stay open awhile, but…"

"Right."

"Give me another!"

What were her options here? "Listen, give me a bottle of whatever he's drinking."

Gabe hesitated. "He's had enough."

"I can see that. But you want him to leave, don't you?" Maybe she could convince Davin to continue his downward spiral at home, and then just shove him onto his bed.

The bartender quirked his lips in disapproval but double-tapped the bar and moved away. Shoshi's hand dipped into her purse. She rooted around, then peered inside. But her wallet wasn't there. *Damn it.* It must have fallen out in her car…or at Rico's. Hopefully.

At least Davin's wallet was lying beside him, so she wouldn't have to search his pockets. Surprisingly agile, his hand caught her wrist as she reached for the black leather. His jaw and neck tensed as he swallowed. Haunted eyes stared up at her, begging for…something.

For a moment, Shoshi forgot to breathe. *So very wrong.* The urge to wrap him in her arms, to offer even a modicum of solace, flooded every cell in her body. Instead she gently uncurled his fingers with her free hand. "I'm getting you more to drink."

He nodded shakily and dropped his hand. What in the world was going on?

She scooped up the wallet and went back to the waiting bartender. A stark state ID—*not* a license—stared back at her from the leather. She slipped out the first credit card across from it and handed it to the bartender. His eyebrows tugged up when Shoshi signed the slip he handed her.

"I'm authorized on the account." *Probably.* The card looked the same as Shoshi's company one. She'd deal with the expense report later.

Gabe slid a bottle of Dimple to her along with the receipt. "Just get him out of here." He didn't wait for a response.

Shoshi slipped the receipt in the wallet alongside a few hundred-dollar bills—which she probably should've used to pay, but too late now—and…

A newspaper article.

Davin was still busy staring into his empty glass, so Shoshi pulled out the small column.

LOCAL BOY KILLED

A tragic accident claimed the life of local boy Micah Hall, 15, yesterday afternoon. Hall was crossing Oak Street on his way to the promenade to meet with friends when he was struck and killed by a car. A police investigation is ongoing, and as of yet no charges have been brought.

Micah was the youngest child of Colin and Vivian Hall. He attended Maple Grove High School along with his sister, Abigail. A memorial service will take place tonight on the Central Quad of the school.

Small print dated the article March 14th. Which made to-day—well yesterday, technically, but today—the anniversary of this boy's death. Breathing past the pang in her chest, Shoshi slid the clipping back into the wallet and grabbed the bottle. It didn't excuse Luc's behavior, not any of it, but he was obviously grieving. Almost twenty years later. *I care who you'll kill if you pass out behind the wheel.*

Luc's head had fallen back against the booth, but his eyes opened when the bottle landed in front of him.

"Come on," she said, taking him lightly by the arm. Rather than his usual suit jacket, he wore a soft sweater that molded to his muscles under her grip. "Let's continue this at your place."

He stared at the unopened bottle.

"This will last you awhile," she added.

His head swiveled so he could peer up at her.

Shoshi tried to wipe the empathy from her expression. She was pretty sure he wouldn't want it. His hand reached languidly for the bottle, but she snatched it out of his grasp, taking a step back. "Let's go."

He pushed against the table to heave himself up, and she exhaled. Upright was good. He left his coat behind on the seat, so she stepped around him to scoop it up. The bartender's reproving stare followed them as Luc stumbled out the door.

"Gimme the bottle," he said a few steps later.

"Come on," Shoshi repeated instead, steering him toward his building. Everything was hushed as they trudged down the street, but at least it wasn't snowing.

"The bottle," Luc commanded several more times, until Shoshi finally closed his apartment door behind them.

"Here." She held out the whisky while Luc groped for the light switch. He grabbed it from her and walked away.

By the time Shoshi saw him again, after pulling off her coat and boots, he was swigging amber liquor directly from the bottle. His sweater was partially pulled off, hanging from one arm. She made her way down the hallway and reached for the whisky.

He pulled it away, stumbling a few steps back into the shadowed living room. Shoshi moved toward him again, stopping in front of him. He tilted the bottle in her direction, looking down at her with that raw hopelessness that sliced into her heart, the rings of his irises nearly glowing in the dim light. She took the whisky, tipping it to her lips as they held eye contact, then swallowed past the light burn.

"Your boyfriend know you're here?" Luc whispered, amazingly lucid for a moment. His breath smelled almost like the open bottle.

"He's not my keeper." Though this was so far outside her job description... But Luc clearly didn't have anyone else, even if it was by his own choice. And Shoshi couldn't help caring, even if she knew she shouldn't. She tugged off his dangling sweater then turned toward his bedroom.

He slapped the wall behind her, steadying himself as he followed the bottle she still held. He plopped onto the bed and held a hand out in a silent command. She tossed the sweater aside and said, "Shoes," passing him the whisky.

Luc squinted as his feet moved, trying to push his shoes off with his toes. That took enough effort that he ignored the liquor, letting his arm droop. He still failed, and his feet stopped moving as he huffed out his defeat.

"Let me." She worked the bottle from his lax grip and set it aside on the floor. Luc fell back on the bed as she knelt to slip off his shoes. His eyes had closed, and she couldn't hear him breathe.

How drunk was too drunk? Obviously, he was wasted, but were they in alcohol poisoning territory? Should she be calling him an ambulance? Shoshi stood but hesitated by the bed. Was his chest moving? She hadn't turned on any light in the bedroom, but some flowed in from the hallway, and some more from the street beyond the angled window past his bed. Despite that, she couldn't see any movement.

Shoshi licked her lips and ran her hand over her scalp, pushing back her hair. Carefully she leaned forward over Luc, bracing one hand on the bed. He didn't stir. Her other hand hovered over his chest, just barely skimming his tee shirt until it pressed more firmly against her palm, then fell away again. She exhaled the air that had frozen in her own lungs, then pushed herself back to an upright position. He was breathing. And breathing was good.

Chapter 29

$\mathcal{P}$AIN PULSED IN LUC'S HEAD. SAND SCRATCHED HIS EYES AS he forced them open, instantly shutting them again. The pounding intensified when he turned his head toward the light streaming through his window. He deserved worse.

His eyes opened again to a glass of water on his nightstand. A white bottle stood beside it, its cap perched on top. Luc squinted. *Advil.* He didn't own Advil.

He tried to swallow past the thickness in his throat. When that failed, he tried to cough, shooting icepicks into his brain. His fingers dug into the bed beneath him as he strained to sit up enough to reach for the pills. He groaned, but this pain was the better choice, claiming all of his attention. He'd almost reached the bottle when his hand stalled midair.

Curled on the armchair in front of the window, Shoshana slept. Had he called her last night? It explained the Advil, and the forethought of the water. Why had she stayed? After everything he'd done, especially lately. Driving her to the brink of collapse with his selfishness. He really was a bastard. And she was the living proof.

Luc managed to pick up the pill bottle, then slogged his way out to the kitchen. He cupped his palm under the faucet to help the pills down. Way easier than lifting the full glass she'd left, even if most of the water never made it to his mouth, dripping down his chest instead. He blinked at the droplets in his sink before making his way to the living room couch. He let his head drop back and closed his eyes. Half an hour for the pills to bring him the relief he didn't deserve.

Shoshi grimaced, then tried to work the soreness out of her cramped neck muscles with gentle movements. It took several more seconds for reality to filter in and her eyes to snap open. Luc's bed was empty, and sunlight filled the room.

How long had she spent watching him last night? He hadn't moved at all, for hours. At some point she'd remembered to turn his head to the side, propping one shoulder up on a pillow—as much as she could manage to keep him from choking if he threw up. She'd gotten up to check he was breathing more than once. The last time she remembered, hazy light had shone through the window. But if he was up, he had to be alive. More or less.

Shoshi unfolded from the chair, stifling a groan. Sleeping with her knees tucked up against her chest had translated to feeling like she was eighty. *Wonderful.* Her first stop was the bathroom across from Luc's bedroom, but its door was open and Luc wasn't curled around the toilet. That had to be a good sign.

Instead he sat on the couch, head tipped back, hands lax at his sides. Shoshi slid her feet along the hallway. Lifting them to step was too much effort.

Luc had to be feeling worse than her. He'd drunk as if he wanted to join the killed boy. *Micah Hall.* Luc's head lifted as

Shoshi reached the coffee table, and he stood, examining her like he was searching for injuries. Almost like he was concerned. "You shouldn't have stayed."

Right. She should have left him with the full bottle of whisky and walked in to find a dead body when he didn't show up for work today. At least now she knew why he'd blocked off the morning.

"Take the day off," he continued. "Go get a massage or something. That chair couldn't have been comfortable."

Shoshi shrugged, then winced at the tug in her muscles. He wasn't wrong. He was also trying to get rid of her. Empathy wasn't exactly in his repertoire. "Are you okay?" she asked instead of leaving.

He hesitated, the lines between his eyebrows deepening. "I've been hung over before." But the comment didn't hold his usual enmity.

Shoshi nodded, even though that wasn't what she meant. He actually didn't look so bad off, if a little haggard, rumpled. Meanwhile she probably looked like a disaster. She wrapped her arms around her waist, and Luc's gaze dropped to the movement. He shook his head slightly and walked past her to the kitchen. Water ran then he stepped back out, glass in hand. At least he hadn't poured himself another drink.

"Who's Micah Hall?" she asked, exhaustion and the stress of last night replacing her filter. She needed to understand.

The glass froze a few millimeters from Luc's lips. He slowly lowered it, eyes suddenly laser-focused on her, fury and panic warring in his expression. "Where did you hear that name?"

Shoshi squeezed her waist a little tighter but then dropped her arms. She wouldn't cower from his misplaced hostility. "The clipping in your wallet."

His knuckles went white around the glass. He disappeared back into the kitchen, and the glass clattered against his counter. Shoshi crept forward. He stood with his back to the hallway, hands braced on either side of the sink, shoulders hunched, his muscles nearly vibrating with the force of his grip.

She leaned against the wall across from him. "Who was he?"

Luc's shoulders twitched, but then he straightened and turned, standing strong despite the torrent of emotion he couldn't hide as his eyes skewered her. "He's the boy I killed."

Shoshi's mouth dropped open with her inhale. If not for the wall, she would have stumbled back. She'd misheard him. He couldn't have *actually*—

I care who you'll kill... Had he spoken from experience?

She forced her lips shut and straightened from the wall.

"Go home," he added brusquely, brushing past her to disappear into the bedroom. He didn't slam the door, but probably only out of deference to his hangover.

She gaped at the empty hallway as her mind tried to catch up to the blunt admission. The clipping had said something about criminal charges, but nothing about Luc. Her sore muscles would have preferred a hot shower, but Shoshi padded over to the couch, pulling the iPhone out of her pocket. It wasn't like she could leave him alone now anyway, no matter what he said. But she could investigate. What exactly had happened all those years ago?

Luc didn't come out of his bedroom until his front door had opened and shut, Shoshana finally leaving. *Good.* He was better off alone.

But his apartment wasn't silent. Plastic crinkled out of sight, down the hall. He followed the sound to his dining table. Two places were set, and Shoshana was laying out containers of delivered food.

"Why are you still here?" He couldn't stand the misplaced compassion in her eyes. Whatever she thought she knew, whatever excuse she'd come up with, she was wrong. And what would compel her to give him the benefit of the doubt, anyway, after everything he'd intentionally put her through?

"You should try to eat something," she said, as if the only thing out of the ordinary was his hangover.

Luc didn't move. Shoshana had turned out to be a more effective diversion than the stream of bodies in his bed, her condemnation at once a distraction from his guilt and the perfect reminder of his reprehensibility. Her care now grated, shredding him raw. "What are you still doing here?" he repeated.

Shoshana slowly withdrew her hand from the container she'd been opening and straightened. "The massage was a generous offer, but I'm fine."

Luc's jaw spasmed, shooting pain into his temples. She was playing dumb. "I *killed* him," he ground out, stalking closer until he towered over her. "Did you not hear me, or are you too stupid to understand what I'm saying?"

Her lips tightened, but she didn't otherwise react to his cruelty. Too used to it by now. "It was an accident," she said evenly, looking up at him. Her large eyes showed none of her earlier derision, none of her disgust. Nothing he deserved.

Luc's hand groped blindly for whatever was on the table, gripping the decanter he'd emptied the night before. His arm swung upward, aiming for anything at all.

Her hand landed on his wrist before he could let the crystal fly.

They froze like that, his arm outstretched above their heads, only the faint pressure from her fingers saving the decanter and whatever it would have hit. Ragged breathing filtered in amid the rush of blood in his head, but Shoshana's shoulders were still. His own chest heaved as he struggled to draw in air, drowning in the depths of her eyes.

He saw her lips move before he understood the words. "It wasn't your fault."

The decanter dropped from his grasp. Shoshana let him go to catch it, and he staggered away.

"You're fired," he informed her and turned back down the hall.

"Luc," she called after him, her use of his name stabbing at him.

"Get out!" he growled and slammed the bathroom door shut. He kept the lights off, staring at the shadows of his reflection as his pulse pounded the unrelenting beat of his damnation.

Shoshi jerked as the door slammed. The crystal decanter remained in her hands, its weight growing with every second that ticked by. She set it down slowly, fingers ready to catch it until she was sure of the table holding it up.

She'd taken so much abuse from him, but this time was different. No amusement or pleasure touched his eyes as he scrambled for an insult—like he was desperate to shove her away. To make her hate him. *Like he hates himself.*

It had taken little effort to find follow-up articles to the one he carried around. Luc hadn't been drunk or impaired as he drove, but when Micah Hall had jaywalked, teenaged Luc hadn't braked fast enough. The papers didn't say if he'd been distracted by something, but that was before the time of teens glued to their cell phones. The boy probably hadn't looked as he stepped out into the street, or maybe he'd misjudged the distance between himself and the car. It was a tragic accident, but officials seemed to agree it hadn't been Luc's fault. No charges were ever brought.

The boy I killed, Luc had spat out. The boy whose death still haunted him—for whose death he so obviously still blamed himself. Was that why he worked with nonprofits like Brighter Promise?

Shoshi shuffled to the mound in the hallway that was her coat tossed over her purse and shoes, then tugged on the boots. He'd asked her to leave several times, and he obviously didn't want to talk about this with her. And he seemed recovered enough to take care of himself.

You're fired. The words had been dispassionate, empty. Hopeless. But his demand that she get out, that was unequivocal. At least she'd had the presence of mind last night to get her car off the street, so it was waiting safely in the garage.

Out in the hallway, she paused. What was she supposed to do now? She fell lightly back against his door. Luc wouldn't be heading to work this afternoon either, most likely. But if she took him at his word, that wasn't her concern anymore. Which meant she could go home.

The bottomless self-loathing beneath his nonchalant, callously uncaring shell... But she hadn't mistaken the pleasure he'd taken in tormenting her all these weeks. And though he volunteered with local teens, there was Kayla. Or had Shoshi misunderstood the pregnant girl's urgent need to see Luc? How did this all tie in with Lacey?

And why did he refuse to speak to his mother?

Because of the guilt. That had to be it—he felt so guilty he...what? Thought he didn't deserve his mother's love? Or maybe anyone's. Was that the reason for the parade of one-night stands—an inability to let anyone get close? Or maybe she was reaching again, trying to find an explanation when his nighttime adventures were just about sex, the women merely interchangeable bodies to be used for his pleasure.

The real question was: what did any of that have to do with her?

Shoshi's phone rang, and she startled. She was home. She'd barely noticed driving back or walking through the door. *Safe, Shoshi.* At least Luc's obsession with car safety finally made sense.

She flipped over the phone she'd dropped onto her bed. The number wasn't registered, but it was an extension from the office. Her former office? Shoshi picked up anyway. "Hello?"

"Shana," Rico said on the other end. "Are you all right?"

Good question. Physically she was fine, or she would be after a hot shower and some sleep. But otherwise?

Chapter 30

$\mathcal{B}$Y THE TIME SHE MET RICO FOR DINNER, SHOSHI STILL hadn't been able to make sense of the muddled jumble in her mind.

"He really fired you?" Rico asked.

She nodded with an affirmative hum and popped another bite of pasta into her mouth. Sleep, eat, shower, laundry, and now dinner. All the necessary steps of living her life while the details worked themselves out in her subconscious—hopefully. Or there was always tomorrow.

"I don't understand," Rico said, watching her as his food got cold.

She sighed and set down her fork. Her other hand fell away from the necklace she'd been fiddling with. The one she wouldn't even have anymore if it weren't for Luc. "I don't either." Why fire her *now*? And had he meant it? Did it matter? Even if he hadn't, Shoshi'd probably be better off taking the out. Assuming she managed to find another job.

"He called you at three in the morning to fire you?"

"No." Shoshi shook her head. "Or, I don't think so." He'd asked the bartender to call her, but did he even remember that? He'd been so far gone, his body so still when he passed out… She shook her head again to clear the memory and picked up her fork, but it paused halfway to her mouth.

"What's wrong?" Rico asked, his own hand hesitating in the motion of putting his drink down.

Shoshi lowered her fork again. "He knows, about us." She hadn't understood the implications of his comment last night, but Luc hadn't been talking abstractly when he'd referred to her boyfriend. How long had he known about them?

"Oh." Rico lifted his glass for another sip. "That isn't why he fired you?"

The anguish in Luc's eyes flashed through her mind again, his hand groping for something—anything—to absorb his rage and pain. She hadn't thought before stepping close to stop him. So close she'd felt both the heat of his body and the agony inundating him. "No." She took a deep breath to drag herself out of the memory. "I don't think so, just thought you should know."

Rico's cell buzzed with a new notification, and he flipped it over, nodding absently. Shoshi speared a slice of zucchini.

What was she supposed to do now? She'd need to go in and collect her things. Plus there would be firing paperwork to take care of. And getting a new phone, since her company one would undoubtedly be shut off soon—or transferred to Luc's new assistant? If he hired one. She'd also need to drop off the company card, and Luc's key, the pass to his garage…

Rico's hand landed on hers to stop it playing with her knife on the tablecloth. His brown eyes watched her with a mix of concern and warmth. "It'll be all right. You'll find something better soon. Maybe even something closer to what you want." His mouth slanted in a reassuring half smile.

Shoshi tugged her lips into a returning smile and nodded. Back to the job search—that definitely had to happen. She'd met so many people in the last months. Would any of them remember her as anything but Luc's shadow? A couple from the Leap party, maybe.

But would anyone other than Luc ever look past her time at Keres Financial? And would listing this position help her at all, after only a few months?

Should she act like he'd never said it, so she could keep the job—and the paycheck? Could she even work with him after this?

Rico squeezed her fingers, prompting her gaze back to him. "Try to take the night off. Figuring out your next steps can wait until tomorrow."

He was right. Shoshi took a deep breath and mentally shook off all the questions. "And it's nice to get to spend some time with you." They'd both been so busy lately.

He winced, withdrawing his hand. "Actually, I have to get back to the office after dinner. Things should calm down soon. Why don't you call Nat?"

Her smile dropped, but Shoshi forced another small nod. Nat was still pissed that Shoshi had put Luc's constant demands first. Only to be left with an impending, likely interminable, job search. And dozens of questions that would probably never be answered.

Chapter 31

S HOSHI DRUMMED HER FINGERS ON HER LAPTOP, THEN pushed the computer away and plopped backwards on her bed. It was weird, not having anywhere to go. Not seeing Luc for days after spending nearly all her waking hours with him. After seeing the boundless torment behind his unfeeling shell.

She'd gone to the office with Rico after dinner Monday to pick up her things while almost no one was there. Of course, "her things" had consisted mostly of a ziplocked bag of Krave, her stash of energy drinks, and some backup hairpins. A good chunk of Tuesday had been spent catching up on sleep, then taking care of some more of those normal mundane chores she hadn't had time for in far too long. Yesterday she'd bought a new phone, taken a walk by the Charles, read a book, and gone over her finances. Luc hadn't commented on her absence, hadn't contacted her at all. So now it was job search time.

At least Rico's schedule should ease up soon. He'd suggested another trip to the ballet tomorrow night. The problem was Shoshi had already worn the one formal dress she owned, and buying something new when she was once again out of a job would be idiotic. Would Rico notice if she wore the same thing? Would he care? And if he did care, what did that say about him? Or her, that she was so focused on a dress instead of finding a new job.

Maybe that every time she looked through job descriptions, her mind returned to the tangled mess that was Luc. What had he wanted from her? Sure, he'd ended up talking through things out loud, running them past her in case she noticed something he'd missed—not that he would admit that—but he definitely hadn't expected to do that when he'd hired her. He'd wanted to push her buttons, to get a rise out of her. All his positive qualities, whatever they may be, didn't cancel out his callous, manipulative behavior.

And yet, it was almost like he *tried* to come off as detestable, to keep all his flaws in the spotlight.

Either way, he wasn't her problem anymore. Still…

Would he pick up the phone tomorrow? What would his mother think when no one answered her call?

Probably that he'd fired Shoshi. She should really stop imagining her brief role in either of their lives mattered. All she and Luc were to each other was a desperate employee and the man who'd taken advantage for his own inscrutable reasons.

Shoshi groaned and lifted off the bed. She'd been stuck in this loop for days, and it was going nowhere. She needed a detox from Luc Davin.

"Anyone know what happened to Shana?" Linda from HR asked, peeking her head into the break room as Rico poured his afternoon cup of coffee. Had Luc not told her?

"She hasn't been in this week," one of the associates answered.

Rico shook his head, but office gossip was inevitable.

"Does this mean she finally quit? Who won the pool?" someone else asked.

Rico's mug hit the countertop a little too harshly, halting the conversation and drawing looks his way. He turned and strode back out of the break room before he said something stupid. Revealing their relationship wouldn't be doing her any favors.

"She *was* looking pretty beat last week," someone commented behind him.

Rico made it to his office and firmly shut the door. No one would come in unannounced, but for once he would have preferred a lock. Thankfully, this week was almost over. Tonight, he and Shana would take another trip to the ballet, and then they could have a relaxing weekend together. He took a calming sip of coffee and sat down.

A missed call flashed on the phone he'd left on his desk. He smiled and called back. "Hola, mamá."

"Rico, ¿cómo estás, cariño?"

"Bien, bien. How are you? How's dad's knee doing?" Rico picked up his coffee and swiveled away from his computer.

"Ai, you know your father. Always complaining, but he's walking better. It's not so bad. How is work? And that new girl of yours? I hope we'll get to meet her."

"Not so new, mamá." Though it had been only a couple months. "Shana's a great girl. I'm sure you'll meet her soon. It's going that way, anyway."

"No, no, Rico. We want to meet her now. You're not so young, you know."

He sat up straighter. "Now?"

"Ai, your father. He did not tell you?"

"You said you wanted to!" his father added in the background.

"Tell me what?" Rico asked before it could spiral into a full-fledged, if loving, bickering match.

"We're coming to visit," his mom announced. "To Boston," she clarified.

Rico chuckled as he shook his head. He swiveled back around to pull up his calendar on the computer. At least they'd waited until after his major deadline. And it would be great to see them. "When will you be here?"

"For Easter."

"Easter?" He must have heard wrong.

"Yes, we want to celebrate with you, and meet that girl. We can go to her church Friday and yours for the Vigil, or the other way. How did you have it planned?"

"What about Easter dinner back home?" Rico asked. He and Shana hadn't really talked about the religious side of things yet, but she probably wouldn't want to spend her weekend with them at mass. And she definitely didn't have her own church. "You always cook."

"Your brother has his family now, and you, you have no one."

"Your mother worries." His dad must have picked up the second handset. "Have you become a heathen?" he teased.

"I wouldn't dare." But he hadn't planned anything other than attending mass. He hadn't even realized Palm Sunday was this weekend, though there it was on his calendar, a reminder to go to church. "When do you get in?" he asked.

"On Wednesday," his dad said.

"You didn't answer about church," his mother reminded, and Rico winced.

"My church, for all the services. And Shana might not join us—"

"Oh no," his mother interrupted. "We travel all that way, you do not hide this girl from us, Rico."

"No, Mom, I meant to mass. Shana's Jewish."

Neither of his parents spoke for a prolonged moment that in another time might have meant the call had dropped.

"Ricardo," his mother said eventually. "Why do you insist on wasting time, again? Won't you ever marry? You promised me, no more. No more of these girls who aren't serious. You think your father and me, we'll live forever? Don't you want us to meet our grandbabies?"

"Mom. This isn't a fling. Shana is wonderful—"

"You cannot marry a *Jewish* girl!"

"Are you trying to kill your mother? This isn't funny, Ricardo." His father's voice was stern, as if Rico was still ten and had been caught sneaking out of Sunday school lessons.

But they'd said themselves, he wasn't that young anymore. "I'm not joking," he said calmly.

"What about your children, huh?" his mother interrupted before he could say more. "What will they think when she does not go to mass? How will you teach them, raise them to believe in the Lord, when your own wife—"

"What wife, mamá? What kids?" He sighed, pinching the bridge of his nose. "We haven't talked about it yet. I don't have answers for you, but Shana is a wonderful girl."

"Are you saying she'll convert?" his mother persisted. "Then she should come to church. And that is where we will meet her or not at all." The line clicked.

"Hello?"

"We'll see you Wednesday," his father said quietly. "You think long and hard, Ricardo. Don't break your mother's heart."

Chapter 32

By Monday, Shoshi still hadn't heard from HR, or from Luc. She had, however, received an electronic notice that her loans were paid in full. She didn't even question how Luc had managed that. So late that morning, she headed back to the office.

The executive half was silent as ever, the desk that had been hers standing empty, but Shoshi veered to the right.

"Wow," Sebastian said as she strode past his desk.

Shoshi stopped and turned back. "Don't get too excited. I won't be here long."

He stood and stepped closer, slipping his hands into his pockets. "So it's true. You quit."

Quit? "Nope. So who won the pool?"

Sebastian glanced around the room and angled his body closer, as if afraid someone would overhear. "Depends. When, uh. When was your last day?"

Shoshi rolled her eyes and started to turn away, but a hand landed on her upper arm.

"Hey, wait." His arm fell away politely. "You look good, you know." His eyes swept down her body as if to corroborate. "Way better."

No undertone of lust accompanied his words, just genuine encouragement. And one of the major perks for this position was supposed to be networking. "Thanks," Shoshi said. "Maybe we could stay in touch, grab drinks again sometime."

His chin dipped with his smile. "Sure. See you around, Shana."

She nodded back and made her way to the HR rep. Connections, a boyfriend, her loans repaid, even her car fixed… On paper, she hadn't come out from this whole thing too poorly. So why did it feel like her life had only careened further off track?

"What," Luc called when someone knocked on his door. He'd been going through Shoshana's ridiculously well-organized notes. She'd streamlined his process even further, and he'd gotten used to not having to deal directly with every call or email. Even let himself start to rely on having someone else to catch things that may slip through the cracks.

Maybe he should hire another assistant. Priscilla had flat out stated she was interested in the job. But it wasn't worth losing her as their office manager. And it wouldn't be the same.

"Sorry to disturb you."

Luc froze, not looking up at the woman who'd come into his office. If he did, he'd see his ears were playing tricks on him. *Stupid.* He dropped his pen and forced himself to lean back in his chair. "Shoshana."

Her eyebrows lifted gently. "Luc."

Their names hung in the air between them. She looked nice in a clingy blue sweater and the skirt that hugged her hips before flaring out. She'd left her hair down, too, the loose dark curls falling around her shoulders like she no longer felt the need to hide them. She always looked most herself this way. Had she actually come back?

She broke their eye contact, glancing down at some papers in her hand. "I, uh. HR says you need to provide written documentation, to officially terminate my employment."

Of course. Rash words, but no surprise she would jump at the chance. He'd incentivized this from the start, caught now in his own trap. "What would it take?" he asked instead of taking the paperwork.

Her eyes narrowed and her head shook in a little confused jerk, but the hand with the forms lowered. "What?"

"I shouldn't have fired you." His jaw clenched, fighting the honest words. "Turns out you were useful, on occasion," he added. No doubt she saw through the blasé comment. She always saw too much.

"I don't understand." She nudged the door shut and took a couple steps toward him.

"We could consider last week an impromptu vacation, compensation for all your overtime."

She didn't say anything, but she didn't leave.

"What would it take?" Luc repeated. Did she know he'd already paid off her loans? Not a bribe, just… The right thing to do. Something to make her life a little easier after all the ways he'd made it worse. And they'd had a deal.

She licked her lips as her chest rose and fell with her breath. Her gaze flicked down toward her hand, which tightened on the papers. Her free hand pushed her hair behind one ear. "Lunch."

Luc couldn't stop his brows from drawing together, but he wiped his confusion away quickly. "Lunch," he repeated, drawing the word out as he searched out the catch.

"During which you have a frank, honest conversation with me. Then I'll consider it."

Luc's heart thumped. Something too soft had filtered into Shoshana's expression. If he were truly honest with her, it wouldn't last long. Weak man that he was, he didn't want to watch it disappear.

"One hour," Luc agreed. Of the two of them, he had the better poker face. He could handle an hour. "But if I'm honest, so are you."

Chapter 33

SWEAT GATHERED ON SHOSHI'S PALMS AS THEY WALKED silently to the elevator. Her hour didn't start until they sat down for lunch. Would she finally get the answers to the dangling threads she'd tried to unravel? Though maybe she should be more concerned with what he wanted to ask her, not that she had any big secrets. With their history, Luc might try to throw her off with overly prying sexual questions, but that didn't seem to be what he wanted. *What would it take?*

Neither of them touched their menus when the waiter walked away from their table. Luc would order the steak tips, as she had so many times for him. Shoshi wasn't really here for lunch. She reached for the glass of water, focusing on the chill between her fingers rather than on Luc's clenched jaw, or the hint of panic that had appeared when she'd asked for honesty.

He raised one eyebrow, the same way he had countless times before, but he sat more rigidly now, on the defensive.

Shoshi swallowed and set her glass down. "Who's Kayla?" she asked. Of everything she wanted to know, this had to be the simplest. She'd met Kayla; he had to know she was curious, and concerned.

"A young pregnant girl," he brushed off.

"That wasn't what I meant by honest."

He reached for his own water. "What is it you want to know?" he asked before taking a sip, his Adam's apple bobbing as he swallowed. This man who handled millions of dollars without batting an eye, unnerved by the mere prospect of honesty.

"How do you know her?" That seemed like a fairer question than what she really wanted to ask.

He scowled. "She's a young girl in a tough spot, who doesn't have anyone."

Wait. "So, it's not your baby? You were just helping her out?"

Luc hesitated, then nodded once, stiffly. Why was it so hard for him to admit?

The waiter appeared, setting down their drinks, and for the first time since they'd met, Luc looked to her to order first. Shoshi glanced down at the menu.

"I can give you another minute," the waiter offered, leaning away as if to go.

"No, we're all set." Shoshi shot him a smile. "I'll have the grilled salmon, please."

"Steak tips, medium." Luc glanced up at the waiter as the young man repeated the order back.

Shoshi expelled her breath slowly. "What about Lacey?" she asked when Luc met her gaze again.

His head tilted back and to the right—a mark of his surprise. How many hours had she spent watching him? Learning to read his every gesture and expression. "My niece."

So the sewing machine had been nothing more than a birthday gift, a sweet gesture. How could she have gotten it—him—so wrong?

But then, that had been precisely what Luc wanted, hadn't it—for her to see the absolute worst in everything about him.

"If all your questions are this easy, I may even enjoy my lunch." But he still reached for his scotch, taking a not-so-small sip. "My turn," he said softly.

With his detached amusement stripped away, unsettling intensity sharpened his gaze. Like there were stakes to their little deal that she still didn't understand. "What's in the storage unit in Philadelphia?" he asked.

Shoshi's chest constricted at the reminder. Her hand lifted toward her sternum, but she'd left the hamsa off today, so she shoved some hair behind her ear instead. "Everything I have left of my parents." From her dad's old stamp collection to her mom's wedding gown—everything that wouldn't fit in that one tiny box hidden in her apartment. Shoshi's wine beckoned, but she reached for the water. The chilled sip was steadying. "How did you know about that?"

"PI report, when I first hired you."

That raised more questions, but none important enough to ask in this hour. Whether he'd been curious or he'd hoped to find something to exploit was irrelevant. Since this lunch had turned into twenty questions, it was her turn. "Is that rumor about the charity fund true?"

"What rumor?"

"That the money for it would otherwise go to your salary."

"Not entirely." This time she didn't have to prod him to elaborate. "It was supposed to be confidential, off the record.

But technically," he said, his jaw tight, "some of it is money I asked to be diverted, yes."

"Some" meaning hundreds of thousands of dollars. Every year. The speculation she'd thought was so farfetched when she first heard it seemed totally believable now, seeing Luc struggle to admit something so many would have bragged about. And given everything, it made sense, him supporting nonprofits that worked with teens.

"Why do you go by Shana at work?" he asked, continuing their back-and-forth. "We live in Boston, *Shoshana* wouldn't exactly stick out."

She hadn't expected that, but then Luc had met her as Shoshana. Even drunk, he'd used her full name—or tried to. "People march through the streets proudly wearing Nazi insignia, spray-paint swastikas everywhere, shoot up synagogues, and you think Boston's impervious to antisemitism?" Shoshi took a measured breath to settle the tremble in her voice. Something like sixty percent of religious hate crimes in the US targeted Jews, but that wasn't technically what he'd asked. "Finance especially deals with clients from other cities, other countries. Implicit bias is everywhere. As Shana, there's one less barrier." The tiniest bit more safety. It wasn't something she was confronted with every day, but it wasn't something she ever forgot, either.

Luc frowned, angled grooves forming between his brows, but he didn't argue with the reality. Shoshi offered the waiter as genuine a smile as she could manage when he set their dishes on the table then melted away without a word. Neither of them touched their food.

Precious seconds ticked away as she hesitated. Still, she was here to get the answers that mattered. "Why don't you speak to your mom?"

Luc stilled. She'd called him predatory before, but those times were nothing compared to now. Had he been a hunter, she would have been terrified. But he was more like a feral, wounded animal. So maybe she should still have been terrified.

His hand clenched into a fist on the cream tablecloth, his pinky knocking rhythmically against the surface.

Shoshi almost backtracked, letting him off the hook, but she needed to know, to understand. These last months Luc had dominated her life, yet she had barely any idea who he really was.

"After the crash… It was a small town." He gazed blankly at the table. What was he seeing? "People knew I was responsible, and they made sure my family knew it, too, driving to the next town rather than shop in my dad's store, things like that. Suddenly my mom's prize-winning pies were deemed inedible. My brother…" Luc sighed. "He probably had the hardest time, going to high school with them all, with…*his* sister, his friends.

"After I left for college, it took a while, but bit by bit, people let up. They started to distinguish between me and my family, realize they weren't to blame." He paused, unclenching his fingers to curl them around his drink. "I could hear it, in my parents' voices. Happiness, normalcy replacing the constant hurt and worry. They're good people." He met her gaze, pulling back to the present with despairing resignation. "They shouldn't have to bear the weight of what I've done."

"It was an accident," Shoshi murmured reflexively, still processing the rest. In his mind, he was protecting them. But that only explained why he had moved away from home, not why he refused to speak to his mother.

"What do you know about it?" Luc asked bitterly, gulping down the remainder of his scotch.

"You weren't drunk. You weren't speeding, you—"

"I was distracted," he spat out. "Fiddling with the radio or something. I should have seen him sooner, reacted sooner. I could have—" He cut himself off with a small headshake and ran his gaze around the room.

His entire life, defined by one moment, one accident. He may not have been charged with anything, but he'd still spent all these years punishing himself, imprisoned by his guilt. Something clicked, and Shoshi took a sip of wine for courage. "I'm sure your parents never blamed you." In his eyes, their support must have been even worse.

"That's not a question," Luc said flatly.

"You explained why you left home back then, but why don't you talk to your family? They obviously want to talk to you."

A faint flush had crept over Luc's cheeks, and his breathing deepened. "My turn," he said brusquely. "What about your family? There had to be someone after your father died. Why choose emancipation, being on your own?"

Shoshi picked up her fork and flaked off a few pieces of salmon, fanning them on the plate. It wasn't a particularly difficult question; she just didn't talk about it, not that anyone had ever really wanted her to. Luc had asked it so casually, as if one of the worst times of her life was no more than small talk.

But then, she wasn't pulling any punches with her own questions.

"There wasn't anyone particularly close," she said. "My grandparents had all passed by then. There were my dad's cousins, I'd met them a few times, but burdening them seemed unfair, and unnecessary when I was so close to eighteen." They were still in touch, sort of—mostly thanks to Facebook—but being on her own had seemed easier than intruding on someone else's life, forcing them to take care of her out of family obligation. Besides, she'd had the local Jewish community, bringing her meals for weeks afterward, checking in on her. Maybe no one had been in the audience for her graduation, but she hadn't felt much like celebrating anyway.

"They're better off," Luc said. "My family," he clarified when Shoshi's head jerked up in surprise. "I didn't want to burden them, either. They're good, faithful people, and I'm…" He exhaled, and his expression rearranged into impassive certainty. "There's nothing good in me."

"How can you say that?" The breathy question escaped her without warning, but Shoshi pressed on. "All the good you do, and you're still stuck, punishing yourself for an accident."

"Shouldn't you know better? You've seen how I live." A hint of that callous, calculating veneer slipped back into place. "Does it look like I'm punishing myself?"

Yes. Cutting himself off from anyone who cared about him, going to such lengths to hide his charity work, making a show of his vices… To convince people he had no morals, didn't feel remorse. Or maybe to convince himself.

"I'm headed straight for hell, but at least I'm going to enjoy the ride," Luc said, confirming the suspicion, fully ensconced once more in that flippant, defiant shell.

"You give thousands upon thousands of dollars to charity, anonymously, rather than living a wasteful, extravagant lifestyle. You donate countless hours of your time to volunteering, helping the community—kids—directly. You take time out of your life to prioritize a young girl in need." To buy a new chain for the hamsa he'd found.

Shoshi set her forgotten fork down and straightened against the back of her chair. She should have realized it then. How many people would have even bothered to return the charm? Or noticed how much it meant to her. "You might want to convince yourself you're irredeemable, but fight it all you like, you can't contain your *good* nature, that you're innately a good person."

Another piece clicked. "That's why you actually offered me the job, isn't it? Because I was desperate, and you wanted to help me." It explained the signing bonus, too. Her car, the phone… Even his work steering various startups was on some fundamental level about helping others succeed.

"You're like a naïve teenager," he retorted, "searching for scraps of goodness where there aren't any, thinking she can reform the 'bad boy.' It's past time you grew up."

Shoshi let the insult slide by. He really was a wounded animal, lashing out. "Believe me, the last thing I wanted was to find any goodness in you. It's just so glaringly obvious I can't ignore it anymore." Another sip of the tart wine washed away the bite of her frustration. "And that wasn't an answer. You promised me honesty. Why did you create a job for me?"

Luc's jaw clenched. He signaled the waiter for another scotch. "For the look in your eyes, all that disgust you didn't really even try to hide. For the daily reminder of how contemptible I am." Over her soft gasp, he added, "Didn't quite go to plan."

Shoshi's eyes tingled as she tried to breathe through the stab of comprehension in her chest. He'd used her to keep punishing himself. And it had worked.

Luc leaned forward, bracing his wrists on the edge of the table. "I *killed* someone. There's no absolution for that, no penance that's sufficient. This isn't something you can say Hail Marys for. No amount of money donated or hours volunteered can even the scale on that."

He must have taken Shoshi's heartbroken silence for agreement because he slumped back in his chair, adding, "The only thing I can do is not drag anyone else to hell with me."

"I'm Jewish," Shoshi pointed out stupidly, as if that mattered. "We don't believe in hell."

Chapter 34

"So, what?" Luc challenged. "No one's responsible for their actions, no consequences?"

"No, of course they are. But it's not a matter of crossing some imaginary line and not being able to find or pray for or earn a way back. With atonement and true remorse, there comes forgiveness."

"How?" Luc couldn't help himself from asking, reflexively clutching at the hope her words offered even when he knew better. Forgiveness wasn't in the cards for him.

A line appeared between Shoshana's eyebrows. "There are different types of mistakes, of sins. If you hurt someone, you're required to make reparations directly to them, if possible, and ask for their forgiveness."

Luc scoffed. "So what, all I'd have to do is apologize to his family." He had, so many times. Nothing he could say would change anything. "And you'd expect them to"—he snapped—"forgive me, just like that."

"Of course not." Her quiet patience grated over his skin. "It's more complicated. It's not really even about the other person. If

258

you are genuine in your remorse, in your apology, in your intention not to repeat whatever the offense, your redemption or absolution isn't dependent on someone else's ability to forgive you."

"And yet on Yom Kippur, you crowd into synagogues and ask each other for forgiveness."

Shoshana's eyes rounded with her surprise, but like he'd said earlier, they lived in Boston. He wasn't oblivious.

"Not quite," she said. "On Yom Kippur, we ask forgiveness for the other kind of sins—for breaking divine law."

"Like 'thou shalt not kill'?" Luc took a large sip from the fresh tumbler the waiter had set down. There was no hope for it, no matter how you spun it. A handful of minutes had damned him, and everything he'd done since proved he didn't deserve any better.

"That's the thing, Luc."

He swallowed roughly at her use of his name. It shouldn't have felt so intimate given all the hours they'd spent together.

"Genuine remorse comes into play there, too. Making amends, like *tzedakah*—supporting charitable work. It'd be different," she added when Luc started to protest, "if we were talking about a serial killer, or cold-blooded murder. Even then that gets too complicated for my understanding, we'd have to ask a rabbi. But in this case, it was an *accident*," she repeated yet again, as if that label solved everything. "A tragic set of circumstances, nothing malicious. You weren't responsible. This agony of blame you've put yourself through has to stop." She sighed, her head tilting as she considered him. "Just imagine what would happen if you stopped fighting your inherent goodness, stopped burying it in your quest to live up to your guilt."

What was penance enough for taking a life? It wasn't even a question worth asking.

Luc dragged his eyes away from her, to the food they hadn't touched as it grew cold. She hated wasting food. He tried to find the waiter to ask for the check, or another drink. Boxes for their plates. Something.

"Everyone makes mistakes, Luc," Shoshana said eventually.

"Yeah? Ever kill someone?" he asked stonily.

Her breath hitched on a little gasp. "Not how you mean, no."

The quiet answer snapped his gaze back to her drawn face. *Her mother.* Not the same, like she'd said. But the thoughtless question had still hurt her. He'd gotten so good at that, he didn't even need to try now.

"I don't think I would have been strong enough, like you," Shoshana continued before he could find the words to clarify.

Not a single trace of sarcasm showed in her expression. How could she look at him and see anything resembling strength?

"Not strong enough, to survive while processing, grieving. Alone, cutting myself off from everyone." Her large, expressive eyes filled not with pity or righteousness, but with compassion, respect. The faintest hint of a lifeline he'd kept trying to snap even as he clung to it…

Movement to her left broke their eye contact as it drew her attention. Her gaze paused on the wall before she turned back to him. "Looks like my hour's up."

Luc pulled out his wallet to toss some bills on the table. "Are you still seeing Rick?" he asked as they stood.

She hesitated before answering, her jacket hanging from her fingers. "Yes."

Luc nodded again, but the selfish part of him, the part he'd been indulging for years no matter what she said, couldn't leave it at that. "You should end it."

She startled, blinking up at him as she forced her lips closed. Her chest rose and fell with a slow breath. "I thought the point of this was to hire me back?"

Having her there, day in and day out… He'd come to rely on her to make it through the day, and not professionally. He'd used her like he'd said, as proof of how contemptible he was. And then, foolishly, for the reminder that despite all he'd put her through, she hadn't lost hope he could be better. Not entirely, anyway, and never for long.

He'd tried to fill the gap her absence had left, but work and even alcohol weren't enough anymore to shut out the quiet of the night that offered far too much opportunity for introspection. Sex with some woman who wasn't her would be even more hollow than all those brief encounters had been before.

Luc forced his jaw to unclench. "The point was to get you back."

Chapter 35

I THINK YOU SHOULD FILL OUT THE PAPERWORK," SHOSHI said when they reached the elevator bank back in Griffith & Moore's building. It was the first time either of them had spoken since Luc's admission. What did he see in her that he wanted around, and since when?

Something had undeniably changed between them. Working for him would no longer mean demeaning assignments or unreasonable demands. But still, continuing to be his subordinate didn't seem like the right call.

He nodded once, decisively. As they'd walked out of the restaurant, a professional veneer had enveloped him. The only difference was now it was solemn, lacking that self-assured, imperturbable amusement.

"I just don't think us working together is right, for either of us," she tried to explain. He could use a friend, an equal, not a shadow. And she needed to focus on finding the right position for her future.

Luc didn't say anything or even look at her, merely strode out the elevator and to his office. Shoshi followed. She couldn't force him to open up, to reach out, not more than this bizarre lunch deal had. But every interaction couldn't be a bargain.

"I don't mean that I wouldn't… I mean." Why couldn't she just say it? *We could try to be friends.*

Luc flipped over the forms the HR rep had given her and sank into his chair, not looking at her until he was safe behind his desk. "I'll take care of these today. You let me know if you need a reference, Miss Glass."

Shoshi nodded numbly and dug into her purse, pulling out his key and then the iPhone. She placed both on his desk.

"You may as well keep the phone," Luc said, like this was all business as usual.

The point was to get you back. It was as if he'd never said those words. As if he hadn't thrown her mind into overdrive yet again. "It wouldn't make sense," Shoshi said, trying—and failing—to match his tone, "continuing to pay for a phone plan—"

"Even with a cancelled line, it's still a computer. Still useful anywhere there's Wi-Fi. Or you could activate it with another number."

"Okay." She forced a small smile and picked up the phone. "Thank you."

Luc watched her for a moment, then tapped his keyboard to wake up his desktop.

"Luc," she said as he entered his password. It sounded like a plea, but even she didn't know for what.

He stiffened, his fingers hovering above the keys.

"You know where to find me," Shoshi murmured before turning away. Each step she took, she strained to hear him call her back. But she made it out of his office and through the glass doors without a word.

Chapter 36

AND THAT WAS THAT. AT LEAST SHOSHI UNDERSTOOD LUC better now—had answers to her questions, and the picture mostly made sense, distorted as it was. Every so often, especially when a phone rang, she'd think about Mrs. Davin, the poor woman's return to dealing with Luc's answering machine, or maybe with Priscilla. And her heart ached for Luc, for his prison of guilt. But unless he reached out, there was nothing she could do. With her termination paperwork in order, Luc was officially in her past.

It should have been a relief, should have felt like freedom. Instead it was like she'd woken up in the middle of a complex dream, or lost a book when she was halfway through. Except there were no other copies, so no matter what she did the story would remain unfinished, with no way to fill in what was missing. Which meant the only real option was to move on, even if she half expected to see one of Luc's bizarre demands every time her phone buzzed.

Still, Shoshi had revitalized her cover letter and résumé and begun sending them out. And things with Rico remained good, calm. There was something on his mind the last few days, it seemed, but she'd been distracted by Luc more than her fair share of times. If Rico needed time to work through something, the least she could do was understand.

Shoshi curled on his bed with a cup of coffee, the sky above her bathed in evening light. It was still a bit too cold and windy to enjoy his rooftop, but this was a very close second. And cozy. She could stay here for hours.

But Rico had suggested an early dinner, and Shoshi needed to go see Nat beforehand, and all of that meant going downstairs and getting dressed.

An hour later, one of Nat's coworkers eyed Shoshi as she got out of her car. "Is Nat around?" she asked, approaching him.

"Who's asking."

"A friend." Shoshi raised one of the bags she'd brought. "Got you guys some donuts."

The guy dropped the wrench and rag he held onto a nearby bench and accepted the bag. He peered inside before calling, "Natalia!"

Shoshi bit back a smile. Nat hated people using her full name.

"*¡Alguien vino a verte!*" he added, then threw Shoshi another look and walked toward the back.

"This better not be—" Nat muttered to the guys, who'd both grabbed donuts, before catching sight of Shoshi. She stopped in her tracks for a moment then strutted over, her chin tipping up. "Well look who remembered the little people."

"That's not fair, Nat." Shoshi held out the coffee carrier.

Nat's jaw shifted, and she dropped her weight into one hip.

Shoshi set the coffee and second bag of pastries down on the workbench. "I'm sorry about your birthday. You know I had to go for work."

"What am I, five? It's not about you leaving early from my party." She scoffed. "Even when you were there, you were hanging out with that hoity-toity boyfriend of yours. Don't need us anymore, right? What are you even doing here during working hours."

"I wanted you to meet my boyfriend, Nat. And he wanted to meet you. I didn't realize you'd mind. And yeah, work was absolutely insane. Rico hated it too, but that was the job." Shoshi lifted one of the coffees from the carrier. Just because Nat wasn't going to have one, that didn't mean Shoshi couldn't.

"Yeah, you're always running off to Davin, aren't you." It wasn't a question.

"So you're, what, mad I had a job?"

"Oh, please." Nat crossed her arms atop her overalls. "That might have started out as a job, but then he'd snap his fingers and you'd rush right over, whatever he wants you to do. All those hours, in his apartment late at night. Does your *boyfriend* know?"

The animosity pushed Shoshi back a step. "What exactly are you trying to say? And even if I had slept with him—which, by the way, I *haven't*—why would that piss you off so much?"

"Sleeping with your boss is just a real classy move, Shosh. Anything to keep your precious job, right?"

"You know what? I'm done here. You want to have a real conversation with me sometime, you know where to find me. My old number, I mean. I'm sorry you're mad I had to work, and that I had a ridiculously demanding boss, but hey, you knew that when you told me to take the job. Sorry the twenty-hour workdays were so inconvenient for *you*."

Nat's arms dropped, her lips pursing in a judgmental pout. Shoshi's nod became a headshake, then she walked back to her car. She hesitated before starting the engine. Nat still stood beside the edible peace offering, staring after her. But when she caught Shoshi looking, she turned away.

"Do you think maybe she was having a bad day?" Rico asked in the face of Shana's frown. The argument sounded a little dramatic, not that he didn't understand being frustrated with Shana's work life. But he was officially out of time to talk to her, and her being upset before he started wasn't going to help.

"Maybe." Shana stared down at her plate, nudging bits of food around.

"You two will work it out now that life is a little less crazy," he assured.

She shot him a halfhearted smile.

"So listen," Rico said, "I need to talk to you about something."

Her eyebrows drew together, and her fork clinked against the plate as she let it go. "Is everything okay?"

"Oh, yes. It's not a big deal." *Hopefully.* "My parents are coming to visit, for Easter."

"That's great!" Her enthusiasm was shadowed with a hint of confusion. "Easter is soon, right?"

"Uh, yes." It made sense, her not following the Catholic calendar, but he still hadn't expected the question. "It's this weekend."

"Oh." She waited for him to go on, uncertainty widening her eyes.

How could he put this? "My parents, they're pretty traditional, religious."

"So…covered shoulders and no sex jokes?" She spoke slowly despite the sarcasm, obviously unsure where he was going with this.

"Look, I hadn't really thought about it, maybe I should have… I, uh. I mentioned you to them."

This smile was tentative, but more genuine.

"And they were a bit…surprised, when I told them you were Jewish."

"Surprised," she echoed, the smile falling away. She sat back, pinching the little charm hanging from her neck.

"My mother asked about meeting you, about the holiday and plans for mass, you know." Rico sighed, setting his own utensils down. "It led down the rabbit hole a bit, questions about the future, things we haven't even had a chance to discuss, and she was a little upset…"

"That I'm Jewish," Shana stated.

"Right. No, well. That you're not Catholic."

"Or some form of Protestant, because if I was, we probably wouldn't be talking about this."

He couldn't argue with that.

A light flush covered her cheeks, and she tucked the necklace beneath her top. "And, what are we talking about, exactly? What did you tell her?"

"I… Nothing." He hadn't known what to say. Shana not even knowing when Easter was kind of underscored his mother's point. "Look, when we met, I hadn't really thought about the possibility of you—" He cut himself off.

"Being Jewish," she finished pointedly. Her shoulders pulled back, the rigid posture like an invisible armor.

"Right." He was saying this all wrong.

"But you've known I'm Jewish for a while now."

"Yes, but I hadn't really thought about what that meant, in terms of the future, if that makes sense. Not until my parents brought it up." They were getting off track.

"What does it mean, exactly?" Shana asked.

"Well, you know, about what traditions to follow, how to raise children down the line—"

"Kids?" She leaned away from the table, shaking her head as her eyebrows climbed up her forehead. "That's what you're…" She trailed off.

"No, look. Listen." All he'd meant to say was that her meeting his parents on this trip might not be the greatest idea. He wasn't even the one who thought there was a problem. "When you've imagined your future, how you'd live your life—in general, not with anyone in particular—I'm sure there were some assumptions. Holidays you'd celebrate, and ones you wouldn't. Traditions you'd pass on to children if you had them." He paused, taking a moment to gather his thoughts. "All I'm saying is my parents made those assumptions about how my life would go. To them, the idea of it being different, of my life not looking like that, was a bit jarring. Unexpected."

"And to you?"

"I—"

"Hadn't thought about it," she finished with him, frustration creeping into her voice.

Rico frowned. Was there a way to turn this around, make it clear? "Shana, wouldn't your parents feel the same way?"

She jerked back, her shoulders twitching up toward her ears. "They're both dead, actually."

What? *Shit.* "I'm sorry, I didn't—"

She cut him off with a little flick of her hand. "So to answer your question," she said, her voice tightly controlled, "I don't know. I'd like to think they would have trusted me to decide what kind of life I want to build for myself and with whom, what lifestyle would make me happy, and they would have supported that." She paused, her head tipping to one side. "What did you tell your parents?"

"I told them we hadn't talked about it." Though he hadn't been able to stop thinking about it since.

Her uneven nod lasted several seconds.

"Look, their flight gets in in a little while. The only thing I wanted to say, needed to tell you, is that it's probably not the right time for you to meet them, it being Easter."

Her gaze danced around the restaurant before settling back on him.

Rico waited as she thought. It wasn't a flattering thing to say, but they hadn't even been seeing each other that long. It was too soon for these conversations, for her to meet his family. Him not knowing about her parents only proved that. But since his parents would be staying with him, and she often spent the night on weekends… "Shana, it's just a few days," he said when her silence drew out.

"You know, I think we should take a break." She paused, tongue slipping out to moisten her lips. "While you think about what you want, about all these questions."

"That *isn't* what I want. I also don't want their trip to turn into a standoff, to cause friction. It's just a weekend."

"That future your mother sees for you," she asked with surprising equanimity, "is that the future you want? Catholic holidays, Sundays in church, everything. Could that picture even have the addition of Jewish traditions, Jewish holidays? I know," she added before he could answer, holding up her palm, "you hadn't thought about it. But you should. Especially if being with someone who doesn't believe in Jesus would mean fighting with your parents. I understand, you not wanting to do that." Huskiness shaded her voice. "Family is so important, and I definitely wouldn't want to be something that alienates you from yours. So that picture, that your parents have…"

Rico shifted, resettling in his seat. What Jewish holidays were there? The only one that came to mind was Yom Kippur, but there had to be more. And could he raise children with someone who didn't believe in Christ? Sure, Shana was new in his life, but he wasn't that young, and he *did* want children. Children who'd go with him to mass, even if not every week, and who'd be baptized and confirmed in the Catholic Church. That was what he'd always expected. But how could that happen without his future wife at his side, understanding and supporting the traditions?

"That's the life you want too, isn't it," Shana said.

Rico cleared his throat but nodded. And if she couldn't be the woman at his side, then staying together seemed unfair, was wasting time like his mother said.

Shana's lips blanched as they pressed into each other. She took a deep breath, then lifted her glass for a sip of water. "I'll get my things from your place while you're at the airport," she said woodenly. "And I'll leave the key."

"Shana."

Her eyebrows rose a few millimeters, her expression the kind of blank he normally only saw in the office, and never directed at him.

"I didn't mean… I didn't want this to end, like this." Though maybe it was better, them being forced to discuss these things, knowing now that a life together wasn't in the cards.

Her composure slipped for an instant. "I know. But you should have the life you want. And I couldn't give it to you."

Rico stood as she did. Should he hug her goodbye? A chasm had appeared between them. Really, what was there left to say?

Shoshi didn't pause to think until she'd made it back to Ricardo's garage with all of her things. Behind the steering wheel, her chest heaved with her breath. She bit down on her bottom lip, fighting the gathering sobs.

It had been fast, their relationship, and she'd gotten too wrapped up. It wasn't Ricardo's fault. They hadn't talked about it, but like an idiot she'd assumed the conversation would be *how* to meld their traditions and beliefs, not whether they should. Sure, Passover and Easter sometimes overlapped, but it wasn't like Easter eggs were made out of bread. And even if Ricardo wouldn't have joined her in saying blessings when lighting Hanukkah candles, he could still have enjoyed latkes and sufganiyot.

That night after Nat's party, Shoshi'd brushed off his initial surprise at learning she was Jewish. In a country where Jesus-based faiths dominated everywhere you looked, it didn't cross anyone's mind that the people they met could be from a different tradition. At least, not if it wasn't easily visible, if some symbol like a kippah or hijab didn't forcibly confront the assumption. The default setting was some version of Christianity, or at most atheism that nevertheless celebrated Christmas and Easter. So sure, when Ricardo'd learned that wasn't true in her case, he'd been surprised. But he'd taken it in stride.

Or so she'd thought.

Maybe this wouldn't have happened if his mother hadn't brought up the future so soon.

But that wasn't fair. Now or later, the question of faith would have been raised. And really, what else could he have done? If he didn't want to be with someone Jewish… Confronting his parents, fighting them, creating a schism in his family for the sake of—what?

Not making Shoshi feel second-class. Unworthy of him, of even meeting his family, because of her identity.

She slammed her hand against the steering wheel, then grimaced at the pain that stung her palm.

What *would* her father have said? They hadn't talked about it, not directly. But she knew, without a doubt. Her dad would have told her to do what made her happy. To be with someone who wanted to be with her, exactly as she was, even if that meant making compromises—on both sides—to build a life together. At the end of the day, Ricardo simply didn't want her.

At least he hadn't brought up conversion, hadn't suggested she sacrifice her identity as some magic solution.

But where did that leave her? No job, no boyfriend, and apparently no friends, after that ridiculous fight with Nat. Shoshi was alone in a parking garage, with nowhere to turn.

And since Ricardo would be back soon with his parents, she had to pull it together. Two deep breaths and quick swipes under her eyes later, Shoshi started the car. Returning to her empty apartment sounded miserable, but she definitely couldn't stay here.

Chapter 37

L UC PAUSED MID-STEP, BLINKED, THEN CONTINUED DOWN the hall. Shoshana's eyes didn't open until he was a few steps away. She sat on the carpeted floor, jean-clad knees bent in front of her. Handles of a plastic bag were looped loosely around her fingers.

He stopped in front of his door. Beside her. When she'd walked out of his office, turned her back on him and stridden out, he hadn't expected to see her again. Some part of him didn't believe he was seeing her now. Luc waited.

Silently, she stretched out the bag of takeout, the plastic crinkling as he took it from her. He transferred the food to his left hand and reached his right one down to her again.

Her large eyes, filled with a loneliness that was only too familiar, glanced down to his hand then back up at him. She hesitated before sliding her fingers forward against his palm.

They froze, hands clasped as Luc's heart pounded in his ears. His fingers tightened and she responded, leveraging her body up until she stood, close, still watching him.

Why here? Whatever had happened, why turn to him?

She exhaled and they dropped their hands, both shifting backward. Her shoulders rose, silently questioning.

"You broke up?" Luc asked, checking the hunch.

Shoshana nodded shakily, her gaze drifting to the ground. "Yes," she said, pulling her shoulders back and meeting his eyes again.

Luc's lungs burned before he remembered to inhale. He turned away, slipping his keys from his pocket, and pushed the door open.

Relief edged her expression as she stepped inside.

Shoshi halted a few steps into the apartment. Behind her, Luc switched on the hall light. He strode past and let the takeout fall lightly onto his coffee table. Shoshi took off her shoes and jacket but didn't follow. Was she making a mistake?

Luc went into the kitchen but emerged almost instantly holding a couple of forks and two tumblers. He stalled as if waiting for some signal, or for her to bolt. For once, hesitation or uncertainty hid in his eyes.

Shoshi took a deep breath and padded past him. She lowered to the edge of the couch and started pulling out the take-out cartons. Luc set down the glasses and forks, then added the bottle of Dimple she'd gotten from the bar, or one like it. His jacket and tie came off before he sat down and switched on the TV. Shoshi swept the empty plastic bag to the floor as he worked the remote.

The clicks stopped, and he looked at her expectantly. On the screen, the streaming page of a TV show she didn't recognize was pulled up. "I haven't seen it," she told him with a shrug, "but whatever works."

What had she expected, coming here? Vegging out with a TV show was something she could have done at home. But she didn't want to be as alone as she felt. This might not be the next *right* thing for her to do, but it was the next thing, and that would have to be right enough for now.

Luc scrolled back through the episodes to the pilot and hit play. The remote didn't make a sound as he set it on the table. He gestured to the food.

Shoshi reached for the chicken fried rice and a fork, then settled back on the couch, tucking one foot under her knee. Luc filled the tumblers then picked up the honey sesame beef.

They didn't speak as they ate, watching the show and trading cartons of takeout, not bothering with plates, this one meal in some ways more intimate than all those ones they'd shared before.

When the episode's end credits started, Luc muted the TV and refilled his glass. Shoshi's remained untouched, but the take-out containers were mostly empty.

"So what happened," Luc asked in the silence.

She glanced at him, pushed her hair back, then reached for her drink. The whisky's light burn didn't do much to counteract the odd combination of numbness and pain in her chest. "He didn't want to be with someone Jewish." She tried to match Luc's detached tone, smothering the bitterness climbing her throat. At the end of the day, Ricardo had rejected her for her identity—for who she had been born as. Didn't she deserve to be just a little bit mad about that? There had to be some kind of irony in this all having happened during the early minutes of Purim, like some cosmic joke whose meaning she didn't feel like unraveling.

"He's an idiot," Luc said after a brief pause.

Shoshi hid her small smile behind another sip of whisky, the drink or the implication sending warmth through her. It wasn't entirely fair of them. "He deserves to live the life he wants." It was true. Within commonsense limits, didn't everyone?

"What did you want?" Luc asked, fixing her with one of those piercing looks.

For a moment, she let herself get lost in that green gaze framed by lush dark lashes. It was easier than answering his question.

"I dunno," she admitted, looking away. She rolled the tumbler between her palms, the amber liquid gently sloshing up the sides. "I guess, I would have wanted him to want a life with me. When it came down to it, we could have found a way to blend—holidays, traditions."

If they'd had children… Well ultimately, no matter what, by law her children would be Jewish. After that, the questions of nationality versus religion, of tradition and culture versus faith… It got complicated. Too complicated, maybe. But Ricardo could have at least made her a part of the conversation rather than deciding it all for them and hiding behind his parents' bigotry. *His* bigotry.

Not that things would ever have gotten that far between them, anyway. If she were really honest, she'd admit that Ricardo's rejection stung for the wrong reasons. Well, one glaring right reason, but a few wrong ones, too. Shoshi would miss the safety of their relationship, of having someone who cared for her, more than she'd miss *him*. The possibility of never seeing Ricardo again, never talking to him again, left her with neither relief nor heartache. Even the antisemitism he'd never admit to elicited resignation more so than true pain. Maybe they were both better off. She sure as hell would be. No matter how daunting the prospect of being so utterly alone was.

Shoshi took a larger sip, draining the glass. The soft burn was growing on her. She leaned forward to slide the tumbler beside an empty container from sweet-and-sour duck. Luc immediately moved to refill it, shifting closer on the couch to reach. The whisky gurgled in their silence. On the silenced TV, a fight in a hospital hallway ended with some creative use of a defibrillator.

Luc replaced the bottle with a soft thump and turned his head to her. They were so close. His lips rested in their gently sloped cupid's bow, his bottom one a touch more generously padded. A hint of shadow covered his jaw like a backdrop showcasing the faint-pink cushions.

It would be so easy to lean closer, to tilt her chin up so their lips could meet. Would that be crazy?

Luc's jaw clenched, those lips tightening disapprovingly, and he leaned away.

Shoshi blinked, shifting back, too. "Sorry." She ran her hand through her hair, her mouth twisting to the side. "I don't know what— After everything, I, well. I definitely know what your type is, and I am so very obviously not it, I know. Sorry." She nudged her refilled tumbler a little further away and gathered a couple empty cartons. Maybe some water would help clear her head.

She'd hardly stood when Luc's hand landed on her wrist, his fingers circling it easily. Shoshi reached deep for that blank expression he'd helped her perfect and turned back to him. He lifted from the couch, barely tugging on her as he rose.

The silence was almost painful as they stared at each other. Luc's thumb swiped lightly on the underside of her wrist. Or maybe she was imagining it. She couldn't pull her eyes away from him to look. His other hand re-centered her hamsa, his fingertips lingering on her skin with the faintest pressure.

"Don't let me ruin you," he said quietly, slowly, piercing her heart in a way nothing Ricardo'd said tonight had.

Luc's fingers fell away, but he didn't move back. Shoshi finished the turn so she faced him squarely. She let the cartons drop back to the table.

"Luc."

His brows drew together, and if his jaw clenched any tighter, he might need dental work.

"I'm not some angel you would desecrate." Her shoulder lifted briefly. "I'm as human as you are."

He reared back, head coming up, lips parting with his denial or surprise. Was it really that crazy a thought? Shoshi looked away, down, to the scattered remnants of their dinner.

But then his hand brushed her hair back, bringing her face to meet his, and his other hand grazed her jaw, and he was kissing her, a nearly desperate crush of lips that managed to remain just gentle enough. Shoshi stretched up into the kiss, but his mouth broke away.

Luc's eyes bore into her as one eyebrow lifted, an unmistakable question. But she wasn't anywhere near Purim-level drunk, and she knew who this man in front of her was. Shoshi leaned closer.

This kiss was slower, a series of soft brushes growing into something deeper but more patient. Less intense, but far more thorough, as if he wanted to taste every bit of her. Shoshi shivered at the idea, using Luc's waist to balance. His hands skimmed down to her arms, and the kiss reverted to a few soft flutters before they broke away for air.

Pale green stared back at her as Shoshi's lungs worked. She slid her palm up to his chest. His heartbeat pulsed against her hand. Tomorrow she'd think clearly, but tonight…

Her inhale ended with the taste of whisky and his lips on hers.

Chapter 38

LUC'S HAND LAY ON THE INSIDE OF HER UPPER THIGH. Exhaling slowly, Shoshi opened her eyes to the light coming through the window behind the corner chair she knew firsthand wasn't as comfortable as it looked. Or maybe it just hadn't been intended for an overnight stay.

Technically, that brought her nights spent in Luc's bedroom to two—one more than most women seemed to get. She'd never quite managed Pepper Potts' flippant attitude toward her boss's mornings after, but Shoshi knew how this went, though she'd be skipping the fast food breakfast.

The thing was, getting out of the bed, any movement really, would inevitably slip Luc's fingers—so dangerously close—up past her inner thigh. And while he'd already done much more than touch, that had been last night. This was morning.

So she could move softly and risk waking him with the contact, or try to bolt out of the bed fast enough that the brush of his fingers didn't stall her in her tracks—and risk waking him with the jolt of movement. Or she could wait for him to wake up on his own, and then—what? A surpassingly awkward good-bye where they dressed silently and avoided looking at each other? One-night stands so weren't in Shoshi's wheelhouse. Last night had come out of nowhere.

Being with Ricardo had been nice enough. Her night with Luc? Electric. Ferocity tempered by an unexpected tenderness, thoroughly attuned to her every sigh and shiver. Now each touch, kiss, stroke, lick was burned into her memory.

Shoshi swiveled her head back to her one-time boss and current…something. All his usual determination, the keen drive that customarily lined his face, even the despair she'd unearthed behind the mask had all been wiped away in sleep. He looked relaxed, peaceful in a way she had never seen. At least sleep seemed to give him respite from his perpetual self-torment.

The calm expression, the unmoving dark crescents of his lashes, it almost made her want to reach out, sweep aside the lock of dark hair over his forehead, and cup his jaw. Tilt her chin closer for a kiss…

But that same calm was all the more reason not to wake him.

Shoshi turned back to stare at the ceiling. Surprisingly blank, unmolded, it was perhaps the only part of his apartment to which she'd never paid any attention.

Luc's fingers flexed, gently digging into her thigh, and Shoshi shut her eyes against the desire to arch into his touch. His thumb shifted, brushing her lightly, and she couldn't prevent a gasp. As if on cue, his other fingers followed, slipping intimately against her, over her. Languid with remnants of sleep but no less skilled.

Luc rose on an elbow beside her. His strokes paused when their eyes met, giving Shoshi a moment to catch her breath. A tiny satisfied smile curved one corner of his lips. A longer stroke arched her against the sheets, and that curve grew a fraction.

Her fingers found his arm, and his movements eased at her grip. But the light touches were their own torment.

And even after one more round—amazing as it could have been—all that would happen was goodbye.

"It's all right," Shoshi said, and his fingers stilled. "I know how the morning after ends."

Luc's smile dropped and his hand moved away, landing lightly on her stomach.

Shoshi let go. "Guess that's my cue." She even managed to add a touch of humor to the statement, but Luc didn't roll away.

"I've been horrible to you," he said, frowning. "Intentionally awful."

Shoshi looked past him to the blankness of the ceiling, straightening her leg to press her thighs together. He wasn't wrong, and yet here she was. Everything he'd done to prove to her there was nothing good about him… Which one of them had been wrong?

"How can I make it up to you?" Luc asked, snapping her back to the present, to him hovering over her, stoic but earnest.

"It's fine," she brushed off. Would they even see each other again after she got dressed and walked out that door?

Could these really be their last moments together, their last words?

His frown grew closer to a scowl. "No, it really isn't. Let me at least try."

Tension seeped from Shoshi with her exhale. There wasn't anything specific she needed him to do, but the fact that he was offering, that he wanted to make amends… Her breath caught on an idea. "Anything?"

"Tell me."

He'd probably refuse. But what did she have to lose? "Go home."

His head shook with his confusion, and his hand slipped from her stomach. "I am home."

"No, I…" Shoshi licked her lips, watching this wounded man whose shell had finally cracked. Even if this was goodbye, maybe she could help him start to heal. "Go home. Go see your parents."

Luc froze, all softness draining from him. He flew from the bed and stalked as far from it as he could get, his back to her. Shoshi sat up, clutching his sheet to her chest. Luc's torso heaved with the force of his breath, and his fingers clenched into fists that left his knuckles white. Sympathy prickled behind her eyes.

He spun back toward her, still breathing heavily. "Choose something else," he ground out from between gritted teeth.

Shoshi nearly choked on the emotion clogging her throat. Causing him pain wasn't what she wanted, but this felt right. Necessary. "That's it. Go home. Talk to your parents."

"I can't." The quieting of his breath belied the anguish in his voice. Everything in his expression begged her to understand, and she couldn't take it.

"Okay." She scooted to the edge of the bed and stood, the sheet slipping away. "It's okay," she repeated, stopping in front of him. "You don't have to."

They watched each other, not touching, for minutes or seconds. Or maybe time had stopped entirely. Shoshi curled her fingers to prevent from reaching for him.

"What can I do," he whispered eventually, "so you'll forgive me." Shoshi shook her head lightly, but he spoke again before she could reply. "I—I need you, to forgive me." He didn't add "please," but it was written in every line on his face, in the desperation filling his eyes, in the rigid tension of his stance.

"Luc." Shoshi swallowed then brought her hand up to his chest, spreading her fingers over his warmth and the beat of the heart he'd still try to deny existed. "I wouldn't be here if I hadn't already forgiven you."

His eyes narrowed as the truth of what she'd said wrapped itself around her mind. Everything he'd done, but he was still a good man. Grieving, torturing himself, but so inherently good he couldn't stop himself from helping others. Including her, when she'd turned up in his office. And last night at his door.

Luc's jaw spasmed, his heartbeat thumping against her palm. Disbelief warred with hope in his eyes.

"It's okay," Shoshi repeated. Air whooshed from her lungs as Luc fell to his knees, clutching her back, head bowed below her breasts. She staggered from the impact, hands falling to his shoulders to steady herself. His breath streamed against her skin. "It's okay," she said once more, brushing her fingers through his hair.

He shuddered against her, and Shoshi shut her eyes against the weight of his grief. He had to miss his family as much as the woman who called weekly missed her son, but Shoshi couldn't force him to go see them. All she could do was offer him the one thing he needed to hear.

"It's okay," she told him again, holding him close. "I forgive you."

Chapter 39

THE DAVIN HOME WAS LOVELY, WITH ITS FADED PINK PAINT accented by light-yellow touches and hanging baskets of greenery that would undoubtedly soon bloom. You wouldn't know it, though, given the terror Luc tried to hide beneath a tight blankness. His neck muscles twitched as he swallowed, staring at his parents' home.

They hadn't spoken on the plane. With Luc engrossed in his tablet, Shoshi had spent the hours gazing out the window. Really, they hadn't spoken much since he'd asked her to go with him. To an outside observer, they probably looked no different now than when she'd worked for him, chauffeuring him around as his silent shadow.

But things were definitely different. Luc had barely glanced at her since she'd arrived outside his building that morning in the car he'd sent for her. Not at the airport, not on the plane, and not when they'd gotten into the rental car and he silently entered his parents' address into the GPS. She'd thought at first he asked her to come along for support, but it felt more like she was his warden as he faced his sentence.

Once he'd decided to go, he hadn't wanted to put off the trip even a couple of days. Now his eyes were trained on the house as if he expected it to reach through the windshield and swallow him whole. And the crests of his cheeks were somehow flushed even as the rest of his face had paled.

Shoshi shot his parents' home a final glance, then turned in the driver's seat as much as the steering wheel would allow. Luc didn't seem to notice the motion until her hand landed on his arm.

He jolted, finally tearing his attention away from the house and looking at her. Fear and yearning flickered in his eyes before he dropped his gaze to his lap. Shoshi let her hand fall away.

She didn't want to push him, but the way things were going, they could easily end up sitting in this car all night. If the police were called because a strange car was loitering near a private property, this wouldn't be the reunion anyone wanted. "We could go to the hotel first." His eyes latched on to her. "If you want," she added with an encouraging nod.

Luc inhaled audibly in the otherwise silent car. "No."

"Okay." The longing to touch him was overridden by the seemingly impenetrable wall of tension that continued to grow around him. They had to get out of this car.

Shoshi turned away and popped open the driver's side door. Sweet, fresh air streamed into the car. Feet already on the ground, she twisted back to Luc. That little muscle ticked in his jaw, but then his eyebrows drew together and he reached behind him. Finally his door handle clicked and he started getting out.

She stepped out as well and quietly shut the door, eyes glued to his rigid profile. *Here we go.*

Luc stopped a couple of feet from the porch steps. This wasn't right. How many times had he considered coming home, at first? But he didn't deserve the comforts of home, his family's stoic support. And they didn't deserve the torture that his return would have brought them. Would bring them now. How had he ever agreed to this?

His family had undoubtedly realized how much better off they were without him. From what he knew, they'd flourished in his absence. Only his mother still went through the motions of reaching out to a memory they would all rather forget.

Pressure on his forearm drew his gaze from the front door. Shoshana's hand pressed lightly against his sleeve. "They don't want me here," he explained.

"Why don't we let them decide that," she suggested, hiding her inescapable pity behind a near-perfect poker face. *Now* she could mask her emotions from him?

Before Luc could protest, she strode up the few steps. Her head swiveled as she searched for a nonexistent doorbell, then her fist was striking the wooden door, unabashedly announcing their presence.

Luc stood glued to the spot. And really, where could he go? She had the car keys. He wasn't in direct sight of the entrance, so maybe he could—

The door swung open, and Luc's mind blanked.

"Hello, there. May I help you?"

He shut his eyes against the agonizingly familiar voice, straining to hear more.

"Car trouble?" his mother added.

"Uh, no," Shoshana faltered.

Luc screamed at her silently to say something—*anything* to draw more from his mother.

"Mrs. Davin, my name is Shoshana. We spoke a few times on the phone. When you called your son's office?"

"Lucas?" his mother gasped. "Is he—"

He couldn't hear the end of the question.

"Mrs. Davin?" Shoshana's voice was filled with alarm.

"Mary?" his father called from inside.

His mother's pale face swam in Luc's vision as she clutched one hand to her chest, the other clinging to the wall. He vaulted onto the porch and to her side, bracing her in his arms before she could collapse.

"Lucas," his father said, halting steps away.

An eternity passed as they stood there, a ridiculous tableau frozen in the doorway of his childhood home.

When he'd stopped short of the house, Shoshi had expected Luc to fight the idea of entering his parents' home. Concern for his mother drew him into their living room and to the sofa at her side, probably before he even realized he'd crossed the threshold. Because no matter how much he fought it, that was who he was. And he missed his family.

Once the older woman had regained a bit of color, he stood rooted to the spot, hands dug into his pockets and shoulders hunched. Shoshi remained by the door. She should have been more careful, introducing herself. She'd never meant to scare the woman like that.

"I'm fine," Mary Davin assured her husband, who stood at her side, hand on her shoulder. Her eyes never left her long-absent son. The men exchanged timorous glances as well.

"I'll get you some water, Mary," Mr. Davin said, his deep voice tinged with a hint of gravel. He passed Shoshi without a glance her way, but if she'd learned anything from working for his son, it was how to remain unobtrusive. Should she go back to the car? She had no place here, intruding on this family's heart-wrenching reunion.

"Are you all right?" Luc asked, hovering near his mom.

Mary Davin pushed up from the couch, and Luc pulled his hand back from its obvious need to help her.

"Oh, Lucas," his mother sighed, tears that hadn't fallen thickening her voice. The older woman hesitated a few interminable moments, but then she wrapped her arms around Luc's torso, repeating, "Thank you, Lord. Oh, thank you."

Luc's lips parted in a silent gasp, his arms flying apart to make room for his mother's embrace. They curled slowly around her shoulders.

Shoshi averted her eyes. Each square tile in the Davin entryway was edged with a pretty floral pattern. How long could she spend on counting them?

Work boots, mostly hidden by lightly fraying denim, stopped at the edge of her vision. Mr. Davin stared at his wife and son, a forgotten glass of water in his hand. There had to be somewhere—anywhere—else Shoshi could look that wouldn't be invasive or rude.

Eventually the water glass thunked against a small table, and Mr. Davin turned to her. He was a rougher version of his son, his shoulders a touch broader, his face weatherworn, his hair a blend from silver to ash. Had he heard her introduce herself? Should she say something now?

"Bill?" Mrs. Davin called from the comfortable room to Shoshi's left.

Mr. Davin considered Shoshi awhile longer. His chin dipped once before he picked up the water and joined his wife. Shoshi puffed her breath out and snuck a glance at Luc. His mother had sat back down but still held on to his arm, as if afraid he'd disappear if she let go—not that Shoshi blamed her.

Father and son stood watching each other like they'd both forgotten how to treat the other man. Finally, Mr. Davin raised one arm to his son's shoulder, and Luc's head dropped. The older man squeezed, head bobbing gently in a prolonged nod.

The trio had barely spoken to each other, but the timid hope that had already taken root didn't need words. Shoshi turned away, ignoring the squeeze of longing in her chest.

It didn't take long for Luc to excuse himself to the bathroom, though Shoshi would have bet it was nothing more than an escape from the emotion of the moment. His parents embraced in the resulting quiet, murmuring their prayers of thanks when they pulled apart.

Mrs. Davin remembered Shoshi first. Her wrinkle-lined eyes trained almost blankly on her son's former assistant. Then she blinked, shook her head gently, and said, "Sorry, dear. It's—" She cut herself off.

Of course, what *could* she say in this situation? "I understand," Shoshi assured.

Mr. Davin stepped closer, saying softly, "Mary…"

She shushed her husband over her shoulder and refocused on Shoshi. Her cheeks were plump in a way that may have once been called *cherubic*. The lines of her decades decorated her face, though perhaps time had gotten a hand from the heartache of losing her son for so many years. Glasses hung on a beaded chain around her neck. "Can I make you a cup of tea?" she asked.

"Oh, thank you, but that's not necessary."

"Please." The woman tried to smile. "It's something I can do."

Shoshi's mind scrambled fruitlessly for words, so she nodded. How could she say no? She followed the couple to their kitchen, a cheery pale-yellow room with pastel accents that nevertheless felt tinged by the tension in the house.

Mr. Davin waited until he and Shoshi sat at the kitchen table and his wife had put the kettle on before asking, "Why now?" The direct gaze he leveled at Shoshi proved it wasn't a rhetorical question. Pale-green eyes framed by silver-streaked eyebrows waited for an answer.

"Bill." Mrs. Davin *tsked* and squeezed Shoshi's hand on the table. "Thank you," she said in that tear-thickened voice. "Thank you for bringing him back to us."

Shoshi dropped her free hand on top of the other woman's, also squeezing gently.

"I prayed, when we spoke…" Mrs. Davin trailed off with a sigh, withdrawing her hand to bring it to her chest, lightly jostling the glasses. A simple gold band glinted on her finger.

"I'm sorry," Mr. Davin said, sounding anything but.

"Bill."

"I'm sorry, we are grateful, yes. But why now? Why…you."

Both Davins trained their eyes on her. "I'm sorry," Shoshi echoed. "I didn't mean to intrude, I— You'll have to ask Luc why, I guess. Maybe he's just accustomed to my driving him around, at this point." It would be foolish of her to assume her presence here meant anything more.

The teapot shrilled, dispelling a smidge of the tension as everyone's heads turned toward it. Mrs. Davin rose and brought down some teacups. Mr. Davin wouldn't meet Shoshi's gaze, so she focused on the stitching of their tablecloth instead.

A renewed charge filled the air, the clinking of the cups and saucers ceasing. Then Mrs. Davin said, "Lucas."

Shoshi twisted toward the archway that served as entrance to the kitchen, where Luc had stalled.

"Would you like some tea?" his mother asked.

The corners of Luc's lips twitched, ever so slightly, and he nodded. "Thanks." Before joining them at the table, he helped his mother carry the filled cups over. Then silence reigned once more. No one touched the steaming tea.

Stray bits of tealeaf swirled in Shoshi's cup, as if agitated by the tension in the room. When she risked a glance at him, Luc was watching her, anxiety rolling off of him. His blink lasted a few seconds too long.

"How—" He cleared his throat. "How's Matthew?"

"Good." His mother jumped on the topic, chin bobbing. "Liza and the kids, too. They're all doing well." She hesitated, the reassuring smile disappearing into worry before she asked, "And you, Lucas? Have you been…happy?"

Pain flashed on Luc's face, his eyebrows jumping up. "I'm fine, Mom," he lied. "Good." He adjusted his sleeves, his suit as out of place in this cozy home as Shoshi felt.

Mrs. Davin brought her teacup to her lips, striving for normalcy, perhaps, now that her son was home.

"And the store?" Luc asked.

Shoshi bit back a relieved smile. He was making an effort.

"It's good," his father said. "Closed early, for the holiday."

The men nodded at each other.

Mary Davin looked between them, both so solemn. "It's good to have you home, Lucas."

Luc's hands cupped together below the table, as if to catch the words.

"Will you stay for dinner?" his mother invited, the yearning in her voice cutting away at Shoshi's composure.

She was about to offer to leave, to come back for Luc later if he didn't want to spend the night, but his sharp look stemmed the words. Dinner would mean hours more, and he wanted out.

"I'm so sorry, Mr. and Mrs. Davin," Shoshi said, falling back into her assistant voice. Luc's mother frowned, resigned to another lie after the apologies that had surely become meaningless. "Luc actually has a work call this evening. We'll have to be on our way soon, to ensure everything's set up at the hotel."

"Of—of course," Mrs. Davin said, bowing her head. Mr. Davin's hand came to her back, offering wordless comfort like he must have countless times throughout the years.

Shoshi stifled the urge to apologize again, tracing the handle of the delicate teacup in front of her, decorated with flowers, of course.

"Come for brunch tomorrow, then?" the tenacious Mrs. Davin invited, her gaze trained back on her son.

"Maybe." Luc stared at his parents, longing overshadowed by his uncertainty. What words was he unable to say? "We should get going," he said instead of whatever it was. His gaze flicked to Shoshi, and he stood.

She followed his lead, rising as well, and swallowed past the combined pain pervading the air, thick enough to choke on. "Thank you for your hospitality," she told Luc's parents.

Mary Davin's eyes were downcast again, her head angled forward. Her husband squeezed her hand, nudging it gently back and forth, before letting go to stand as well. "I'll walk you two out."

Chapter 40

*L*UC STRIPPED OFF HIS JACKET AND TOSSED IT ON THE HOTEL bed. Six strides to cross the room, but the carpet had survived countless pairs of feet. It could take his pacing.

Shoshana hadn't said much since they'd left his parents. He'd waited in the car as she checked them in, even though they were staying at the Best Western outside of town and not at the Baxters' White Ash Inn. She'd gotten them adjoining rooms and disappeared wordlessly into hers. Luc threw another glance at the connecting door, then strode over to the mini fridge. Tiny bottles lined the inside of its door.

What had she expected from him? What had they? After all this time…

He let the fridge door drift shut. He deserved every clear-headed second of this misery and more.

Several trips across the room later, Luc's hand reached for the bolt on the adjoining door. Instead he flattened his palm against the cool, smooth surface. Shoshana's touch had been so soft yesterday, fingers running through his hair. She'd held him as he fell apart, whispering her forgiveness. What would she say now?

He flicked the bolt and pulled the door open. Whatever he saw in her eyes, it couldn't be worse than the heartbreak he'd put in his mother's.

Silence greeted his knock. Luc shook his head, banishing the foolish glimmer of hope. He'd already dragged her all the way out here. The least he could do was leave her in peace now.

But the second door swung open, and there Shoshana stood. "Hi," she said, her hint of a smile overwhelmed with exhaustion, or sadness.

"Hi."

She waited a moment then stepped back, angling her body toward her own room. Luc exhaled and stepped through into a room that was a mirror image of his own but felt immeasurably lighter.

"Do you want to find somewhere for dinner?" she asked.

His head jerked toward her. "No, I—" His parents were one thing, but the rest of the town? "I probably shouldn't leave the hotel." Outskirts or not, it was a small community.

Shoshana's eyes widened, but she nodded and stepped away, looking for something. "Maybe they have a list of places that deliver."

"Shoshana."

She spun back toward him, the hair she'd let down bouncing around her shoulders. "You can call me Shoshi, you know," she offered in his silence.

"I can't go back."

A small groove appeared between her eyebrows.

"Tomorrow…" Luc trailed off, forcing air through his lungs. His hands fisted in his pockets. "I can't."

"Okay." Her jaw shifted, mouth opening then closing, and her head shook gently.

Car horns and other sounds of life floated past outside the room.

"They love you," Shoshana said eventually.

Luc's teeth ground against each other.

She looked down, blowing her breath out through pursed lips and blinking rapidly. When she looked back at him, her eyes were redder. She sniffed before continuing, "I just—" Her breath puffed out. One hand brushed through her hair, shifting the dark mass. "You've lost so much time. Someday…" Little gasps punctuated her words. "You're going to wish for every possible moment." A tear beaded under one eye. "For even a second more with them." She sniffed and shook her head again.

Luc covered the few steps between them. Tears made her eyes glisten even as she tried to blink them back. He reached for her shoulders and nudged her closer, until her head dropped gingerly against his chest. Her arms wrapped loosely around his waist, her breath moving through her torso in ragged bursts.

Luc twined his fingers in the soft curls of her hair. What did he know about comforting her, or anyone?

Shoshana pulled away quickly, a slight sheen still in her eyes, her lips reddened from the pressure of fighting her own pain. Luc slid his hand from her hair so he could cup her jaw. She didn't have the luxury of choice when it came to seeing her parents. And on top of everything else he was guilty of, he'd taken the choice away from his own.

His thumb brushed away the hint of moisture on her cheek. "Okay," he breathed. "Brunch, if you'll go with me."

New tears welled in her eyes.

"Just please don't cry," he pleaded.

A gasping chuckle burst from her lips, tightening her cheek against his palm. "Deal." Her head dropped back against him, and they stood in the embrace, her arms offering all the comfort he hadn't been able to give.

Luc's fingers played with a lock of Shoshi's hair, so lightly she barely felt it. Remnants of their dinner—barbecue with an assortment of sides—still lay spread out on the bed. As the credits started, he muted the hotel room TV.

"It's getting late," Shoshi said. It had been such a draining day, and tomorrow wasn't likely to be any easier.

Luc's hand dropped to her shoulder. "Do you want me to go?"

She'd almost forgotten about the second room. Once again they hadn't spoken much since ordering dinner, but this time the silence hadn't been uncomfortable. More like a reprieve from the raw intensity of the day. Still, curling up together while watching a movie wasn't the same thing as sharing a bed. It wasn't that she wanted him to leave—staying in his arms sounded nice, actually—but were they in a place where sleeping together without *sleeping* together was an option? Was he looking for an opening to leave? "Up to you," she hedged.

He shifted so they faced each other, no longer touching. "What you want isn't up to me."

They'd jumped so deep, so fast, but technically they'd only had the one night together. If he wanted to go, but she told him to stay… Was she overthinking this like she did everything else? "What do you want?"

His lips slanted into a wry smile tinged with sadness. "I'm asking you." When she still hesitated—why did this one choice feel so important?—he added, "We can write it down and exchange answers, if you want."

Shoshi's exhale was part chuckle. One of many major changes between them, for him to even care what she wanted, and they'd all happened so fast. Her mind was still catching up. Luc didn't take his eyes off her, waiting for her answer. She'd spent so much time worrying only about what she needed, what she had to do. Beyond the obvious—her parents back, a secure job, and world peace for good measure—what *did* she want?

"I… I want to pay you back, for my loans," Shoshi admitted. It had seemed like such a good idea at the time, a battle of wills with ridiculous stakes, a way to pay off her debt through sheer stubbornness. To make him pay for underestimating her.

Now it just seemed wrong. Not like he was buying her off, exactly, but still leaving them on unequal footing, whether the money was his penance or her winnings from a bet they never should have made or both. If they were going to be in each other's lives, as friends or whatever else, they couldn't have this standing between them.

And if they were going to part ways after this weekend, then she definitely didn't want this to stay unresolved.

Amused confusion flashed across his face. "Not what I was expecting." His palm skimmed up and down her arm before landing on her hand. "Don't worry about that."

Shoshi moved her hand away, tracing the abstract multi-colored pattern of the bedspread. How could she explain so he'd understand?

"Hey." He pulled his hand back too. "Listen, if it'll make you more comfortable, we'll figure something out, all right?"

Relief let her shoulders drop. Had he always been able to see through her like that? *Took you long enough,* proclaimed the unhelpful voice in her head. Luc never missed anything, while she'd missed so much. But the point was, he'd agreed. "Okay, thanks."

"But," he said, self-assurance threading into his tone. Of course he'd find money easy to talk about.

"But?"

"Let's put a pin in it until you find a new job."

He was trying to help her out, to take care of her. She should probably have expected that at this point. Still… "That might take a while."

Luc frowned as Shoshana started gathering up the containers they'd left scattered on the bed. "Anywhere would be lucky to have you."

She scoffed, getting up to put things away. "You don't have to say things like that."

"Wait, Shoshana." He got up to follow her, turning her around with a touch on her elbow. She looked up at him, uncertainty trying to hide beneath her calm. "You are capable, intelligent, tenacious. Determined, with a spine of steel and enough integrity for all of Griffith & Moore." Luc sighed. It was almost a relief to tell her what he really thought. He hadn't realized how much she needed to hear it, too focused on himself as always.

He stepped closer, bracing her shoulders so she wouldn't look away. "You're insightful, and compassionate to a fault."

"I think you meant 'almost,'" she joked, her throat constricting as she swallowed.

His lips quirked. "You're stubborn and resilient." His fingers tugged on her earlobe as they both grew serious again. "And beautiful."

Her lashes lowered. "Now I know you're lying," she exhaled, trying to play the self-deprecation off like another joke.

Luc skimmed his thumb over her cheek then tilted her chin up. "You spend so much time hiding behind who you think you're supposed to be. It did take me some time to see past it, to really see you." Which mostly proved he was a blind idiot. "You were probably most yourself when you were pissed at me, you know."

A small chuckle curved her lips, but the shadows of every time his words had hurt her lingered.

"I meant everything I said tonight." He tucked a curl of her hair behind her ear before letting his hands drop. "But the things I said before…" He trailed off, unable to get the words out.

"Don't worry about it," she murmured, starting to move around him, back toward the bed.

Luc stepped in her way, and her gaze jumped back up to meet his. "I needed you to hate me," he admitted in a whisper. He still didn't deserve anything else. "But it became more than that. If you resented me, anything more was impossible. Wanting it wasn't an option. And I could use it as an excuse to keep you close, all those late nights. I could tell myself it was to punish you so you'd quit, have even more reason to hate me. But mostly I wanted you there."

For years he'd distracted himself from the specter of his guilt with a combination of work and alcohol and sex. With a succession of women whose faces eventually bled together.

And then with Shoshana, who'd surprised him and challenged him. Then captivated him, the buoy he'd held onto as he floundered in his own self-hatred, torturing himself with her nearness, knowing he'd never be able to touch her.

Luc stepped back, giving her the space she'd wanted a moment ago. "Regardless of all that, you were incredible at your job, even though I definitely didn't make it easy on you." Understatement of the millennium. "But I can help you find something better. Call it networking, if you want." After years of forging her own way, she hated depending on anyone else. He of all people could understand that. But using professional connections wasn't the same thing, and this was something he could do. Easily, even. "You don't have to do it all alone."

Silence pressed between them as she thought, her eyes still trained on him. Did she see the broken man she'd led home, or the one who'd tormented her at work? Could she see anyone else in him?

"No," she said finally.

Luc nodded, stepping away. It made sense. After everything he'd done, she didn't want his help. She didn't want to feel beholden to him, even if he didn't see it that way.

"No," she repeated. "I don't want you to go."

Chapter 41

THEIR ARRIVAL BACK AT THE DAVINS' THE FOLLOWING morning was strained. Neither brother seemed to know what to say to the other after so long apart, keeping their distance on opposite sides of the living room. At least Luc had chosen a dark-green sweater rather than a suit jacket today, keeping things a little less formal. And the children helped break the tension.

The young girl, Lacey, was a lovely little version of her mother, minus the adult reserve. Both had blonde hair and gray eyes. Had Luc even gone to his brother's wedding—had he met his sister-in-law before? It didn't seem like it.

Lacey timidly thanked her uncle for the sewing machine. At her grandmother's prodding, she swept out the edges of her skirt, which she'd sewn herself. The little girl stood there, eyes wide, waiting for her uncle's approval.

Luc threw Shoshi a terrified glance.

"It's lovely, Lacey," Shoshi told the girl, kneeling down beside her. "Right, Luc?"

The direct question startled him enough that he took half a step back, but then he looked at his niece, and finally his lips curved lightly. "Beautiful," he murmured.

The weighted silence of witnessing this first interaction pressed around all of them. None of the Davins seemed able to move, so Shoshi added, "And this stitching." There were swirly patterns mimicking waves stitched into the blue fabric. "You did this all, too?"

Lacey nodded, shyness contending with her pride in the skirt. "My momma showed me how."

"Wow," Shoshi said, shooting Luc's sister-in-law a quick smile. "That's awesome, having a mom who can teach you how to sew."

"Oh, well, I'm nothing compared to Grandma, right honey?" Liza stepped closer and dropped a hand on her daughter's shoulder.

Shoshi stood to meet her gaze, though the woman still had a couple of inches on her. "Lucky little girl," Shoshi said quietly despite the pang in her heart. This moment wasn't about her.

Luc's nephew, Aaron, a toddler young enough to be oblivious to the tension in the air, chose that moment to say, "Mister Luc?"

"Luc's your uncle, buddy," Matthew Davin corrected gently, not looking at his brother.

"Oh." The boy with sable hair, dressed in a precious little argyle sweater and jeans, paused a moment before saying, "Uncle Luc?"

"Yes?" Luc forced out, as wary as if he faced a feral tiger rather than a little boy.

His nephew was unfazed. "Are you gonna have pancakes with butter, or syrup?" he asked seriously, like it was the most important question in the world.

Shoshi's lips twitched with her suppressed smile.

"Oh, I uh…" Luc trailed off.

"Someone sounds hungry," Bill Davin said.

"I like 'em with syrup. Gramma makes the best pancakes." Aaron twisted to look over his shoulder. "Right, Dad?"

"Best in the state, I'll bet." Matthew Davin's smile crinkled around his eyes, wiping away all the grim tension of a moment before.

"I remember," Luc said quietly, staring at his mother.

Mary Davin's brows drew together, the pain of missing years still evident as she zeroed in on Luc.

"What's your favorite?" Aaron asked, blissfully unaware. "I like blueberry. But sometimes I like choc'ate chip. On special days, Gramma makes both. Is today special, Gramma?"

"It sure is, Aaron." After a small sigh, she offered the room a determined smile. "Guess I'd better get started on those pancakes."

Brunch went better, the frenzy of setting the table, and wrangling the kids, and holiday-themed conversation relieving some of the Davins's trepidation. Sharing a meal made everything better, or at least took a bit of the pressure off. Even Luc's anxious hesitation lessened as the conversation turned to the everyday community news, shifting the focus from his unexpected return. Though sometimes he pressed his knee against Shoshi's under the table, like that little touch was enough to keep him from bolting.

As the family settled in with some iced teas following the meal, Shoshi excused herself and veered off into the kitchen. Luc needed the space to reconnect with his family, and she had the iPhone with its digital library to keep her company.

"Oh, dear. Cookies after pancakes?" Mrs. Davin's voice, laced with humor, carried to Shoshi's seat a short while later. "I don't think so. But we can see if there's some lemon for our iced tea."

Aaron ran into the kitchen, heading straight for the refrigerator. Mrs. Davin soon followed, her smile dropping a bit as she caught sight of Shoshi. She sliced up a plate of lemons then handed them to her grandson. "Do you think you can take these out to everyone, Aaron? Careful, now."

The boy bit his lip as he took the plate, then made his way back toward the dining room, placing each step with exaggerated care. Shoshi's lips split into a grin at the sight.

"I hope you're not hiding in here on our account," Mary Davin said when the boy was out of earshot.

"Oh, no, of course not." Shoshi let the iPhone drop down to the table in front of her. "I wouldn't want to intrude on your time together, any more than I have, I mean."

The older woman nodded, contemplating Shoshi as if trying to place her. "You're good for him, with him." Her eyes narrowed the same way her son's did when he was piecing something together. "The two of you, are you…involved?"

Shoshi's mouth popped open, and her head twisted toward the other room, as if she could suddenly see through walls. When she turned back to Mrs. Davin, the older woman watched her with a wary curiosity. "Luc? I work for—worked for him." Whatever they were now, it was too complicated to put a label on it for his mother. And she'd hate to say anything that might somehow add to all the hurt this woman had shouldered. Shoshi exhaled, aiming for a pleasant smile as she added, "I think I'm mostly here to drive."

"You brought him back to us," Mrs. Davin said hoarsely, then cleared her throat.

"It seemed past time."

"We could never repay you. But then," she added before Shoshi could protest, "I think you did it for him, did what was best for him. That's not a small thing."

Shoshi caught the attempt to stare through walls again, preventing the motion. Luc had needed the push, and unquestionably it was good that he had come home. But had she truly been the impetus, or had he used her as an excuse to do what he himself had yearned to?

His mother nodded again, smiling gently this time. "We'd truly like it if you both would join us in church tomorrow, and for Easter dinner."

"Thank you," Shoshi said on autopilot. "That's very kind of you."

Did Luc's mother realize Shoshi was Jewish? Would the offer be rescinded if she learned that was the case?

"Luc probably won't come to church, but." Mary Davin's gaze trained vaguely on the wall to the living room. Staring through walls must be contagious. "Well, you're welcome here any time, Shoshana."

The confession that she wasn't who Luc's mom seemed to believe clogged Shoshi's throat, mixing with an aching desire to accept the invitation, to be welcomed in this family. But none of this was about her. So instead she said, "Luc's trying."

"Thanks to you." Mary Davin's hand patted Shoshi's lightly then landed with a soft squeeze. "Your parents must be very proud."

The casual comment stole her breath. She'd been so focused on the pain the Davins were facing in this reunion that she hadn't foreseen all the ways this trip was dunking her in fresh waves of grief. Too late, she managed to return his mother's smile, her face feeling like it would crack as she forced the muscles into position.

"Well. Like I said, don't feel like you have to hide." Another little pat later, Mary Davin left to rejoin her family.

Shoshi closed her eyes and curled her fingers into loose fists, silently counting down from ten. The secondary meaning in Mrs. Davin's parting comment had clearly been unintended. Had any of the Davins connected Shoshi's blatantly Hebrew name with the possibility that she wasn't any flavor of Christian? Not that it mattered. Who knew if she'd even see them again after this trip? With her eyes open, she counted back up. She had to stop taking every little comment or polite invitation so personally.

When she could move again, she picked up the iPhone and switched to Kakuro for some mindless distraction.

Wanting to have a family to belong to, to be welcomed like Mary Davin's words had so nonchalantly dangled in front of her, didn't change anything. Shoshi was only there for Luc. And if having her sit there in his parents' kitchen somehow helped him reconnect with the family whose loss he didn't have to keep grieving, then that was what she'd do.

Chapter 42

"YOU'VE REALLY DONE WELL FOR YOURSELF," LUC TOLD HIS brother when they stepped outside. A good wife, two great kids, and by all accounts a solid career in web administration over at the university. Their mother had sent a smattering of photos and cards, of course. Wedding announcement, birth announcements, Christmas cards. They'd all piled into a spare shoebox that was far from full. The man his brother had become, without the specter of Luc's transgression hanging over him… That was exactly as it should be.

"So have you," Matt said, "if all the reports can be believed."

Luc forced a small chuckle. "Don't believe everything you read." He turned to the slightly overgrown backyard, bracing himself on the porch rail. Liza had taken Aaron for a nap, and their parents were setting up the egg-painting supplies for Lacey. Shoshana had inconspicuously disappeared a while back, leaving Luc alone with a Matt who was a far cry from the depressed teen he'd last seen. They were virtually strangers now.

"When are you leaving?" Matt asked, jerking Luc's head back toward him. "We both know you aren't moving home," he elaborated, but the animosity that had slipped out in the question wasn't unexpected. Or undeserved. Of course he'd want life to return to normal, as they'd all pretended it had been while they ate.

Luc's head bent. The paint on the porch rail was chipping, and a handful of persistent weeds curled their way around the wooden columns. That was what he was here: an invasive weed.

"I meant, are you staying for…the holiday? Mom won't ask, but you know she wants you to."

A frown tugged Luc's eyebrows together. Every time the word *Easter* came up, his parents had thrown concerned glances his way. Everyone talked around the plans for tomorrow. A hand landed on his shoulder, jolting Luc upright.

Matt's arm dropped away, but he met Luc's gaze. They had to be about the same height now. "We all would," he added.

Luc grit his jaw and forced air through his nostrils.

"Look, even if you hate the idea," Matt said, standing strong, "can't you do it for them? Put off breaking their hearts again for one day."

Luc's lips parted to speak though no words came.

"You could probably still make it back to work Monday morning."

"Matt…"

Luc's brother shook his head, resignation bracketing his mouth. "Forget it. Just don't make them any promises you don't intend to keep." He turned to head back into the house, but Luc's hand snaked out, catching Matt's arm. A question formed in the line of his brother's brow.

"I left for you." The words scratched out of his throat.

Matt reared back and Luc let go, stuffing his hands into his pockets. He hadn't come to explain or for any kind of absolution, and yet the temptation was too strong. He forced a swallow past the dryness in his mouth. "I left for all of you," he repeated. "And look at the life you've built."

Matt turned back, facing Luc squarely. "We didn't ask you to."

"Daddy, come see!" Lacey called from inside the house, snapping the chain of history between the brothers.

Matt glanced at the patio doors then hesitated. "But I am asking you to stay. Give Mom one Easter." He didn't wait for a response before going inside to his daughter.

Which was for the best since Luc didn't have an answer to give.

Easter meant church, and a community egg hunt, and family dinner. Sweat beaded on the nape of Luc's neck. He moved further away from the doors and sank onto the top porch step. Easter meant staying.

He'd done the right thing, leaving so they could lead their lives. And going to church tomorrow was unthinkable. No one had mentioned them, but the Halls had to still be in town. Reappearing in their lives, on a holiday… Even he wasn't that much of a bastard. He'd done the right thing, letting them all move on.

Maybe he shouldn't have stayed away so long, or cut himself off so completely, but it had been the only way. The only way he could free them from him. Now, seeing his family again… What was right this time?

A softer touch swept over his shoulder, and bits of grass he'd torn fluttered from Luc's palm as he looked up into Shoshana's face. Her hand slid away, and she lowered to the step beside him. She didn't speak, watching him with that solid support she'd shown the entire time they'd been here. And maybe a hint of sadness.

"I think, I might stay," Luc heard himself say. She'd never see her own parents again. He could handle dinner, even if church was out of the question.

Shoshana's brows jerked up, but then her lips curved into a gentle smile. "I'm glad."

"For a little while," he clarified. More needed to be said with his family, but Matt was right: Luc had no plans to leave Boston, or his job. Still, he could stay an extra day, or maybe two.

Shoshana nodded, folding her arms atop her knees.

"You don't have to, though. If you don't want to, I mean." He could figure out another way to and from the hotel. "You have your life to get back to." He'd stolen more than enough of her time.

She hesitated then leaned away, trailing her fingers through the long blades of grass reaching up toward them.

Luc reached for the sinewy stem of one especially long weed, twisting it in his fingers. Last night, this whole week, had put them on the path to something. He'd barely slept, hours ticking by, nothing else mattering as much as the feeling of her, nestled close. He didn't want to let her go. "Shoshana."

Her head swiveled to him, her hands coming back to rest in her lap.

"I am not a good man," Luc said.

Her posture softened as her eyes filled with that unpitying compassion.

"I am nowhere near the kind of man you deserve. And I'm not someone who can make promises." He paused, plucked a tiny daisy hovering at his fingertips. "But I'm a selfish bastard. And I want to ask you to wait, Shoshi. Wait for me to figure myself out, to try to be better."

A smile rounded her cheeks but disappeared almost as quickly. Her chest rose with her breath, dropping suddenly with her rough sigh. "I'm never going to convert."

"And I'm never going to ask you to." The whole issue of his faith was part of the mess for him to figure out. Therapy would probably have to be involved. But no matter where he landed, it would never be about needing her to change.

Emotions he couldn't quite decipher flowed across her face. "What about your parents?"

"My parents? They'd probably say you walk on water if it wasn't bordering on blasphemy."

Her frown didn't budge. Rick's rejection clearly still weighed on her, the wound too fresh regardless of everything that had passed between the two of them since. Anger that the other man had caused this pain, hadn't appreciated Shoshi exactly as she was, warred now with perverse gratitude that Rick's ignorance had cleared the way to bring them here. Luc might not have grown up around many folks outside the church, but his parents had never modeled anything other than respect for other cultures. If time had somehow changed that, no matter how he wanted to reconnect, to rebuild, Luc knew what his priorities were.

"We could go inside and tell them," he offered, "and you'll see that they won't care. But it's not about them, anyway. I know who you are, and what I'm asking."

He swallowed roughly. Asking her once had been tough enough. He hadn't expected to have to do it a second time. But as he was learning, sometimes doing the hard thing was worth it. "Wait for me, Shoshi. And if that ever becomes an issue, we'll figure it out, too."

Slowly, warmth replaced the wariness in her eyes. "Almost sounds like a promise," she teased.

Luc held up the fresh little daisy ring his fingers had made practically on autopilot, like he had countless times as a kid, so long ago. Shoshi's gaze fell to the movement, and amusement puffed softly from between her lips.

He took her hand from her lap to slide on the delicate circle, then laced their fingers together. The little flower bore up well under the weight of everything he wasn't able to say. Shoshi squeezed lightly, letting it be enough, and her head dropped to his shoulder. Luc lifted their joined hands and brushed his lips on the underside of her wrist. Tendrils of the breeze that swayed the tips of the grass washed over them, carrying away a tightness that, in all those years, never had quite left his chest.

Luc inhaled, savoring the fresh air of home, then kissed the top of Shoshi's head, and smiled.

Chapter 43

PRISCILLA'S NEUTRAL WELCOMING EXPRESSION TRANS-formed into surprise when she realized it was Shoshi walking through the office doors. "Are you back?"

Shoshi smiled apologetically. The edge of hopefulness was quite a change from her first few weeks here. "No, sorry. I have a meeting with"—she barely caught herself in time—"Mr. Davin."

Priscilla's eyes flicked down to her phone console. "He's on a call."

"That's all right, I can wait. How've you been?"

"Believe it or not, we're surviving just fine without you," she quipped, but there was no malice behind the words.

"I have no doubt," Shoshi answered as the office phone lit up.

Priscilla tipped her head toward Luc's office, holding up her chocolate stash. "You know the way." She didn't wait for a response before picking up the call.

They hadn't gotten rid of her old desk, so Shoshi walked over and perched on the chair, popping a little chocolate kiss into her mouth. Luc had mentioned he'd be hiring someone new, but since he'd only gotten back to Boston last night, that process hadn't started yet. With the computer off and the surface completely clear, the space felt odd, like it had never belonged to her. So much had changed since she'd first sat here. Even the silence was calming rather than oppressive. It hadn't been long enough for her to quite *miss* it, but maybe she should give coming back some real consideration before the option stopped being available.

"Shana." The voice snapped her out of the contemplation, and Shoshi shot up, quickly swallowing down the remnants of melting chocolate on her tongue.

"Rick," she said before realizing it. "Mr. Mora," she corrected.

He shook his head, palm splayed toward her before his hand dropped back down. Keeping the desk between them didn't seem right, so Shoshi circled it, stopping beside him.

His hands slipped into his pockets as they watched each other. "I'm sorry," he said, a tinge of sadness filling his eyes. "How things ended…"

"Don't. You deserve to live the life you want." Rehashing how hurtful his and his family's rejection had been wouldn't help anyone. She was the one who'd let their relationship matter too much, longing for someone to care, even a little. But he hadn't wanted Shoshi. He'd wanted Shana—the mainstream version, with the objectionable pieces of her identity stripped away. Unlike Luc, who'd always seen all of Shoshi and refused to pretend otherwise.

Ricardo's gaze fell to the vacated desk chair. "Are you coming back to work?"

"No," she assured quickly. They'd both be spared the awkwardness of daily run-ins. "No, Luc offered to sit down with me, give me some pointers for an interview I have coming up." One of the applications she'd sent out had actually gotten a bite. Luc had also offered to recommend her for a startup's CFO position, insisting she had the skills no matter how daunting the title sounded. And for a small company just building, maybe he was right, but she hadn't taken him up on it. At least, not yet. Either way, considering how her last interview had gone, some practice was definitely in order. Although in hindsight, things hadn't turned out too badly.

"Least he could do. And hey,"—Ricardo's hand brushed her arm—"feel free to use me as a reference, any time. Or if you need any other help finding something new."

"Thank you," Shoshi said, even if he wasn't exactly her first choice. Then again, if his guilt helped her land something better, maybe that wouldn't be the worst thing.

His lips edged into a bittersweet smile. "I mean it. I hope eventually we can find our way to being friends."

"I'm sure, with time," she said politely. They would probably never end up close after what had happened, but she didn't want to burn any bridges unnecessarily.

On the plus side, she'd managed to start patching things up with Nat over dinner Tuesday night. Turned out their fight had more to do with Gerardo and his boss than with Shoshi. Nat lashing out made sense, and hopefully they'd get back to normal quickly now that Shoshi's schedule would be more predictable.

Getting drinks with Sebastian was also on her To Do list. No matter what else had changed, she could use all the friends she could get.

"Shoshana."

She swiveled to face Luc, standing in the doorway to his office.

"I don't have much time," he said stiffly, as if their plans were a nuisance, a commitment he felt obliged to keep. Not quite what she'd expected upon his return.

"Of course. It was good seeing you," she added to Ricardo, who nodded back.

She fell into step beside Luc as they walked out to the elevator. It was tempting to slip her hand in his—or it would have been, if not for the cold tension radiating off him. "You all right?" Shoshi asked quietly as the elevator chimed.

He nodded curtly, and they stepped inside. They didn't speak as they descended then strode through the lobby, tacitly agreeing not to cross any professional boundaries. Or was she misreading him?

Now that he was back, it was like last week hadn't happened. Maybe they'd both underestimated how much time it would take for him to be able to move forward, how difficult it would be for him to open up to her, to a future together. If he still wanted that at all.

His trip home, all those overwhelming emotions, had ripped something open in him. Had exposed so much of her, too. But was that why he'd let her close, her literal proximity the only reason he'd turned to her at all? Had distance in turn made him decide to sever their tenuous connection?

"Luc," Shoshi said once they'd made it outside, nudging him out of the stream of pedestrians. Warm sunset colors bathed the buildings around them, but the coolness between them persisted. Her questions stayed trapped in her chest as they watched each other in a silent standoff.

Luc's jaw ticked, then shifted. "Are you back with him?" he asked quietly.

"With who?"

An eyebrow arched sardonically.

The undercurrent of his hurt answered the question for her. *Oh.* "Rick? Of course not. I was waiting for you. Rick happens to work there. We made awkward small talk." Shoshi stepped closer, her hand landing on Luc's forearm.

His stance eased, but a trace of uncertainty remained. "I thought you'd changed your mind."

"Nothing's changed." She swallowed then added, "For me, anyway."

Acceptance rippled through him, his chest rising and falling with his breath as if he'd been holding it this entire time. He used their light contact to tug her closer, hands coming to her waist. "What do you say we skip drinks? Head to my place instead, order in some dinner."

The transformation was instant, throwing her off balance. The simplest question came out first. "Do you have the time?"

His confusion cleared as quickly as it appeared, replaced by a smirk that managed to be sheepish yet self-satisfied. "I lied. Wanted to get you to myself."

Shoshi shook her head with a small chuckle. The confirmation tingled over her skin—he hadn't changed his mind, either.

But as he opened the door to his apartment a short while later, insecurity trickled through her again.

Luc toed his shoes off and disappeared into the kitchen, like it was completely normal for her to be there. And in a sense, it was—how many hours had she spent here as his employee? Both legitimately and when he'd been trying to antagonize her. But things had changed, and there was so much left to figure out.

He stepped partly back into the hall to ask, "Everything okay?"

Shoshi nodded with a hum of confirmation.

His head tilted toward the living room. "Make yourself comfortable," he said before disappearing again.

She slipped off her shoes and forced herself deeper into the familiar apartment, the only visible difference a tin colored with pastel eggs that stood on his coffee table.

Shoshi sank onto the couch, and Luc joined her with a bottle and two glasses. He set them down and loosened his tie, then started to remove his suit jacket only to freeze and slip it back on with a small frown. He circled the coffee table to sit next to her and opened the bottle with a small *pop*.

With the bottle tilted over a glass, he hesitated. Maybe he was a little nervous, too. "Would you like some sherry?"

Her chin bobbed up and down. "Sure."

Once he'd poured, Luc's eyes zeroed in on her again with that prickling intensity.

Shoshi intertwined her fingers on her lap.

"I, uh, I have something for you." He reached into the inside pocket of his jacket and produced a small jewelry box, which he set in front of her.

Her eyebrows shot up, then kept going. "Luc—"

He cut her off with a small wave. "Open it."

"You're going to have to stop bossing me around," she teased breathlessly, not touching the box.

His cheek twitched as he flipped the lid open. Inside, a delicate ring with a twined band, pale-green like his eyes, featured a tiny daisy replicated in stone. "I don't know how long it'll take me," Luc said, lifting the ring out. "I wanted you to have one that'll last."

"Oh, Luc." Emotion swelling in her throat prevented her from saying more.

His free hand cupped her face, thumb skimming over her cheek. Shoshi's chin tilted up and his lips met hers, the kiss as gentle as his touch. As he pulled back, his fingers tugged on her earlobe.

"You deserve something perfect," Luc said, huskiness coloring his voice, "and I'm not sure I could ever give you that."

She slipped her hand up his torso, stopping over his heart, fingertips digging lightly into the warmth beneath his shirt. "This is better than perfect." Shoshi paused to steady her breath, and her voice. "It's something real."

They might have a ways to go with the day-to-day, but they'd already bared so much. Perfection was nothing but a false shell they'd already seen beyond.

Luc remained still, searching for something in her eyes. Then he lifted her hand away to tuck the ring into her palm, his head dipping to kiss the underside of her wrist. He let go, the implication unmistakable—the choice was literally in her hands. The band slid smoothly onto her middle finger.

With an audible exhale, he stripped off his jacket and tie, like now he could finally relax. His arm curved around her shoulders, fingers teasing her earlobe again as she leaned into his embrace. His other fingers twined with hers, tilting her hand to display the ring. So many people thought daisies were weeds, overlooking the little flower's ability to thrive in harsh conditions, missing the touch of beauty it brought to neglected places in its determination to survive. The road ahead for them might not be the smoothest or simplest, but they could be each other's resilient touch of beauty.

"I'm glad you're back," Shoshi said, letting their hands drop to his lap.

"Oh." Luc straightened, his arms slipping away as he leaned to pick up the tin on the far end of the coffee table. "Has Passover started yet?"

"No." But the thoughtfulness of him asking was no longer surprising. That was just Luc. "Why, what's that?"

"My mom made these for you," he explained, setting the container in her lap.

Shoshi focused on prying off the lid so he wouldn't catch the faint sheen the gesture had brought to her eyes. "She did?"

Luc squeezed her shoulder, seeing through her anyway, of course. Gooey pale squares with touches of amber were layered inside. "Caramel s'mores bars. Sent with strict instructions not to touch them without your permission," he added, his exaggerated dejection eliciting a chuckle.

"Maybe if you're on your best behavior." She tore the corner off one square to pop it in her mouth, moaning as the blend of marshmallow, salted caramel, and chocolate hit her tongue, mostly to tease Luc.

Heat seeped into his expression as his gaze fell to her lips. "Scout's honor," he assured, hand creeping toward the tin.

"You'll spoil your dinner," she joked, sinking back onto the couch and popping another piece in her mouth.

An easy grin she wouldn't get tired of seeing flashed across his face. "You're right. Maybe..." He set the tin aside and twisted on the couch, angling his torso above her. "I should just have a taste of yours," he finished, stroking his knuckles down her cheek then tipping her face up.

His lips brushed hers once, twice. The third time Shoshi's hand drifted down, careful to keep the gooey square away from Luc's shirt. Her lips parted and obligingly he deepened their kiss, tasting her patiently, thoroughly. As if he really did want to lick up every lingering trace of the s'mores bar, except the kiss went on long after there remained any taste but the two of them. Shoshi arched up into him, her free hand gripping the muscles in his back to pull him closer or maybe keep herself anchored as he savored her.

When the steady warmth of awareness had suffused every inch of her, Luc leaned back. "See?" he murmured, his expression sending a tiny shiver through her. "Who needs dinner?"

"Totally superfluous," she agreed.

His shoulders dropped with his exhale, and his lips found a rueful slant. "Interview's tomorrow, huh?"

Right. She'd actually forgotten for a moment. But he hadn't, because he knew it mattered to her. "Yeah," she sighed. She wasn't quite as desperate for work as she had been the night they'd met, but that didn't mean she could throw away this opportunity.

With one more light kiss, Luc shifted back so he was sitting beside her. "Nervous?" he asked.

"Not really," Shoshi murmured, leaning away to set the remainder of the s'mores bar on the lid from the tin. Sure, professionally she was right back where she'd started—unemployed, with a less-than-stellar résumé. But her car was running and her rent was covered, for a little while at least. And now she had Luc.

"Good," he said as she sat up. "Be yourself and you'll blow them away."

Shoshi rolled her eyes but couldn't hold back her smile. Because the thing was, he really meant it. The woman he saw when he looked at her was enough—determined enough, smart enough, capable enough. With his faith in her, his support, it really did feel like she could handle whatever came next.

"Ready to get started?" Luc asked, opening up the job description on his phone.

Shoshi ran her thumb over the promise he'd made in ring form. "Yeah," she said, not really talking about the interview. "Let's do this."

Catch up with Luc and Shoshi in a bonus Hanukkah short!

Grab your free copy:

latkes.ariaglazki.com

Some stories are harder to write than others. For many years, I didn't feel ready to tackle this one, with the depth of emotion and subtleties it required. And even once I did, the first draft was a far cry from the story you read because I wasn't prepared to dive deep enough. I hope now I've nailed the complexity that allows Shoshana and Luc to come together in a healthy way—after they no longer work together, and only once Luc has committed to making amends.

Please keep in mind that throughout the story the characters speak only for themselves and their personal understanding of any topic. This is especially true when it comes to religion and faith. No character's words should be seen as representative of an official stance, nor of my personal views.

For those wondering or who know the intricacies of tax law, I admit I took artistic license with Luc's arrangement with his company. In the book, this allows for thousands more dollars to reach nonprofits doing important work in their community. In the real world, to my understanding, this arrangement would make the IRS rather cranky.

Researching believable ways in which Shoshi's boss could make her life difficult required reading some truly awful examples from the real world. Worse, I couldn't use them, since it was critical that Luc never cross a line that would make him truly irredeemable. (Did you catch him shielding Shoshi from Fuller?) I will note, however, that the moment with the *Playboy* magazines was inspired by an FML from 2013. While some progress has been made in the last decade, protections for employees—particularly young women working for powerful men—remain insufficient at best.

This story took place in a time when none of us had ever heard of COVID-19, but these last years have been excruciating for so many of us. On a personal note, 2021 nearly destroyed me, physically and otherwise. I am so fortunate to have had the support that has kept me going, and grateful for this book to finally be out in the world despite it all.

Thank you for taking the time to read it.

Acknowledgments

A note in the back of a book hardly feels like enough to offer in exchange for the help I've received with taking this story from inspiration to published work. Nevertheless, it feels critical to get these words right.

So, thank you to:

> Rachel, whose enthusiasm for my early drafts somehow hasn't abated. Thanks for always making the time even as life grows ever crazier.

> Jim, for lending your artistic eye to the cover art, but mostly for your consistent support in the face of my unending uncertainty.

> Susan Litman, whose generous feedback helped shape this story. It definitely wouldn't be the same without your notes.

> The Jew(ish) Binders, Romance Binders, and Wide for the Win authors, who never hesitate to share their experience and expertise.

My Patrons, who kept the faith through my extended hiatus. I finally have a book for you!

And the friends and family, including those already mentioned above, who steadfastly encourage and support both my writing and me. You know who you are—so do I.

Love wounded characters healing
as they build a love that lasts?

Read on for an excerpt from:

Tasting

Temptation

One

"Zip me up?" Gina asked, coming out of the dressing room in her maid-of-honor dress.

Roger dropped his cell phone beside her purse and stepped up behind her. "Can you *believe* Sabella's getting married, and we don't even have dates to the wedding?"

She shot him a chiding look over her shoulder. "Sabella deserves her happily ever after." And being date-free suited Gina just fine.

Roger tugged the zipper up then resettled her hair. "I know! She does. But, seriously. Us? Stag at her wedding?" He plopped back onto the plush cream bench across from the angled trio of mirrors. "Unacceptable!"

"Ever the drama queen." Gina stepped onto the raised ivory platform to assess the alterations, trying not to look too hard at her reflection.

Roger actually stuck his tongue out at her.

"Weddings are supposed to be great for meeting people," she reminded, turning toward him.

"Easy for you to say, Miss 'I can pick up any man I want without even crooking a finger.'"

Gina shrugged the sudden tension from her shoulders. The last thing she wanted was to be tied to another man. "There are worse fates than a trip to Sonoma for a wedding, Rodge. Even without a date."

His lips found the impeccable pout that always made Sabella jealous. "You're grouchy today."

"That's 'cause you're extra whiny today," she shot back lightly, trying to sound normal.

He sighed, twisting open the cap to his diet iced tea. The salads they'd picked up for lunch on their way to the boutique waited patiently beside him. Gina swept her hands out, silently asking about the dress. Roger's nod of approval ended with a head tilt.

"Look," she said, checking the hemline in the mirror one more time before stepping down, "you're the one who broke up with his hottie boyfriend because he got bored."

His shoulders and eyebrows lifted with choreographed innocence. "What can I say? I'm hard to keep satisfied."

"Well, then. Good thing you work for me and not the other way around." She softened the comment with a smile. Roger's mouth still dropped into a nearly perfect "o." Rolling her eyes at his dramatics, Gina turned away and swept her hair to the side so he could undo the zipper. He obliged silently, and she walked back to the dressing room to change.

"Speaking of work," he called from the other side of the heavy brocade curtains. "You leave Saturday, right?"

"You just can't wait to get me out of the office." She paused, smoothing her palm over the dark-purple chiffon. Sabella and Kane's wedding was something *good*. And Gina couldn't wait to see her best friend outside of a computer screen again.

"I like being in charge," Roger admitted, drawing her back to the present.

"Good thing we're wrapping up the layout today," she said, slipping the dress off to change back into her knotted skirt and Rebecca Taylor top. "So you'll only be in charge of brainstorming ideas for the next issue." She was mostly kidding. Roger was a fantastic assistant, and he was really developing a good eye.

"And what have I ever done to you?" She would have bet he was pouting again. "Anyway, I was *going* to say that you could use the break."

"Well that's true." Gina tucked back a flyaway strand of hair before taking the dress and rejoining him in the main room. "But since I don't particularly want to lose this job, we better get back to work."

"Yeah, yeah. It would be nice though, snagging a hunky millionaire at the wedding. Just think of all the clothes we could buy… Oh, and fashion week!" He fixed her with a solemn stare. "Promise me, if you ever marry rich and go to fashion week in Paris or New York, you'll take me with you."

A chuckle bubbled from between her lips. Roger might be fickle with men, but he was undeniably devoted to fashion. "I'll think about it," she said. Not that she would ever date a wealthy man again.

"You're cruel," he accused, holding out her purse.

"Have to keep you motivated. The department gets strong enough, we won't need some benefactor to pay our way to fashion week."

"And meanwhile"—he sighed—"we settle for Sonoma."

"Wait 'til you see this place, Rodge. It definitely beats New York."

Two

"Okay, I am officially stealing you away," Gina declared, steering Sabella away from the bevy of cars that had somehow managed to arrive all together. Gina had driven up with the bride-to-be's sister, Trisha. They'd beaten the rest of the bridal party by a half hour, but then Gina had learned to drive in Boston.

Sabella craned her neck toward all the activity behind her. "What about my dress?"

Sighing, Gina stopped, pulled her sunglasses from her nose and into her hair, and scanned the milling crowd until her eyes landed on a curvy blonde in paint-splattered jeans. "Hey, Trisha?"

She spun toward them while everyone else continued unloading.

"Would you please make sure that no disaster befalls Sab's dress between here and our suite?"

Trisha nodded vigorously, rolling her eyes for good measure, and shooed them away.

Sabella laughed and looped her arm through Gina's. "Okay, what about your dresses?"

"We already hung them up. And anyway, you shouldn't be worrying about that." Gina led them to the terrace where various employees were setting up round tables and chairs. They skirted the bustling activity, keeping close to the wrought-iron fence that blocked off the overhang. Gently rolling vineyards splayed out beneath them in a blend of greens.

Sabella's shoulders dropped as she exhaled, leaning over the railing. "It's almost quiet here."

Gina chuckled. They'd spent five days surrounded by Sabella's and Kane's families, and Kane's bandmates, all in a lovely four-bedroom home in Mountain View. "Cramped" didn't quite cover it. The craziness of last-minute planning hadn't helped, adding to the chaos. The drive up had been the most relaxing time Gina'd had all week, until now.

She inhaled the crisp air, letting the peace envelop her. "It's so beautiful."

Ignoring the bustle behind them, they gazed out at the neatly organized rows below, glinting under the sun. Sabella'd fallen in love the second they saw a virtual tour of Cavaliere Vineyards. "Chivalry vineyards" she had not-quite-translated when they'd found it online. With the large yet secluded terrace opening onto this breathtaking view, it was an undeniably gorgeous setting for a wedding.

"You know?" Sabella turned toward her, smiling. "I'm kind of excited."

"Kind of? You're *kind of* excited for your wedding? Maybe we should call it off."

Sabella's head tilted slightly to the side, her lips pursing. "You know what I mean. Everything has been so hectic lately, but now that we're actually here... This is really going to happen."

"I can't believe we pulled this thing off in less than a year."

Sabella hummed her agreement.

A breeze wound its way around their shoulders, and Gina straightened, exhaling. "All right, I'd say it's time for a welcome to Sonoma drink. Unless there's something you need to tell me?" she half teased.

"A glass of wine sounds lovely," Sabella answered, trying to keep a straight face at the suggestion.

Elbows linked, they strode up to the secluded balcony bar with its own magnificent view. A few of the winery's patrons surrounded them, seated at wrought-iron tables with partially filled glasses and tiny cubes of cheese.

"Riesling okay?" Sabella asked. "Or a white Zin? They have this really interesting one with a bit of a raspberry flavor."

"Shouldn't I be the one buying?" Gina offered, picking up the tasting menu.

"I think the least I owe you is a glass of wine, Gi, with all your help, and putting up with everyone."

If anything, Gina owed Sabella—everything. "Your family's a piece of cake compared to mine, as you well know," she brushed off. "Or have you blocked any memory of the trauma?"

"Oh, shush you. Your family's wonderful."

"Loud. Overbearing. Completely nuts."

Sabella crooked an eyebrow.

"And, yes, wonderful," Gina agreed. "But you didn't have to invite them, you know."

"Of course I did. And anyway, it'll save you at least one of your mother's guilt trips about visiting home."

She had a point. Maybe.

As the bartender set out a couple of glasses, efficiently filling them with Riesling, Sabella added, "You know she's cooking brunch tomorrow?"

"You're kidding." Not that Gina was all that surprised. Her mother was physically incapable of not feeding everyone around her. "How did she bully you into it?"

"Bully me into accepting her free labor and delicious food?" They moved toward a lonely table in the shade, resettling a pair of chairs to face the view before lowering into them. "Maybe we'll get lucky, and she'll even make truffles," Sabella said after tasting the wine.

Gina took a long sip rather than answer, letting the pleasantly crisp white flow over her taste buds before swallowing.

"I tried to talk her out of it, since she's our *guest*, and Kane offered to help out, of course, but she wouldn't have it." Sabella smirked. "She said it'd be good practice."

"Oh? Is Donny getting married?" Gina asked, deadpan.

Sabella chuckled. "It's too bad your brothers couldn't make it."

Gina hummed noncommittally. Annoying as he was at fifteen, Donny always made them laugh. Her older brother, Gerardo, wasn't half-bad either. She did love and miss her family. She just usually loved them most in small doses or when they were on the other side of the country. But her best friend wanted them here, and the least Gina could do was ensure this weekend was all about Sabella.

"Gina, you've barely eaten. Are you sick?"

She'd had two servings of everything. "Ma, I ate plenty, I promise. And it was delicious. I've really missed your cooking." She squeezed her mom's familiar hand. "Sabella's lucky you made brunch."

"We all are," Bobby, Kane's bass guitarist, chimed in from across the table, picking up an empty bowl. "Thanks, Mrs. Sabatino."

Her mother's cheeks rounded as a blush spread over them. This wasn't that big a group by her mom's standards, but brunch really had been amazing. Gina would have bet everyone ate too much, unable to resist the tantalizing assortment. Their tables were still covered in nearly emptied dishes, which the groomsmen were slowly clearing.

Trisha broke away from the bride's and groom's families and swished over. "So everything's set for tonight, right?" She popped a lingering truffle into her mouth.

"I think so. Could you just confirm the limo one more time?" Gina asked.

"Oh, yeah. No problem."

"Beatrice, are you coming?" Sabella's mother called. She never seemed to shout, though her voice always carried as far as it needed to. It was as impressive as it was intimidating. Nothing at all like Gina's mom, who preferred to rely on guilt trips.

Trisha forced a smile. "Family bonding time." The families were heading up to Calistoga for the afternoon, though Trisha had promised to ensure they'd be back before Sabella's surprise bachelorette party. "You sure you're all set with treats and the cards and everything?" she asked.

"Treats? What treats?" Gina's mom interrupted, stacking empty plates for Kane's bandmates to take away.

"For the bachelorette party, Ma. I need to run out and pick some stuff up, but it'll be taken care of," she assured Trisha.

"Okay. Thanks again, Mrs. Sabatino. Brunch was unbelievable," Trisha said before hurrying off.

"I will come help you, with the treats, Gina," her mom declared.

"You didn't come here to work, Ma. You should take Dad, and go explore. It's beautiful out here."

"I can spend some time with you, and help you, and your papi and I can explore tonight, when you girls are out. Or do you not want to spend any time with your mother, even though you never come out and visit."

Gina didn't even pretend that was a question. "You know I'd love your help. I just don't want you to miss out on seeing

Sonoma. But I bet everyone would love it if you have some more of those truffles stashed away somewhere."

"I have extra chocolate, I'll make more for you girls, but I need sugar. We finish here, and we go to the store, okay?"

"You're leaving me?" Gina's dad chimed in with a smile, coming back to their table, drink in hand.

Gina threw her arm around his sturdy shoulders. "I'm stealing her away, just for a bit."

He chuckled, returning her embrace. "Mi passerotta. Why haven't you been home? Ci manchi."

"I know, papi, I miss you guys, too." She'd spent the December holidays with Sabella's family, to help plan the wedding. And because after last summer, she'd needed more time before facing her family's overly perceptive gazes. "I'll come visit soon, I promise."

"Ai." Her mom's hand landed on her shoulder, squeezing gently. "She was busy, planning all this. And now, I'm here to help. So, let's go."

The groomsmen had already insisted on taking care of the dishes, and there wasn't a point in arguing anyway. Gina kissed her dad's cheek then looped her arm through her mom's. Sometimes, it was more than nice having them around.

Three

Two hours later, Gina had changed her mind. Logically, she knew her mom meant well, but the poking and prodding questions about her life, and settling down, or moving home were enough to drive her up a wall. And then she'd been kicked out of the borrowed kitchen! Not that she didn't have plenty to do before tonight, and it was undeniably sweet of her mom to make all those chocolate-dipped snacks for them, but still.

Gina stalled in the vaulted entryway and debated—hallway one would take her back to the guest rooms, all filled this weekend with the bridal party, plus Gina's parents and Kane's manager; hallway two opened onto the main tasting room. It wasn't like having a glass of wine in the afternoon in the middle of wine country would be particularly notable. And she could use some time to wind down, so she didn't destroy tonight's goodies when putting them together. *Tasting room it is.*

The room was empty, but with the gorgeous weather, most visitors probably preferred the outdoor terrace. Gina chose a stool by the bar, absently tapping her fingers on the wood as she waited. Various wine-themed knickknacks covered display tables and shelves around the room. The faintest smell of wood somehow still lingered, though the construction was lacquered and far from new. Maybe they pumped it in for atmosphere.

She flattened her palm on the bar and sighed. Maybe the emptiness was a sign that a drink was a bad idea.

Before she could make her mind up to leave, a barman came out of the back room, carrying a fresh case, which he set down with a clunk. His eyes raked over her torso before his lips pulled into a crooked smile. "You look like you could use a drink."

"How extraordinarily perceptive."

His smile grew, crinkling around his eyes. "Maybe if you're nice to me, I'll pour you one."

Gina exhaled, focusing on the man before her. This was a game she'd mastered long ago, even if she was a bit out of practice. "Maybe if you're nice to me, I'll let you."

He strode closer. "What'll it be?"

"What are you offering?"

He picked up a towel and wiped off his hands before running his fingers over the bottlenecks arrayed between them. His faded tee shirt stretched slightly across his chest and shoulders as he moved. Deftly, he spun a glass from its spot out of sight and placed it silently on the bar. He uncorked a fresh bottle with a pop. A deep red gurgled into the glass.

Gina lifted it and took a long sip.

The barman's eyebrow crooked. "Glad I didn't pour you the good stuff."

She set the glass back down, half-drained, and shrugged. "I'll be paying you for it, regardless."

"Wine isn't about the money. It's about the experience." He fitted the bottle with one of those tops that control how much is poured at a time.

"Or the goal."

Friendly eyes caught her in their gaze. "There are better ways to de-stress, you know."

"Are you saying I seem stressed?"

"You're part of the bridal party, aren't you?" Another smile tugged at his lips. "Stress comes with the territory."

She leaned slightly over the bar. "And you're offering to make it all better?"

He sobered as his eyes trailed over all the skin exposed by her summery top. "How could I deny you?"

Gina traced the stem of her wineglass with her fingers, knowing exactly where his mind would go. "Is this a service you frequently provide, then?"

"Maybe I should start." He leaned onto his elbows on the bar, so their faces were almost even.

Gina's lips parted as she considered the man before her. Dark hair lay tousled, with stray locks drifting over his forehead. Symmetrical eyes demanded attention, easily holding their own with the strong line of his pronounced nose that drew her gaze to gently curving lips, set in a wash of stubble that flowed over a crisply defined jaw. De-stressing definitely didn't sound like a bad idea, if they played on her terms.

His eyebrows lifted in challenge.

She stood, picking up her wine, and scooped her purse off the stool beside her without breaking eye contact. He straightened and gestured to the far end of the bar. Her heels clicked on the stone floor as they moved toward it. The door he'd entered through was still open.

"After you," his voice sounded next to her.

"Aren't you going to get in trouble for this?"

Amusement or something like it flashed in his eyes. "I'll risk it."

Keep Reading:

temptation.ariaglazki.com

About Aria

Aria Glazki's first kiss technically came from a bear cub. Though no fairytale transformation followed, she still believes magic can happen when the right people come together— if they don't get in their own way, that is. So now Aria writes heartfelt romances about hurt people healing as they build a love that lasts. Sometimes she adds a magical twist.

Aria Glazki

Relatable People — Remarkable Love

www.AriaGlazki.com